D0984220

HALFWAY MAN

Wayland Drew

ISBN 0 88750 740 9 (hardcover)
ISBN 0 88750 741 7 (softcover)

Front over: "Winter Fishing." Copyright © 1987. by Michael Robinson. Book design by Michael Macklem.

Printed in Canada

PUBLISHED IN CANADA BY OBERON PRESS

Dedicated to the memory of Alfred Foster Higgs (1910-1964). *Ludens in mysterium*

Neyashing

My name is Travis Niskigwun. I belong in the north—on the shore of Lake Superior and in the Shield beyond. I belong where lakes are still the eyes of the earth, and where the shadows of invisible beings move on the snow in moonlight. I belong where there are bears and spirits still....

This story comes out of the Lake and returns to it again. It's many stories. It has as many beginnings as the Lake. Jenny says I should start with the Friday night when we met Michael Gardner. "After all," she says, "it's his story." But she knows that's only a little bit true, like one grain of sand in a whole beach of truth. She knows it doesn't matter where I start; I'll always come back to the Lake, and to the way Neyashing was before he came.

Jenny is the woman I love.

I'm a labourer. A few years ago, when I came back from university, I picked up whatever jobs were around, and I've done that ever since. I've worked in the pulp camps, and on the highways, and on fishtugs, and in between jobs I hunt and trap. I won't do surveying. I won't work for the government. Lots of offers for steady jobs have come because I work hard and I know what whitemen think of time. But I've said no. I don't want money, I want space. I need to be able to go down the shore. I need to go back into the bush, sometimes for a few days, a few weeks.

There was fog on the lake when I got home from work that night, and I was glad of it. I wanted it to move right in. I wanted it to cover us so I couldn't look at Neyashing and think about what was coming. When I drove through the dunes behind the village it was already swirling around the western point, filling the bay like milk in a dark green bowl. I waved to it. "Biindigen awun," I called out the window. "Come on in, fog."

I parked and walked up the hill to my cabin without look-ing back. I said hello to Guaranteed, got my soap and towel, and went along the path to take a swim in the creek. When I came back, naked in the warm spring evening, the fog had rolled all the way in and covered Neyashing. "Miigwetch," I said. "Thanks."

I went inside and dried and dressed.

Other years on the first warm evening of spring, I would have stayed out in the last of the sun, watching the fog wrap the cabins of Neyashing one by one, first Aja's place tucked in behind the western point, and then the twelve other places between the beach and the dunes, and then what was left of the old fish plant, and cemetery in the meadows, and finally the spit that curved like a big arm from the east end of the beach. I used to love to watch all weathers move over and through my village, including fog; but not this spring. This spring I was seeing everything for the last time, and I was too tired, and bitter, and ashamed to watch. Even that night. Even though it was a Friday and Jenny was coming.

When I finished supper I put on my cap and whistled for Guaranteed, and we went back down the hill together, into that clouded world.

"Station," I told him. "We'll go get Jenny." And he grinned and thumped his tail against my leg. "Nimoo," I said. "Good dog."

He looks more like a wolverine than a dog—enough to make people nervous. He has the same colour and the same rolling gait, and the same squashed look. He even smells like a wolverine after he's been out overnight. When I got him in Beardmore five years ago I asked the guy, "You guar-antee that's a dog?"

"Close enough for this far north," he said.

I gave him his case of Blue and took Guaranteed home.

He was one hungry, gritty, skeptical dog, but he still had his spirit. I could see that. It was there in the core of him like a hard little flame. I fed him and washed him in the

6

creek and he stayed. He's been dirty lots of times since then, but he's never hungry anymore.

He ran ahead to the truck and jumped into the box and slung his forelegs over the side so he could watch me in the mirror and see ahead at the same time, and I drove through Neyashing and then up out of the fog and onto the highway, toward Schreiber.

It was a quiet night. A good night. Too early in the year for tourists.

When we got to town we parked where we always do, at the far end of the station platform where the concrete stops and a strand of old cobblestones lies like a grey beach. I shut off the engine and we got out and waited, listening to little sounds in the stillness. There was a raven calling in the twilight above the hills, and the gasps of a monster diesel idling on the far side of the yards, and a burst of laughter through the open door of the pool-hall across the road.

And then, the whistle of the train from Thunder Bay, bringing Jenny.

It brought Michael Gardner too, but I didn't see him get off. I was only watching Jenny, Jenny coming across those cobblestones in her sweater and jeans, with her pack crammed full of mail and essays to mark, and her sunglasses pushed back on her head, and her long hair the gold of autumn tamarack.

She reached up laughing and grabbed my cap with both hands and pulled my face down. Two kids inside the train cheered and rattled beer cans against the window, and the conductor applauded before the door clanged shut, and Jenny gave them all a little wave, kissing me.

Guaranteed chased around in circles, sneezing and snuffling until she greeted him. "Nimoo," she said, rubbing his ears. "How are you, flat dog? Up you go. In you go."

She dropped her pack into the box beside him and climbed into the cab from the driver's side and shifted over. "So," she said, slapping her thighs, "what news?"

"Nothing." I got in beside her and started the engine.

"They haven't started?"

"Not yet. The ground's still too wet. We'll have another week or two."

"Have you decided where you'll go?"

I shook my head. "North," I said, and started coaxing my transmission into reverse.

"Well, *I've* decided something." She was nodding with her lips pressed tight, the way she did when something was absolutely final.

"Can it wait till we're home?"

"No."

"Out of Schreiber?"

"No. It's very important. It will amaze you."

"Better tell me then. I could stand some amazement."

"Travis," she laid both hands on top of mine on the gearshift. "Travis, I want..."

"Hello there!" A stranger was bending down to the open window on her side, smiling, "Can you help me? Can you tell me how to get to McDonnell's Depot?"

Right from the start I didn't care for Michael Gardner. For one thing, he interrupted Jenny. For another, he was smiling too much, showing too many teeth the way some people do when they want something. Worst, he said "McDonnell's Depot." That's the shaganash name for Neyashing, the map name. We never call it that. Nobody who lives there calls it that. Only people who come in cars or in big white boats, people who want to take something away ever call Neyashing "McDonnell's Depot."

I leaned over and inspected him from under the brim of my cap. He was 50, maybe 55, with grey hair carefully trimmed over his ears and a four-day grey stubble on his chin and cheeks. He had on a plaid shirt and a khaki jacket, and carried an old knapsack on one shoulder. No hat.

Horizons, Mother told me when I was little. She drew a finger across her eyes. *Look for the horizon, here. If you see it,*

8

trust the man. If you don't, don't.

I've always done that. I did it then. The horizon was there all right but far back, miles away in his blue eyes, and I could hardly see it over the rubble piled up in the foreground. Wreckage was strewn all over in there, as if buildings had collapsed and the pieces hadn't fallen out yet. He was a man held together by his will and his skin, by whatever kept him smiling.

"Know how I can get there? McDonnell's Depot?"

I looked down the platform. Everybody else had left or was leaving. The VIA office was already dark. There was no point telling him to call a taxi because if Clem Watson wasn't already there he was drunk. It was starting to get cold; a little wind came sneaking under the fog.

The last thing I wanted was someone else in the cab with Jenny and me. I just wanted to hear what she had to tell me. I wanted to put my arm around her on the way home. I wanted to kiss her. So it would have been easy to leave that man right where he was.

But I knew who he was. And I knew who had brought him.

I said, "We're going that way. Unhitch that door and climb in. Throw your bag in the back." I leaned out the window and told Guaranteed in Ojibwe, "Don't eat that man."

He dropped the old knapsack into the box. He unwound the coathanger that held the right door shut and climbed in beside Jenny. He offered his hand. "I'm Michael Gardner."

Yes, this is his story. Jenny says I should begin with that night, but she understands now why I have to go back two weeks to the last Friday in March, the weekend before Easter.

Jenny knows I have trouble with beginnings because I have trouble with logic. I know the more you move around something the more of it you see. I know thinking like that takes time, and that logic wants to speed up, straighten out, simplify, line things up and count them. Logic is what builds roads or draws lines on maps with no care about hunting lands, or water paths, or burial grounds, or anything else.

"You think in circles," Jenny says.

"I have to look at things."

"Like a child drawing. Around and around and around."

"And you think like a soldier. Marching."

"Oh dear. Is there hope for me?"

"Only if you stay here for treatment. A very long treatment."

Usually we'd be in bed when we talked like this. It would be Sunday and she'd already be worrying about going back to Thunder Bay and into school next morning. That's what she meant by logic. That necessity. I'd tell her it might be logic but not good sense. It would be more sensible, I'd tell her, if she stayed in Neyashing so we could be together every night, her skin white on my brown, listening to the Lake, making good babies....

Two weeks earlier: the last weekend in March.

Ice was moving in the bay, and if you listened you could hear the floes brushing against each other in the night like big soft hands. Already seagulls were screaming and swooping in the mouths of the rivers. There was that spring smell in the air, warm-cold, living-dead, water-ice, clean and pure. North. Full of promises, like the skin of a woman in winter, when you're warming her.

Guaranteed and I drove over to Schreiber station as usual to pick up Jenny. We were a little late that night, and she was waiting alone on the platform. She hugged me and kissed me, as usual, and bent over to let Guaranteed lick her face, as usual, and we drove back to Neyashing with the windows open, letting our arms trail through the wind in long waves to nothing and no-one in particular. To Spring, I guess. To the Lake.

We turned off the highway and went through the bush to the crest of the long hill, and Neyashing lay below us in the dusk.

From there, Neyashing looks like a lot of other hamlets in the north—just a few cabins clustered at the east end of the beach, and a few more scattered across the hillside and through the dunes to the west. Half a mile north, behind the highway and the tracks, the cliffs of the Palisades rise straight for five hundred feet; and beyond the spit to the south, lies the endless grey of sky and Lake.

It looks passed over and forgotten. There are no gas stations in Neyashing, no supermarkets. There isn't even a store, except for the few shelves in the corner of Bobby Naponse's living-room where he keeps canned food in case somebody needs something quick. There's no dentist, no plumber, no school, no post office, no church, no phones, no electricity. There are only our places, pretty much as they've been for a long time.

Neyashing means *the spit* in Ojibwe; no, it means more than that. It means *the place of the spit, where people live.* We've lived well in Neyashing. We don't have much, but what we have we share. We look after one another.

At the top of the hill, coming home, I used to get a sinking feeling in my stomach that had nothing to do with height or speed. It came just from seeing how tiny Neyashing was compared to Thunder Bay, or Nipigon, or Schreiber, from knowing how vulnerable it was. But since Fall the feeling has been worse than that; it's been like knowing someone you love is going to die soon, but not knowing when. All winter I haven't looked at Neyashing, coming home. I've looked out at the Lake instead.

We drove down through the village and behind the dunes to the western end of the beach, where Jimmy Pagoosie and my brother Cutler and I park our trucks. The evening sounds of Neyashing came with us as we walked up to my cabin—kids playing on the beach, dogs and seagulls crying, somebody laughing, somebody splitting kindling, an outhouse door banging shut, Jimmy Pagoosie hammering something on the *Bad Loon* down at the mooring—and underneath everything the slow rhythm of the Lake, like Earth breathing. Spruce smoke and pine scent filled all of Neyashing.

The three of us stayed on the Council Rock in front of my place awhile, listening, watching the afterglow fade and the first stars come out. Guaranteed sat on the very edge where he could see all of Neyashing, moving his nose across the breeze. Jenny stood with her arms around me and her head against my shoulder. She didn't say anything. She didn't have to.

Inside I put fresh wood on my two fires—fireplace and stove. I lit the lamps and we drank tea and talked for a while. Usually we'd have a sauna, but the stream was still too fast and too cold to wash comfortably, and the last of the snow was too littered with twigs and bark, so that night Jenny used the bathtub.

In February, hunting, I found an old lumber camp 40 miles or so to the north. Only one building was still standing, held up mainly by snowdrifts, and on the wall was a big copper boiler with oak handles on the ends. Hanging beside it was the copper bathtub, a hip-bath, round, with a broad sloping lip all around and a little seat inside. By spring that wall would collapse and those interesting items would be gone for good. They were too big and awkward for me to haul out on snowshoes, but a week later Tommy Espaniel and I mushed back with his team and gave them a new lease on life. I fixed them and cleaned them. I polished them until they glowed like big coppery jewels.

Later that Friday night I watched her take her bath, watched the reflections play over her. In summer, when Jenny and I take the canoe and move out into the wilderness, her skin tans almost as dark as mine, but that night at the end of winter she was the colour of clouds, a pale spirit moving between fire and shadows, moving against the smoke-dark log walls, against my packs and snowshoes and guns hanging on their pegs, across my grandfather's drum and my canoe on the rafters, the line of its hull like a grey horizon. She was a spirit blending everything I owned. I watched her with my eyes half-closed so the lashes became a screen, as if I were hunting low in the underbrush on a shore, watched the chairs and table and bed move over her and through her, watched the water slip across her like northern lights, with a sound like wind in aspens....

But I haven't come back to that Friday night because of a woman's bath; I've come back because of the Sign.

It came then. Right then.

While she was drying I carried the tub outside and emptied it over the railing. I planned to go back in, close the door, and take Jenny to bed and make love with her for a long time. I wanted to fall asleep with her, listening to the fires and the Lake. But just as I was hanging the tub on its peg, the birds came: geese. Three flocks.

Of course there's nothing strange about Canada geese returning in the spring. You hear them laughing in the night, riding the updrafts off each other's wingbeats. Sometimes they're so loud they wake you up. You might hear a wedge of them passing right over Neyashing, and then another far down the shore or out over the Lake; but very rarely do two come close together, and almost never three. So what happened then was very strange.

The first flock came clamouring low across the water to the east, crossing in front of the half moon like ragged brush strokes, their cries breaking against the Palisades and tumbling back on Neyashing.

I ran off the porch and out onto the Council Rock to see them better, hear them longer. Even before their sound had faded another flight came in on the west side. They were even louder, more urgent, filling the whole bay with their calls. Laughing I answered them, called goose-sounds like a child, and I was still calling with my arms raised when the third flock came.

They came so low off the Lake that their honking reached up the hill like arms, so low that in the moonlight they looked like airborne fragments of the spit. I thought their leader had made a terrible error, mistaking the Palisades for a cloudbank, and I waved and shouted to warn them off. But there was no mistake; they were coming for me.

They rose as they crossed the beach, rose up the hillside to the Council Rock and then were on me, buffeting me with their sound, sweeping me into it and lifting me over my cabin and up across the spine of the Palisades, and I was one with them flying on, feeling only their surging power, seeing only North below, and the glint of Ningotonjan Lake far ahead in the moonlight....

Jenny called me from the cabin door, called me back, "Travis? Are you all right?" and I was kneeling on the Council Rock with Guaranteed beside me, waiting. "Fine," I said.

"Are you coming in?"

"Yes," I said. "Soon."

I was waiting for the fourth flock. There had to be a fourth because three of anything is incomplete, like an invitation. Only a four is whole.

But there were no more flights of geese that night. Long after we had gone to bed and made love I kept listening. Long after I had fallen asleep with Jenny's head on my arm a part of me kept listening. But there was only a barred owl calling on the western point, and loons in the bay. The fourth flock didn't come till morning, and they weren't geese, after all.

So, the summons of the three flocks is another beginning for Michael Gardner's story. For me it spanned all time since that night even as those life-mated birds spanned the Shield, sweeping through the darkness with the surge of fertility in

14

their blood and the promise of salt marshes in their nostrils.

Somewhere on the edge of sleep I whispered a question to Jenny about our baby, the one I wanted to have, but she didn't answer.

Next morning, Aja moved.

We were still in bed when it happened. Birds knew it first. Their calls woke me—loons and gulls, black ducks and whiskyjacks—all making the same announcement.

I got up and went out onto the porch, but thick fog had moved in overnight and I couldn't see past the Council Rock. I kept checking while I lit the fires and washed, and by the time we finished breakfast the sun was burning through and I could see right across the bay, almost to the end of the spit. All the beach was clear except the mouth of the creek, and there, moving through the last tendrils of fog, was Aja.

She was headed east, toward the sun and the spit. She was unmistakable. No-one else had hair so white it shone. No-one else moved so slowly, with such hunched determination or such gnarled pain, like a rock or a tree being drawn out of Earth. No-one else was so indifferent to the separation between land and Lake, was so careless of the cold water washing sometimes right over her leaky boots, almost to her knees. And no-one else stopped so often to rest, to wave a greeting to her companion birds, to look for omens in the patterns of the beach and hear news in the swirling foam.

I felt a rush of joy to see her there in the spring, and I raised my arms to her. I was glad that she was still alive and could attempt that long traverse of beach, and I was glad too because Aja's journeys to the end of the spit were good omens; Aja moved when people needed her to move.

I watched her all the way down the beach, until she reached the base of the spit and started up the trail. Then I went inside.

"What is it?" Jenny asked. Her mail and students' essays

were spread all over the table, and she was starting to work. She had tied her hair with a red bandanna and she was wearing a pair of jeans and a loose blue T-shirt that let her nipples brush around inside. *Fondue Me, Quiche Me,* it said. I wavered but hauled out the telescope, folding the tripod and propping open the screen door with my elbow.

"Aja. She's going out to the spit."

I knew I'd have time to get the scope set up and focused before she reappeared, and I went about doing that, extending the legs to their fullest so I could stand up to watch. Sometimes I keep the legs low so I can sit down and let the dewcap of the scope just clear the porch railing. I watch the Lake for hours like that, sometimes. But I couldn't do that with Aja. I wanted to be on my feet, watching Aja....

I bought that telescope because of her, because of what she taught me about the stars. I paid $200 for it in Duluth, the night I decided to become an astronomer. It's a good one—a ¾-inch refractor with a rock-steady equatorial mount.

What happened was that my brother Cutler, Jimmy Pagoosie, Maynard McTavish and I went down to Duluth one weekend just to raise hell. We were young and feeling pretty rich after a summer's work. So we thought, why not find a nice big hotel with rugs on the floor, and some rum, and some women?

We did that. We went down in a '65 Chevy that Jimmy bought with his share from the season on the *Bad Loon,* hauling trout and whitefish, and we had no trouble at all finding the hotel or the rum or the women. Our only trouble happened just after we arrived, in a bar where we shouldn't have gone anyway. You could tell from the outside what kind of place it was. You could tell it'd be full of dockworkers all beered-up by that time, 6.30 on a Friday night. It was one of those places with red neons in the window that say *Michelob,* or *Budweiser,* or *Stroh,* so old they've gone pink and flaky, and under the signs were chintzy waterstained curtains with dead flies dangling from the hems.

We went in out of sheer bravado, I guess—nineteen and Indian with a fat wallet in your back pocket and new muscles all over. The place was full of guys wearing hardhats or talking caps that said things like *Toledo Police,* or *Stolen From Amy's Whorehouse.* Some of them had cigarette packs pushed up into the sleeves of their jerseys, like rectangular growths on their biceps. They were sitting at little chipped arborite tables with beer puddles and empty bottles huddled in the middle. The smoke was so thick that when we went in Jimmy cut an imaginary doorway with the side of his hand and walked through it, laughing his silly laugh, and Maynard McTavish, who was half French, clutched his throat and staggered around a bit saying, "La brume! La brume acide!"

We were already a bit drunk and thought all this was pretty funny, but the hardhat regulars didn't think it was too damn funny. The place went still. A lot of little eyes peered out from under those visors, and a lot of mouths opened just enough to sip beer. I could see they were just itching to beat the shit out of somebody, some foreman-surrogate or boss-surrogate, and here we were, four clowns, an answer to their prayers.

I kept grinning along with the others, saying through my teeth, "Let's get the hell out of here," but the others were already sitting down, giving orders.

Things got worse fast. Jimmy called the crewcut waiter "my man" three times in a limp-wristed way, and Maynard fixed a pretzel in his nose and started into his bull imitations, staring red-eyed around the room, and Cutler spewed a mist of made-in-America beer across the floor and said, "Moose piss!" loud enough to be heard back in the Lakehead.

I pulled a chair close with my toe and put my boots up on it. I kept saying, "For chrissake!" behind my teeth, but it was too late, way too late.

Two customers detached themselves from the rest and

17

ambled over. Their friends began to smile unpleasantly and shift around so they could watch. I said, "Here she comes, boys."

The bigger guy I might have gotten along with or even liked in another time and place. He looked willing to follow simple instructions—pick up a small building, say, and put it where you told him to, or deal with half a dozen Hell's Angels. But the little guy I disliked from the start. He was downright mean, quick and mean, like a weasel hunting. His eyes were set too close together and he was chewing a toothpick, shifting it from one side of his mouth to the other. "You-boys-from-up-north-are-yuh? Huh?" He talked fast like that, running his words together and then grunting, just making sound.

He didn't want an answer and we didn't give him one. We watched.

"Well, we-gotta-tell-yuh-we-don-like-your-kind. Nosir. Not-here. Unh-uh."

Maynard took a swig of beer, worked it around in his mouth a little and swallowed. "So, what kind's that, exactly."

"Injyuns," the big guy said, flatfooted, rolling his shoulders a bit. "Yuh stink like goddam injyuns."

We set our glasses down slowly, and Cutler shrugged and lifted one arm and stuck his nose under it. "Stinks like whiteman to me. Here, *you* have a sniff."

He was half on his feet when the big guy came at him, and he clamped an arm around that thick neck and held on. The big guy went right over the chair, right through it, trampled it to kindling, and then he and Cutler were travelling at considerable speed toward the wall, Cutler backward, screaming a war-whoop that has been known to turn people the colour of cold ashes, conjuring as it does visions of feathered heads and painted faces coming through the mist.

Maynard booted the big man just below the knees as he

18

passed, and Jimmy Pagoosie danced sideways and hammered his kidneys twice with a beer stein.

I heard Cutler hit the wall but I didn't see any more for a few minutes. I was busy myself. The little guy kicked the chair from under my feet and dove. He wanted to get to my face while I was off-balance, but I was not off-balance. I was ready. When the chair went spinning my boots came back into my butt and then out and up, steel toes hitting his gut just under the breastbone. He went down hard, skidded a yard or so and sat with his eyes and tongue bulging out, turning a nice shade of purple.

There was enough silence for Dolly Parton to belt a few bars of "Nine to Five" out of the jukebox, and then every man in that room was on his feet. The whole bar turned into a many-legged, single-minded animal. I thought: our one hope is that there will not be enough room in the doorway for that moving mass of meat; it will jam, and we can say goodbye before it gets unjammed.

But the others never got to me. The little man stood up, wheezing, waving his friends back, saying, "Leave-im! Leave-im, goddammit!" And I saw the knife in his left hand, one of those little flip-spring things.

I lifted my hands and looked hard at him. I said, "You don't want to do that, friend. You really don't." I backed up but he kept coming, turning the point of that blade in little circles. "Honest," I said, "you don't want to do that."

I backed up until I felt the wall behind me, and he kept coming.

We were brought up with knives, all of us on the north shore. By the time we were seven we could clean a fish with two flicks of the wrist, and fillet it with a couple more. We played with knives all the time, tossing them to each other, tossing them into walls or trees, or into the decks of boats. By the time we were eight we could put a knife wherever we wanted it. They weren't just tools for us, they were appendages—fish-knives, jack-knives, crooked knives.

Crooked knives: tools of the old North. One-handed draw-knives, curved to gouge.

When I felt that wall behind me, when he kept coming with that blade aimed at my cheekbone, I reached down and slid my crooked knife out of my boot and scooped a chunk of flesh out of his hand.

It was not a large piece, but big enough to make a wet sound when it hit the floor.

He looked at the bone glistening in his thumb. He looked up at me and then down at his hand again. "Mutherfukker," he hissed. "Injyun mutherfukker!"

I wasn't angry until then. When it happens, crimson haze comes down like little curtains over my eyes. I see red. It takes quite a lot to make me angry, but it happened then. I didn't like that man, I didn't like his idea of a good fight, and I didn't like what he called me. Most of all I didn't like what he called me.

The little red curtains came down. All I could see through them was that mean little mouth spewing more filth, and I took a step forward. I was going to make that mouth bigger, big enough to say *Ojibwe*. Maybe even *Anishnabeg*.

Cutler grabbed me before I got to him. Cutler knew. He says that you do not see the red from the outside. All you see is black. He says my eyes go shiny black, like obsidian. And the little man's friends also knew, because they wrapped up his hand and got him quiet, and no-one seemed ready to come at me.

Jimmy was holding the door open, and Cutler and Maynard were pulling me, "Come on! Come on, Travis!" The big man was flat on his face, but his arms and legs were beginning to twitch a little as if he'd soon be thinking about getting up. So they hadn't killed him.

We backed out and ran. We were in a street, and then a parking-lot, and then Jimmy's car with Cutler driving and Jimmy upside-down trying to stop his nosebleed, and all of us weak with laughter. Then somehow we were in a park

20

with the Lake right there, close enough to reach into it and wash, and the lights of moored freighters in the harbour, and Maynard was looking at his hand saying, "Hey! *Hey!*" and holding it up so we could see the little finger at right angles to the others. "Busted! Busted on that dumb shit's skull!"

He claimed it didn't hurt much, even when we pulled it back into place and wrapped it up with sticks and electrical tape from Jimmy's car.

That was the night I bought the telescope. The others told me I spotted it in a pawnshop window and hoofed in and laid down the cash. They said I wandered around Duluth for quite a while with the tripod over my shoulder, looking at the lights. I don't remember doing that. I remember only sitting up in bed at 2 AM and seeing the telescope on the other side of the room with a big yellow tag still dangling on it, and the woman with me laughing, saying, "What d'yuh want to look at you can't see with the naked eye?" and offering one or two things to my naked eye. She had a husky voice, like Lauren Bacall's in those old movies.

"Want to be astrOMomer," I said. "AstrOMomer."

"Later," she said. "Let's have a drink first."

She was a fun-loving and considerate woman. She left me $20 out of the $200 or so I think I had in my wallet. Cutler and Maynard got cleaned out completely, and my twenty and the ten Jimmy always kept in the split in his boot were all that got us home.

That was how I got the telescope. I've never regretted buying it, though later at university I didn't take a single course in astronomy. I just read some books. I listened to Aja.

Aja came up out of the woods and onto the trail that wound along the spine of the spit, pushing first on one knee and then on the other, hoisting herself the way old people do on stairs. She was bent over so far that through the scope I

21

could see her shaman's otterskin bag, her *pindgigossan,* swaying out from her body.

At the top she just stood for a while, bent, her shoulders heaving. Then she lowered herself on a rock and slowly turned to look at me.

I was half a mile away. Even if her eyes had not been clouded with cataracts she could not have seen me in the shadow of the porch. But she knew I was there. She knew. I felt her gaze come right into me through the telescope. Hairs prickled all over me. "Zhawendagoziwin," I whispered. "Go in peace, old woman."

Aja smiled. She lifted her hand. She looked toward the end of the spit where birds waited, and she raised her face to the unfinished moon.

Jenny came out behind me. "What's happening?"

"Aja's moving."

"Where is she?"

"There. On the spit."

Aja rose then as if something had lifted her away from the rock and carried her toward the end of the spit and the Lake. I swung the scope up and saw a flight of black ducks circling, whirling above her in a widening vortex until they vanished in the fog. A heron, then an osprey followed, then smaller shadows swooping and darting as she moved.

"Let me look."

I moved aside and Jenny bent to the eyepiece. She groaned softly. "Oh Travis, she's so old and sick! Why is she doing this?"

"Because it's important. Because it has to be done."

I shielded my eyes against the sun and saw Aja moving steadily toward the smooth slope at the end of the spit, her pindgigossan swinging—a bent and tiny figure, but huge.

"It's about Neyashing, isn't it?"

"Yes."

"What will she do out there?"

"She'll call..."

22

"Spirits," Jenny said, watching Aja. "Say it. She'll call spirits out of the lake. Out of the sky and the rock."

"Yes."

Jenny left the telescope suddenly, folding her arms and turning away from the spit.

I watched Aja until she had reached the end and began to descend the slope. She would keep going right to the water's edge, perhaps beyond. She would go out where the footing is most treacherous, where the icy water would swell over her ankles and her legs. She would raise her arms....

Dozens of birds flocked above her now. Hundreds.

I watched until I could see her no more, and then I turned away.

Jenny was leaning on the rail, frowning, wearing that expression I had seen many times, the expression that said, *I love you, I really love you, Travis Niskigwun, but when you and Aja...*

I held out my arms. "Quiche me. Fondue me." She stayed where she was, so I went to her. "Sorry," I said. "Don't be afraid."

"I'm not afraid. I just don't understand."

I took her in my arms. I told her that I was frightened too, but there were many things we could never understand, should never understand. I told her that was what faith was for and love was for, to carry us over when there was no sense. I held her and kissed and smoothed her hair, and she nodded yes, but then without looking at me she said, "I have to finish this marking," and went back inside, leaving me alone on the porch with the telescope and the flocks of birds soaring over the place where Aja was conjuring at the end of the spit.

Three Women

I love Jenny, but she is very nervous in the presence of mystery. Many white people are like that. Mystery is either an emptiness that they must fill or a cloud they must disperse, and if they can't destroy it they'll hide it, pretend it isn't there, give it another name.

When you deal with the shaganashag, especially when you love them, you must be very careful. I've read about it. People made a big mistake with the first who came—the Norse, the Basque whalers and cod-fishers, Cartier and Champlain and the rest. They thought they were ignorant and innocent children. They showed them how to survive, how to hunt, how to forage and blend medicines. Before they knew it, the shaganashag were here to stay, straightening all the mysterious curves of life and death into lines, into fields and corrals, into square barns and houses and rectangles on maps, into all the numbers that so reassure them.

Even their language has to line up nouns and events, must become print and history, whereas ours floats in verbs and rhythms still, shifting and circling, blending into tales and possibilities.

When I was little I loved to hear my grandfather tell me stories in Ojibwe. He told many. He didn't wait for winter, the time when the spirits were asleep and could not hear and be offended. He told stories whenever he felt like it. He told stories walking, and paddling, and working in the little garden behind his cabin. He told me stories coming back from the hunt, and while we were cleaning pelts, and in the long evenings beside the stove.

Once he told me a story that took four days, a story about his childhood and a journey back to Ningotonjan Lake where his family had always wintered. We were sitting on an old black boom-log high on Neyashi beach. It was early morning when he began and I listened all day until Mother called me for supper, listened to how his voice rose and fell with the cadences of the lake, soft as foam across the sand. The next morning I ran down to the same log, and he was waiting there for me. He lifted me up beside him and went on with the tale.

It was like a river that I had left overnight and re-entered in the morning, that story, and like a river it passed over me and through me on its way to the Lake. Like a river it meandered and ebbed, meandered and flooded, always altering the land. Often Nimishomiss would describe a place I thought I knew, but as his tale swirled and rose behind some dam in memory or imagination the topography mysteriously changed and what he told me became narrative and landscape both.

I think I know now what he was doing. He was telling both the land and me into being, teaching me that the real world is not substance but story, that tales contain the only world we'll ever really have. He was saying that around the haven of our tales lies a great mystery.

On the evening of the fourth day Nimishomiss' story returned to Neyashing, and he drew a map on birchbark of the strange journey we had made together. I have that map still—a maze of river-curves and lake-circles, full of spirits, like nothing from any government.

When I use this map to tell our child, Jenny's and mine, my story will not be the same as Grandfather's. It will change again and again. Each time it is told the story will change, and the land with it, and the children who listen; and so, growing, they will be part of the land, at peace with mystery. They will not be afraid any more than the land is afraid, and will never want to reduce that mystery to something measurable, weighable, or countable. They will know the spirits of the land; they will know that the land is Spirit.

Jenny did not yet understand that, although she wanted to. It is probably harder for teachers than for others, because they feel they must cherish history, must keep it roaring along like some crazy train they haul students into. I used to tell her to do what we do—draw back, fade, absorb things the way an amoeba absorbs food, or Shield wetlands absorb misbegotten expeditions. But that advice often provoked outbursts. She'd accuse me of being soft and indifferent, or not standing up for my rights, of putting feelings ahead of principles.

Sometimes after one of her lectures about the need for continuity, I'd go out and stare at the Lake and tell myself that it looked the same way 7000 years ago, when somebody with skin the same colour stood on the same rock, before the pyramids, before the Babylonians and Minoans, 4000 years before the Trojan War.

I knew how she felt, why she wanted to run. I know how history and philosophy and pure reason can get such a shaganash stranglehold on you that you start eating yourself like a wendigo, from the inside out. And I know there are alternatives. I remember reading that line of Wordsworth for the first time, "a pagan suckled in a creed outworn." I loved it! "Hey," I said. "That's me!" If he'd been alive I would've phoned him right then: "Come on, Willie. We'll take a few days, go back into the bush and have a look at the spirit world. I'll show you how outworn it is!"

A lot of people worked hard to send me to university and keep me there. J.C. McTavish, first of all.

I guided for him when I was sixteen, seventeen. He was one of those sportsmen who hated to kill but who needed some excuse, some disguise like a rod or a gun, to get out into the bush. He used barbless hooks and never hit what he shot at. I liked him a lot. For two years he came up from Pittsburgh, and both years I guided him, four trips in all.

Often I'd look up from whatever I was doing on the camp-site and he'd be watching me, his eyes just slits. I didn't know then that he was dying. At the end of the last trip,

26

before the boat came for him, he asked me to take him to see my guardians, and he walked very slowly up the hill and said to Cutler and Barbara, "I am going to give this boy a sum of money. I am asking that you look after it for him. It will be enough to put him through university, provided he is careful and works hard. My lawyers will make all the arrangements, and you will hear from them."

I said, "I'll pay you back, Mr. McTavish."

He put his hand on my shoulder. "I know you will," he said. "You will pay me back in ways that neither of us can imagine."

And there was Steve Papovitch, my physics teacher in my last year of high school, when I was thinking about buying out Sally Dewney's trapline after Sam broke his hip and froze at Jeebish Lake. One afternoon Papovitch took me into the locker-room, and grabbed the throat of my shirt and twisted, and said, "Travis, I am going to talk to you straight in the head. Today is the deadline for filing university applications. You haven't filed one. You are going to do that now, even if I have to kick your ass all the way down to the guidance office, because I will not watch you waste your life on a freaking *trapline!*"

And there was Dr. Sinclair in my first year of university, when the city had just about destroyed me, when I had started to let my hair grow long again, started to hold it out of my eyes with a bandanna, who kept me after class one afternoon and said, "Mr. Niskigwun, I must tell you frankly that you make me nervous the way you stare at my scalp, bald though it is. Is it me, personally, that you hate?"

"No sir. But you talk of poetry and freedom, and there's no poetry in this place, or freedom either."

He looked at me a long time, saying *hmmm,* rubbing the back of his neck. Finally he said, "Do you have a bicycle?"

"A *bicycle?*"

"No? Well, here's my address. I want you to come to see me after supper tonight, because I have one to give you."

An old ten-speed. Rusty, dusty. "Needs work," he said, "but it's yours."

I cleaned it up and learned to ride it, wobbly at first but smoother each night. It became freedom for me, that bike. It was grace and flight, and sometimes in the dusk, coming back after a long ride through the parks, along beside the rivers, I would whistle the *kree kree* of a redtail hawk soaring on an updraft, because that was the only sound for the feeling that bicycle gave me.

At Christmas I asked Nettie Naponse, Bobby's grandmother, to stitch and bead a pair of moccasins for the Sinclairs' new baby, not the lumpy things you find in souvenir shops, but smoked deerskin, hand-worked and sewn so finely you could scarcely feel the seams. Nettie was nearly blind by then, but she didn't need to see. She said she thought maybe those moccasins would be the last pair she'd make, and she liked doing it for the people who had been kind to me. She wouldn't accept the meat I took over later on. She said she had enough. She said I should give it to Sally Pagoosie, who was having a hard time just then.

And there was Cutler, who got guiding jobs for me in the summers as the costs rose and the money Mr. McTavish left wasn't enough anymore, and Barbara, who sent packages every two or three weeks, tied with saved bits of string and containing many good things from people in Neyashing. Jimmy Pagoosie would always send down a smoked trout. Once a postal clerk made some crack about the smell as he handed me the package. Red haze came down. I grabbed his shirt and picked up the little sponge for wetting stamps, letting it drip across his counter and into his drawer of stamps, and I told him that if ever, if *ever* he laughed again about a package from Neyashing he wouldn't smell anything because that sponge would be somewhere up his nose.

A lot of people helped to send me to university. They meant well, but the city was awful. Sometimes I found I was holding my breath the way I would going by something dead on the trail. Sometimes I felt as if I were going through a disaster area where I couldn't do anything to help the survivors except not get too close, not catch what they had. Sometimes looking through my window I'd think, If this had happened overnight *everyone* would see it for what it is, *everyone* would understand! And that was the most horrible thing of all—the way people had adapted, accepted, collaborated.

I had grown up with sounds, not noises. Sounds dropped randomly into a great pool of silence. Moose-cough, bear-grunt, gull-shriek, raven-squawk, child-laugh. And underneath them all, the heartbeat of the Lake. I never got accustomed to that concrete-and-steel roaring, that blaring and screeching of traffic that never stopped. Once in the middle of the night I lunged awake shouting, "Cutler! Look out!" groping for my axe, reeling back from that noise coming at me like wendigos. Then there were smells. I knew the smell of death. I had grown up with that odour of flesh returning to Earth, nourishing fresh life as it went. But the city was pure carbon-stink, pure chemical, burning my eyes and throat, burning and eating everything it touched. Even the food tasted antiseptic. Even the water.

Most of all I missed colour. The city I remember is all grey—grey in its buildings, grey in its sky and its streets, grey in its very soul. Grey rain falls on it. Grey sewage spills out of it into a lake that was once green, long ago. People said, "But there are movies! There are plays and concerts, galleries and museums! There is clothing! Look at the clothes! Look at the colour!" But all of that was not real to me. It was like some crazy, swirling dream, or pathetic efforts to make up for something lost.

I missed real colour, tangible colour. In the bush, the plants are there always, saying, "Do you need red berries? Touch. Take. Do you need good medicine today? Some of that green leaf? This brown root? Take!" And all the hues of bushes in the wind, and pastel flowers so frail you have to brush them with the backs of your fingers to feel them at all, and shaggy spruce bark, and cones and needles, and mineral soil glinting, and millions of pebbles on any beach, each one a world of colour, and the quicksilver hues of water cupped in the hands to drink, all touchable....

I remember the first time somebody said, "Ugh!" when I went past. I spun around: three laughing students, one prancing in a little whooping dance. I went back so fast they didn't know what was happening until I had that man by the shoulder, spinning him around, saying, "What kind of asshole *are* you?"

People usually backed off and apologized, but a few times when someone commented on my colour, or my way of walking, or my father's cap, I had to take things further. A few times there was blood from noses and from places where teeth had been.

No, if I had not met Jenny I wouldn't have lasted in the city. I would have come back at the first of the winter, despite everyone who had tried to help. Jenny was my sanity in that labyrinth; Jenny led me through it, helped me out.

I met her in the museum. I went there often, that first autumn. It was a safe place. Those stone walls kept city noise at bay, and in the silences there was room for sounds—the footsteps of a guard, a child calling down a stairwell in the distance, the shuffling of a tour group led by the voice of the guide like toddlers on a string.

I liked most of what was there, except for the mummified animals. What a terrible thing, those rooms full of static agony, desiccated skin, dusty fur, glass eyes, cracked and painted lips. I felt the same about the Egyptian mummies, but I liked the rest of that gallery, and the Greek and Roman galleries. I spent a lot of time in pale sun that angled through high and dusty windows, listening to plundered relics whispering, "What happened? What happened? Are we *all that's left*?"

The medieval galleries bothered me, too—all those doughty pikes and breastplates, all those shields and swords and wiggly daggers. "See those things?" I said to a guard once. "That's what happens when people get crowded. They invent things like that." He looked hard at me and fingered his walkie-talkie, and followed me for a while, keeping his distance.

The totem poles I saw like huge dowels holding the place together. I loved to spiral down the stairs around them, down to the little airless rooms where they kept Indian artifacts. And when I listened there I heard something different from the whispers of the other rooms. I heard laughter, soft laughter spreading right through those walls and into Earth itself, spreading forever.

One afternoon down there I heard someone lecturing two rooms away in a clear, nasal voice. I walked through and found myself at the back of an anthropology class. One or two students glanced my way but most paid no attention. They were absorbed in making notes of what their lecturer was telling them. She was about 30, and she looked as if she were girded up for some serious trowel work deep in the dig. No nonsense. If necessary she was going to brush away every speck of nonsense with that toothbrush voice and leave only what was clean and measurable.

I listened. She had brought a tray of artifacts to illustrate her lecture on the Laurel Culture, and she pointed to others in the cases as she spoke. She was tracing trade routes, usuing stone tools and incised rim sherds to illustrate her point, which was that women moved with the traders, taking their styles with them like signatures, and it was therefore possible to reconstruct routes fairly accurately.

Then she moved on to other cultural influences, and as she did so she reached into the tray and brought out a birdstone, drilled lengthwise. She called it an atlatl weight. She said that such weights had been used effectively by the Aztecs against Spanish armour, and that later their use spread north.

I started forward. *Be patient,* some of the old people say. *Wait. Keep invisible. Watch and listen from the other side.* I say to hell with that. The shaganashag aren't going to go away, we aren't going to go away, and we're all learning. So, I moved. She stopped lecturing when I took the birdstone out of her fingers, and she made little incredulous noises. "Ex*cuse* me!" she said finally, and held out her hand.

"Birdstone," I said, giving it back. "Nice one. Jasper."

"Do you mind very much if I go on with my class?"

"No, I don't mind. But that's a birdstone, not a weight for a spear-thrower."

"Really? Well, perhaps then you'd like to explain its *real* use."

"Sure. They were for..."

But it was wrong, wrong. The *real* use. The real *use.* How could I explain that? Fool! I grinned, scratched my head, started backing up. In that right-angled place with the woman holding the birdstone like a weapon, in that place where time was being measured out, how could I say *spirit* without demeaning the word? How could I begin to tell then and there, on command, about the loons and cranes and whiskyjacks who were guides and guardians, about the ravens who were message-bearers, or the owls who were keepers of the soul? How could I tell a woman who was looking at her watch about the grave-markers in Neyashing, or about the bird-poles older even than the paintings at Lascaux? How could she or any of that amused class understand how one might perch birdlike high on a cobble beach, freed by hunger and by cold to soar into vision? How could I talk about amulets borne on journeys, about being magically lifted out of peril?

"Sorry," I said, backing away with my palms raised in surrender. "Sorry."

You see? the old ones said to me, out of their things in the cases. *You see what happens when you try to cross? Now you know.*

Now you will watch. Now you will be quiet.

I stayed in another room until I thought the class had gone. But when I started back toward the stairs someone was waiting for me—a girl with broad frank eyes and a smile like a cool drink. She was wearing a white shirt with the cuffs folded outside the arms of one of those pleated jean suits. One hand was in a pocket, the other held notebooks against her breast. Her glasses were pushed into her hair. She said, "Would you tell me about birdstones, please?"

Jenny.

What chances! If I had never met her I might never have known what love was. All my life I might have believed that love is what happens in Thunder Bay hotels.

That first summer she took a job at a lodge in the cottage country near the city, where every bit of the shoreline was owned, and squabbled over, and built on. It was awful, she said.

I worked on the highways that summer, and I worked hard, sweating the city out of me. Every morning I'd hike three miles along the back trail out of Neyashing to the work yard, and I'd climb into a half-ton and start the day. We'd clear rockfalls, repair washouts, do cold-patching and fix the guardrails where drunks had driven through. The only part of the job I hated was cleaning up the bodies of dead animals. It was such an empty way to die, alone there on the road, blinded by lights; I used to take the corpses into the bush so they'd fertilize something, go back into life again.

But all day I was close to the Lake. I could see it, smell it. At lunchtime I'd stop in high, quiet places where I could watch it for an hour undisturbed, never the same from one day to the next.

Sometimes at five o'clock I went out with the other guys, but not often. Their idea of a good time was to go into the pub in town and drink some beer, or maybe go down to Thunder Bay and find some girls. I didn't enjoy that much; I

33

was thinking of Jenny most of the time by then.

Usually, I'd hike back to Neyashing. I was living in Tommy Solomon's place. Tommy didn't own it, of course, because nobody in Neyashing owned anything. Tommy just used the place for 30 years or so after the old guy who built it died. By the time I left to go to the city, Tommy was pretty old himself. He used to spend a lot of time just sitting out on the Council Rock, looking at the Lake. Sometimes he'd go down the trail to Aja's, leaning on his stick, and the two of them would sit on a log and watch the waves roll in, not saying anything. That fall Tommy just disappeared. When nobody had seen him for two or three days, Cutler went over to see if he was okay, and found the place just as neat as Tommy always kept it. But Tommy was gone. On the night of the full moon he had taken a walk into the hills behind the Palisades, and he never came back.

"Might as well live in Tommy's place for now," Cutler said when I came back that spring. "Tommy won't mind."

So, after work I'd come home to that cabin. I'd have a bath in the stream, in the pool under the falls, and put on fresh clothes, and sit for a while just listening to the sounds of Neyashing bloom in the silence, out of the hum and whisper of the Lake. I'd hear gulls far out over the spit, or above the beach if there were fish guts to be had, if Jimmy Pagoosie's *Matchi Maung* was coming in. I'd hear Cutler's truck rumbling home behind the dunes, and maybe Cutler's kids shouting and laughing up in the woods, and someone calling among the other houses, a long slow call like an animal longing for her mate, and someone else splitting wood, and a hawk crying in little circles, high up, and the breeze humming in the pines. Sometime before dark I'd eat and read any letter from Jenny and then, thinking about her, take my telescope out on the Council Rock and find the Pole Star and the dippers with Draco twisting up between them, and then Arcturus and Bootes, and then Alphecca and the Corona, and then I'd begin my travels for that night.

34

I missed her. I missed that woman. I wrote many times asking her to come. Then without any warning one evening at the end of August I saw Cutler's truck coming home as usual, only this time when it pulled into the parking-place both doors opened. He'd brought Jenny from the station. She lifted her pack out of the box and brushed her hair back and looked where Cutler was pointing, up the hill at my place, telling her something, and there was a fresh sound in Neyashing—Jenny's laughter.

I didn't go to work the next morning. Cutler dropped into the yard office and told them I was in bed and probably would not recover from what I had caught before I'd have to go back to school. He asked them to send my cheque to his box in Schreiber, and they did that.

Her first day was one of those cool, still ones that is no longer summer and not quite fall. I showed her all of Neyashing. I showed her the bathing-place, and where I thought I might build a sauna, and what repairs I planned for the cabin. I showed her every one of the houses, and told her who lived in each of them.

We walked the beach, and then out to the end of the spit. She shaded her eyes and looked out across the Lake, and over the bay to Neyashing nestled on its slope at the base of the Palisades. "It's wonderful here," she said, turning to me. But she didn't see the spirits there, and I didn't show them to her.

It was dusk when we walked back. I took her up behind the beach to the old campground, and then to the graveyard in the meadow. I showed her where Mother was buried, and the headboard with the little bird that Cutler had carved for her.

Holding my hand she bent down to read the dates, shaking her head. "But she wasn't even 40! What was it? How did she die?"

"TB."

"But Travis, nobody..."

"I know. Nobody dies of TB anymore. But she did."

"Were you with her?"

I nodded. "She was in the hospital, but she wanted to come back to Neyashing at the end, so Cutler and I went and got her. There were some doctors in our way. Nurses too. They had different priorities than we had, I guess. Different obligations. Anyway, we brought her back." Suddenly, remembering that, I sat down like a child beside her grave. "The last thing she said to me..."

Jenny kneeled beside me, held me, her lips close to my ear. "No," she was saying. "No."

"Was..."

"It doesn't matter, Travis."

"Yes, it does matter. She said, 'Travis, I would like a drink of water, from out there, please.' And she was looking at the end of the spit. I took a jug and ran out there, and reached down as deep as I could to get the cleanest, coldest water for her. And when I was coming back Aja met me on the path, and she said, 'Travis, your mother doesn't need that water, now. But I do. I am a very thirsty old woman who has walked all the way out here to be with you. Come. Let's sit for a while on this rock and admire those carefree spirits.'"

"Travis," Jenny said, holding me and rocking me. "Travis." And then, when I was able to stand up and put my cap back on, "Do you think your mother would have liked me?"

"She would have loved you. You would have been laughing together in five minutes. She would have said, 'Travis, something terrible has happened to this woman. Look how pale she is, like she's been living in a cave all winter. Her skin is like chewed doeskin, her hair is like dead grass in November frost. Travis, you must take her out into the sun! Take her into the wilderness and make her well again!'"

"I'd like that," Jenny said, walking home through the meadow in the dusk. "A canoe trip."

36

Next morning I carried my canoe and gear down to Cutler's truck, and he drove us 30 miles up-country to Joe Five-Foot Lake. "When are you going to grow up, n'sheemenh?" Cutler asked as he helped us unload at the glittering edge of the lake. "When will you become a responsible man like your older brother, who is now going to get back into his family truck and drive to work. You think life is a game? You think you can just play in the woods forever? Don't you know it's much more important to *suffer?*"

He wrapped us both together in his big arms, kissed Jenny on the forehead, and pulled my cap down over my face. Then he walked back to the truck with one hand raised, goodbye.

It was the time of the first frosts. Already a few tamarack and poplar were beginning to turn, rich gold against the dark green of the spruce. It was the time when geese were moving, and when the smoke from campfires spread like cool mist across the water. During the days we travelled; during the nights we listened to wolves, or to moose trumpeting in the marshes, or to rain drifting across the roof of our tent. And all of that for Jenny was like coming home, a confirmation that Earth was healthy still, in spite of everything, and that there was a place for her in the heart of it.

She had profound doubts and dreads about the Earth. Sometimes I would find her curled into a shivering little ball, knees pressed against the bridge of her nose, saying, "We're not going to make it. It's too late." And I would hold her and tell her that it was not too late at all.

"But anything we can do is so *trivial.*"

And I would say, "Not trivial, just small. The way all life begins."

Later, the morning Aja moved, we went out on the Council Rock together. The fog had gone completely and all Neyashing lay in sun. The bay sparkled. There was no sign

37

of Aja, but clouds of birds still wheeled above the end of the spit like a shimmering question. Children called like sand-pipers below, chasing each other in circles around the beached boats, splashing through the shallows. As we watched, one small boy went off by himself and sat in the sand, shading his eyes against the glinting sun. He pointed to the end of the spit and called to the others, but they were absorbed in their game and paid no attention. He wrapped his arms around his legs, rested his chin on his knees and stared.

"Who's that?"

"Vincent Misabi."

"And there's Tega. And who's that?"

"Where?"

"That one. There."

"Marilyn Pagoosie."

"And that one? With the red cap."

"Snubber Naponse."

"God, Travis, these kids are growing *up*!"

"Know what I think? I think we should put a little Travis down there with them. A small Jenny."

She turned and laid a finger on my lips.

"We should not delay. I am getting senile. Impotent. Next week might be too late."

"At 92 you'll be impotent, maybe."

"Jenny..."

"I'm afraid, Travis. I'm just afraid. You know that."

"Look, the Lake's open now. The rivers are open. Let's take the canoe down the shore for a few days, maybe go inland awhile."

"I have a job. So do you."

"To hell with the jobs."

She shook her head.

"This is more important than jobs. You know that, Jenny. You know it is."

She shook her head again and started back toward the

cabin with her arms folded. I called her but she kept going, and again we were apart, two people troubled by the crying of an unborn child, a child lost in a place of too little faith.

We should have gone into the wilderness. That is where healing is, and sanity. When you go into the land you go into yourself also, in dreams, in memories, in talk with the spirits and the dead. Things get clarified in the wild. That is why wise people go back, go in, when they are troubled, and why men like McTavish sometimes pretend to hunt or fish. That is why youngsters fasted in vision pits long ago, and why, in the end, men like Tommy Solomon return alone. And that is why, if a person is calling for help, some friend, some guide prepared to be as close as self should take him back to the wilderness where the wendigos inside him can be freed.

I should have taken Jenny right then. Along the shore and up one of the rivers. Deep enough to lose ourselves, deep enough for Jenny to be assured again that Earth was good and there was hope for children in it.

But she wasn't ready. She shook her head and folded her arms and turned toward the cabin.

Then, at that moment, the fourth part of the Sign came—the flock I had listened for all night. I heard them, or felt them, turned, and saw a glittering shape lifting from the end of the spit, like a frenzy of minnows when a big trout rises. Gulls, I thought. But they were not gulls; they were not swooping and diving like fretful gulls. They were one purposeful body spiralling up in ever-wider circles.

"Jenny!"

She looked where I was pointing, shading her eyes with both hands. "Oh, beautiful! Swans! Whistling swans!"

Without speaking we watched them diminish to a radiant cloud, and then to a white speck far over the Lake, and then to nothing. Long after they had gone and the thin clouds had shifted like veils behind them, we kept watching the place where they had disappeared. Jenny held my arm in

39

both of hers. Finally she whispered, "Travis, they're going south.... They're going *back*!"

It was noon before Aja came off the spit and onto the beach. I waited for her, splitting wood. Her progress was agonizingly slow, and at last she sank down on an old boom-log. I put on my jacket and cap, and Guaranteed and I went down through the meadow and across the dunes.

She was rocking a little, smiling, listening to something I couldn't hear. She did not open her eyes when I sat beside her. "Aniin, Travis."

"Bojo, Ajawac."

I sat beside her in silence, listening to the Lake-talk, the wind-talk around us. At last I said, "You have made a long journey."

Her eyes were thick clouds with specks like stars shining through. Her hand groped for mine and closed on it. "There will be more travelling yet."

"Another day, Aja."

"Yes. Another time."

"You should rest now."

She felt for my shoulder, and I stood up and raised her very gently. She groaned as her knees straightened. We started down the beach to her cabin. She stopped often, reaching down her open hand whenever she did so, and Guaranteed laid his cold muzzle in her palm. When we moved he stayed close beside us, guarding her other side.

Inside her cabin, bending low under the dried herbs and tubers hanging in clusters from the ceiling beams, I lit a fire and warmed soup for her. When it was ready she stayed where she was on the bed and took the mug in both hands. "Miigwetch, Travis."

"Aja, it is possible to give too much."

"Never. There are always fresh streams, always rivers filling me."

I sat beside her, held her, helped her sip the broth. "You

40

must rest then. Until you are filled again."

She nodded, drinking. "A little rest, yes."

I started to get up, but her bird-claw hand clutched my sleeve, and her eyes like speckled shells sought my face in that twilight under the dried herbs. "I will need you, Travis."

"Aja, I'll be leaving. When they begin I'll be going..."

"No. You will not leave."

"Aja, Neyashing's..."

"You will not." Her fingers tightened, shook my arm gently. Her voice was a whisper. "I need you."

"Aja, I can't help. I've thought, Aja. All winter."

"There is a place you must cross for me. Do you hear, Travis Niskigwun?"

"I hear you, Aja."

She grunted, nodded. "Good. Go now. Giga wabamin miinwa."

"Giga wabamin," I said. Guaranteed got up and left with me. I closed the door softly and we went down the path together, back to the beach.

Ajawac.

In my childhood memory she is always old. Always she looks like the old-woman-Indian on postcards, all seams and wrinkles, beyond further ageing. Always she wears the same bandanna across her forehead, the same felt hat—maybe a fedora, once—on her white hair, the same moccasins sewn so fine and tight in the old fashion that you could hardly feel the seams, or the same leaky rubber boots tied on with twine around the ankles. Always she has the same way of looking, her eyes clouded, her nostrils flared a little, searching the breezes like an animal's, her mouth always ready to loose soft and toothless laughter. Always she is nodding and trembling. Always her lips work with songs or charms that no-one else will hear. Always she is stiff and bent, like copper twisted into a lump of grotesque pain, pain beyond all curing.

Usually she moved little; she watched. She watched from the pile of driftlogs in front of her cabin at the western end of the beach. She watched over all our childhood. She watched us play, she watched us fight, she watched us come and go from school. Later, she watched us make love. Nobody cared; there was no point in trying to hide from her, even if we wanted to. She was Ajawac; she was everywhere, always. Having her there was like being watched by the sky, by the Lake, by four hundred million years of rock.

She was a centre, Ajawac, a living centre.

That was why her moving was so momentous when it happened. All play would cease. We would stand close together watching her slow passage up the beach, hearing her laughter like the coughing of the Lake in the caves on the western point, hearing her anger hiss like a breeze in aspen.

Always, when she moved to the end of the spit, the birds moved with her.

No-one knew where she had come from, or exactly when she had arrived. The story of her appearance floats above time and logic as buoyantly as the little craft that brought her. I have heard it many times, and each time differently. Perhaps in the centre there is a kernel of fact. Perhaps not. Perhaps facts have long since been layered-over by the forgetfulness and invention vital to truth. Think of an agate. Think of those many-coloured bands that formed as the magma cooled. The beauty of the stone is there, in them, not in the core of fact....

Long ago, perhaps a century, children were playing where the boats were drawn up, at the base of the spit. Some claim that it was not the children who found her, but fishermen setting out. Others say it was neither, but a young woman and her lover. Still others, a wise fool, a shaman chanting to the dawn. But in the version I prefer there are children playing among the boats....

It is early morning, early summer. There is fog in the bay, the kind of fog that moves through the spruce forests even when the Lake is still. It beads on the moss and bunchberries, glistens on spiderwebs in the spruce and on the old-man's-beard hanging from dead birch.

The children run barefoot like bobbing sandpipers across the beach, gathering wood. Suddenly one of them pauses. Something is strange. Something has changed during the night. The child raises a hand against the glare of the new sun and calls out, pointing to the end of the spit, now just visible in the wraiths. Something lies on a rock ledge there. Something stranded. What? A small, dark shape, not a log. Birds hover above it.

The children run for a canoe, and in moments they have launched it and paddled out. They find that the strange object is itself a small canoe, less than five feet long. From it come birdlike sounds. They lift it onto the higher safety of the ledge and cluster around.

Inside they see a tikanagan, a cradleboard, wrapped in white doeskin such as some of their grandparents keep only for special ceremonies. The boy who first saw the canoe reaches in to draw back this doeskin, which hangs like a veil from the bar of the tikanagan. Under the dangling talismans lies an infant. She is smiling. The faint sound they had heard was not a cry of fear or discomfort, but laughter.

All those things—the cradleboard with its charms, the exquisite doeskin, and the little canoe itself—were eventually stored in the rafters of Willie Joseph's house. But not before everyone in Neyashing had minutely examined them, and puzzled over them, and experienced their strangeness. Neither the small canoe nor anything in it had been made within two hundred miles of Neyashing, the women could vouch for that. See the fastenings on the tikanagan? How finely they were sewn! See the charms? How peculiar they were—the loon's foot for grace and power in the Lake; the tern's wing, wrapped in otter skin at the joint, to give magical fleetness between the breakers and the storm; the bear's ear, to listen for the safest landing; and the tiny woven spiderweb dangling on its thong, turning all ways to entrap evil. Even the tiny moosehair-embroidered pouch was strange, for there was no umbilical cord inside, as there should have been.

No, no-one in or near Neyashing had made those things; no-one, perhaps, on this side of the Lake.

They folded them into a parfleche and laid them in the little canoe in Willie Joseph's rafters, and there they would remain untouched until the girl herself was old enough to reclaim them.

In time, they held a naming feast, and several elders spoke. Each had considered carefully. One suggested that she be called Nenegean, One Who Frightens Children, because of the strangeness and fears surrounding her arrival. Another, pointing to the significance of the place where she had landed, suggested Nawajibigokwe, Central Rock Woman. A third, remembering the fog of that morning and the mystery from which she had emerged, proposed Gagewin, Everlasting Mist. But it was a child who offered the name finally agreed upon: Ajawac, Wafted Safely Across.

In later years, Ajawac would wave away the suggestion that she had crossed the Lake in that tiny canoe, borne on gentle south winds. "Not across," she would say. "Out of. Out of the Great Body." And she would gesture outward, lifting and spreading her arms to show the majesty of the way the Lake had given birth to her.

Ajawac: girlchild delivered precisely to Neyashing, precisely to the end of the spit. What a miracle! She had not been swallowed by a cresting wave, or dashed against the cliffs, or snagged in the thickets of some cove to be gnawed by blackflies, pecked by ravens. Not only had she survived against all odds, but she had survived laughing. And by this fact alone they knew that spirits watched over her, and that her life was magical. Henceforth, the future would reveal itself to her in talismans leaping from a heated scapula. Cast beaver bones would bring her news. In certain places, the four winds would speak to her alone. At certain times, she and the Lake communed.

She grew. Her laughter flowed like glancing sunlight in Neyashing; everyone there was young again in the childness of that child.

One morning, to their horror, the Josephs awoke to find a family of otters sitting placidly outside their door. They were terrified because to discover an amphibious mammal on land, especially in front of one's house, is the surest harbinger of death; and there were five of them, waiting, braced upright on their webbed feet! Everyone was paralyzed but Aja, who laughed when she saw them and went out to them, extending her arms in welcome. And, the story goes, when the otters saw the child they began the peculiar dance they often perform in water, stretching their necks and weaving from side to side, hissing and uttering guttural cries of welcome. She knelt and offered her hands to them, and they came to her and laid their muzzles in her palms.

Some say she was eight when this incident occurred. Others say six; still others, five.

Later, the same homage was paid by other creatures, the amphibians, the mammals and finally the fish. There are many stories about the fish. In one, the whole eastern half of the bay shimmered at dusk with the undulating bodies of trout and whitefish like an immense, three-quarter moon in the water. And the child bent and dipped her hands while they swarmed close. Another story tells how a sturgeon, an ancient nahma larger than anyone had ever seen slid half its length onto the beach and lay docilely while she spoke to it, and caressed its barbelled snout, and helped it return into the depths of the Lake.

In yet another story, the little girl stood in a wild storm on that point where the Lake had given her to Neyashing, and gazed serenely upon a terrible cat, a primeval horned creature with eyes of fire.

And there were always the birds. For hours they would surround the child—waterfowl and shore dwellers, birds of the marshes and the forests, seed-eaters and raptors. All came. Loons bobbed silently, wild eyes fixed on her, bills touching her fingers. Eagles and ospreys rested beside her. Warblers and whitethroats perched on her head and shoulders. All came; all waited upon her.

Some said they obeyed her commands and often flew on errands to the limits of their endurance, but others claimed that she caused spirits from the rock to possess them, investing them with unnatural

45

splendour and vitality. And, it was true, the end of the spit swarmed with spirits. White and black, orange and pink, green and blue, they lived in the labyrinth of veins in that metamorphosed gneiss, energies old and as sublime as Earth. When the sun blazed they hovered like shimmering clouds of insects; when the Lake rolled they gambolled in its green translucent flesh....

When we were children we would venture right out on that glass-smooth slope, searching for the spirits in the rock. Sometimes they were near the surface and clearly visible; sometimes they were pale and undulating shapes in the dark folds of the Lake. When we got older their grotesque anatomies gave much earthy merriment, and when we laughed we heard myriad tiny voices laughing with us. Later on, disappointed and bitter and mauled by life, some of my friends stopped going to the end of the spit. They had reasons: those spirits would pull you down, they said; those rock creatures would twine sinuously about you and drag you into the deepest caverns of the Lake. But the truth was that they had grown afraid of the spit as they grew afraid of life.

I have never been afraid out there any more than I am afraid of Aja. I go in all lights and weathers, but I am happiest when the great Lake is rolling, roaring, sliding frothy paws across the spit. I love to be there then. I go right out into the wind and the spray, right down among the frolicking spirits on the slope, where the footing is most perilous.

Men Between

Jenny talked to the man in the truck with us. I drove.

We were clear of Schreiber and on the highway when I realized where I'd seen that broken-up look he had, as if something had crumbled inside and the pieces were starting to fall out. As if the man were held together by skin and guts.

In veterans. Combat veterans.

Baraga Naponse, Bobby's grandfather, had that look. He had been a sniper at Passchendaele, and until the day he died 50 years later his eyes were half-full of rubble. And Weass Faille's Uncle Selim had the look from Sicily, and Harry Trowbridge still has it a little bit. It's the look of men betrayed.

Joe Weiss had that look. I met him working on a Domtar cut near Minnitaki Lake. He had trained rangers in Cambodia in the sixties. He didn't sleep much. He worked harder than any two other men, but the slightest sound in the night and he'd be on his toes and fingertips. Anyone with sense could tell you should keep lots of quiet and distance around that man.

In our crew that summer was a young guy in his first year of college. Very big, very loud, not too smart. He thought it was funny to sneak up behind Joe one coffee break, getting pretty close because of the noise of diesels idling nearby. Nobody knew what he intended to do because he never got the chance to do it; one minute he was creeping forward with his arms spread like a sumo wrestler's, and the next he was on his face unconscious.

He was in the hospital for a long time, in traction. He had a broken leg, some cracked vertebrae, and a crushed testicle. He was lucky it was daytime, lucky Joe caught himself in time.

Joe used to walk a lot in the night, and that was all right up in the bush where he didn't bother anyone and nobody bothered him. Even when he went into town it was usually all right. But one night in Thunder Bay two cops in a prowl car hassled him because it was early morning and he looked rough and had no ID. One of them pushed him, and they both grabbed his arms. Joe told me later he didn't remember anything after that until he was in the police station giving car keys and handcuff keys to a desk sergeant who was getting up very slowly. The cruiser was outside with the two officers in the back seat, handcuffed together.

Some Vietnam veterans could *feel* people getting close, as if their skin had grown special sensors. They had to be away from the crowds, away from the streets, back in the bush. Way back. A few went up into Oregon, and northern Washington, and British Columbia. A few came across the Lake.

Twice when we were boys Cutler and I found abandoned boats—tanks, motor, everything—swamped and half-buried on beaches east of Neyashing. They were old battered things that guys had bought for next to nothing somewhere on the south shore—Grand Marais, Duluth, Marquette—and had driven across on a fairly calm night. When they hit the beach they just kept going straight north, up toward the height of land and sometimes a long way beyond, I guess. Into the taiga. Into the tundra.

One of those boats was at the mouth of Nanabush Creek. It had been there for awhile, and the Lake had twisted it like a pretzel and ripped it open. The only reason we saw it was that the camouflage paint had peeled off the bright edge of the hole. There was no trail left by then, so there wasn't anything we could do. We stood for a while looking at it, looking at the bush, thinking about the guy back in there somewhere.

The second boat we found about 40 miles east of there, moose-hunting. A fresh trail led back from it and we followed it, although the police had told us after the first boat—when they'd traced the motor back to us—that if we ever found another we were to let them know immediately and under no circumstances follow any trails. Under no circumstances, they said.

We followed the trail; it was easy, even in the dusk. Up the creek about four miles Cutler crouched suddenly and held his arms out like you do when you know something's wrong but don't know what it is. He went lower and lower, feeling carefully ahead of him in the near darkness. I knew there was something, too. No animal. Nothing natural.

Cutler's nose kept working back and forth across the breeze, lower and lower until finally he was looking at his boots. He reached out with two fingers and drew them toward him about a foot off the ground, like a priest giving a slow-motion blessing. He grunted. He reached back for my hand and brought it forward gently until I felt what he had felt: nylon monofilament, tight across the trail.

Then, aged twelve, I learned what a trip-wire veteran was. I learned how afraid a man could be. The monofilament stretched around a perimeter, with feeder lines leading into the centre. What they carried were impulses, touches, the slightest trembling of that outer line that would indicate that something or someone had touched it.

In the centre was a man.

We worked in and saw him, sitting in a tiny clearing in the moonlight. He was very long, maybe six-six, six-seven. His hands were laid on their backs with the fingers curled up, and his bare feet rested on their heels. Across his knees was a weapon like nothing we had ever seen. It was stubby, and instead of a wooden stock it had a triangle of black tubing. In fact, everything about that man was black—gun, clothes, skin. But it wasn't a natural black on his skin; it was smeared on.

All those lines led in to him, each one tied to a finger or a toe, and by tensing them just a bit he could keep the perimeter line taut. He could sense twenty different places on it, like a spider in the centre of a web. The gun, that was for anything that touched that monofilament.

He wasn't asleep but he wasn't awake, either. Something in between.

We watched him for almost half an hour, and then Cutler gave me the sign and we faded back out of his web, back down to the beach and into our canoe and out onto the Lake.

When we were around the first point I said, "That guy, he woulda shot us!"

"Fuckin' right," Cutler said.

"Why?"

"Spooked."

"Should we tell?"

"Naw." Cutler stopped paddling and bent down and scooped up some of the Lake to drink. "Nobody's gonna go back there, Travis. Nobody's been back in there twenty years. Leave 'im be." After we started to paddle again he said, "Might keep an eye on 'im, though. Over the winter."

Cutler's three years older than I am and he had a lot more experience then. He knew abut Vietnam and assassinations, and tortures, and mass killings. "They call it history," he said. "Social studies."

"But there must have been a lot of good, too. Must have been. Or else we wouldn't be here."

"Oh sure, but that's not history. They call that something else. History's just the bad stuff."

I thought about this. "But why remember it?"

"Progress," Cutler said. "The idea is you're supposed to remember what's gone wrong so that you won't do it again."

"That's the *only* reason?"

"I think so."

We paddled in silence for awhile. Clouds hid the moon. The Lake was beginning to roll from a storm in the west, and the wind picked up and whipped spray off the crests. I dropped down and sat on my heels with my butt against the rough cedar of the ribs. It was comforting to paddle that way, safe in the Lake with the canoe rolling. But I kept thinking about what Cutler had told me, and after a while I said, "It doesn't work, does it."

"What?"

"What you said about history. That we're supposed to remember, and not make the same mistakes. If it worked, there'd be less bad stuff, not more."

"Yeah," Cutler said. "I guess."

"Maybe there're so many mistakes they can't miss 'em," I suggested.

"Maybe they like 'em."

"Maybe they just can't tell the difference anymore."

"Maybe," Cutler said.

We landed and carried the canoe up and overturned it beside the tent so it would give some protection from the wind, and then we got inside, into our blankets. We lit a candle and ate some supper there, listening to the Lake crashing and the storm rolling in like loads of big pine timber at the mill. It was a good thunderstorm, all right, what the old people called a *mekumiguneb,* an ice-bird, the last thunderstorm of fall. Behind it would come the snow. I lay with my chin on my fists watching the whole scene through the front flaps, the Lake churning white and the storm driving into it, absolute black, full of roaring and lightning flickering like snakes' tongues.

"Might be here awhile," Cutler said. We were chewing jerky and Mother's special bread baked with beer and molasses, thick as Christmas cake. "Might miss some school."

"To bad," I said.

Rain lashed across us like somebody flinging buckets of water on the tent. A moment came when all the lightning in that storm gathered in the bay in front of us and danced there, bolt after bolt crackling into the surface so fast we couldn't count them, and in the afterflash of every strike thunderbirds took flight out of the water, trailing fire and water, and we heard them scream.

I felt magical, watching that. Immortal. I wanted to go out there into the midst of them. I wanted to fly with them. I even started to put my boots on, but Cutler held me back. "Don't be a goddam fool. We're close enough to getting fried right here."

So we drank lukewarm tea out of our thermos, and we watched. The storm lumbered off to the east. A tree on the far shore got hit and blazed for a minute like a huge torch, and then the lightning moved on to the next bay, and the next, and soon we were left with only the wind and the rollers crashing.

We were dry and warm, but I kept thinking about that guy up in the bush, hunched like a black spider in his web. He'd be drenched and cold, and hungry, maybe. On the edge of sleep I said, "Cutler?"

"Mm."

"You asleep?"

"Not now."

"What does spooked mean?"

"You know what it means, Travis. You know how a moose acts when he scents you."

"I now, but it's more, isn't it?"

"Yeah. Yeah, it is." After a minute he said, "Remember what happened to Emmet Shabogesic when we were in Grade 5?"

"He got lost."

"That all you remember?"

"Unh huh."

"Well, the whole school was called out to look for him. Jimmy and I picked up his trail pretty soon. He was kind of simple-minded, Emmet. Didn't know enough to wait in one place. He started running, across creeks, streams, rivers even. Through thick bush. The trail went in a big circle, and it was *fresh*. Jimmy and I couldn't figure it out. We'd be right on top of the kid, so he couldn't help but hear us, but we wouldn't catch him. Finally Jimmy said, "He's scared of *us*!" And he was right. *Emmet was running away from us.* When we realized that, we caught him easy. Angled him off and tackled him running across a slope. He screamed like a bobcat. Scratched like one, too. Screamed gibberish, wild-eyed, like he didn't know any of us. He was looking at us but not seeing us. Seeing something else, wendigos maybe. Not us. He was spooked. That's what spooked means, n'sheemenh. It means not knowing your friends from your enemies."

I woke once in the night. The wind had died and the Lake was calmer but still rolling. I wiggled my head under the wall of the tent. It was cold and clear, so clear the stars were a thick blanket of light. I found the stars Aja had taught me, beginning with Keewaydnanung in the north, and then up to Chiogima-anung right above me, and then down to Shawananung in the south. I fond Ojeeganung, and Maung, and Makwa-shigun, and then I drifted beyond them into other dimensions, deeper and deeper into space and dreams.

The next day we took the canoe up Splitrock Creek and found moose-sign in the new frost, a cow and a calf. We tracked them and shot the calf at mid-morning, and by noon we had him cleaned out and cut into four pieces and slung on carrying poles. There was a lot more good meat in him than Cutler and Mother and I could use before it spoiled. We'd give some to Aja and other people in Neyashing who needed it, but we took some up to the guy in the hills, too.

It didn't take long. He was only four miles in and we carried just fifteen or twenty pounds of tenderloin, just a little gift, a reminder that not everybody was out to kill him. When we got to his perimeter we heard chopping, so we figured he'd started a cabin and might be all right for the winter. We set the meat down and gave the nylon a couple of little tugs, and then we faded.

We went back a few times that winter just to make sure he was getting along all right. I guess we felt responsible because we hadn't told anybody he was there, and we couldn't be sure that he even knew what winter was. He might have been from down south where they have little floppy flowers all year long. Here it gets so cold you can hear the northern lights hissing. So cold wolf calls hang like pure ice and trees split like gunshots.

We usually went before dawn, fast, on snowshoes. Always we took something and left it where he'd find it, and always when we came back what we'd left was gone; so he knew someone was helping him. He knew he had friends. He'd built himself a pretty good little cabin, with a chinked roof and a fireplace made of stones hauled out of the creek, tucked under trees, so if you weren't looking for it you'd never know it was there. Somehow he got mortar, and tools and winter clothes. He must have had maps and money; he must have found his way out to the highway and flagged the bus to Thunder Bay.

Once we saw him in a snowstorm. He was standing in a little grove with his back to us and that ugly gun on his arm. In February we told Tommy Espaniel about him. Tommy's trapline ran within ten miles of the cabin, and he could side-track and be down there in less than an hour with his dogs. He had a team of seven purebred Siberians, Tommy, and on the trail they were the fastest, quietest things you could imagine. Like ghosts. And Tommy's like them. Just nods or shakes his head when you speak to him. Moves like a shadow. He is probably the quietest man I know, but he wasn't always that way. Years ago he used to be very sociable, very attractive to ladies. One winter up north of Nipigon he fell in with a crowd that thought he was *too* sociable with their ladies. So when they were drunk one night, they castrated him.

After that Tommy got very quiet—just worked his trapline and ran his dogs. Sometimes he'd be gone two or three weeks, and when he came back to Neyashing you'd never know it unless you saw smoke from his cabin or heard that high-pitched growl Siberians make when they're hungry.

Tommy nodded when we told him about the guy in the woods. He'd keep an eye on him. That man would never know he was being watched unless he ran into serious trouble—split his foot with an axe, say, or got real sick.

He stayed two winters. One morning in the spring of my fourteenth year Tommy tapped softly on our door, lifted his chin to the northeast, and said, "Fella's gone. Pulled out."

Cutler and I went back on the last of the snow. We found all the trip-wires cut and the cabin emptied of everything except the carbine and a few boxes of ammunition. "I think," Cutler said, looking at the gun on the table, "he's telling us he's not so spooked anymore. I think maybe he's saying thanks."

"What'll we do with it?"

"You want it?"

I shook my head.

We got rid of it. Going home we dropped it into a river pool where fresh, strong currents had worn the ice away.

"Years ago," the man beside Jenny was saying. "I was just a boy."

"Why did you come?"

"My father brought me. He and some other men had a hunting-camp on an island off Rossport. I went there for a week one fall. I've forgotten everything about it except the dead moose. And that." He nodded toward the Lake. Most of it was hidden under fog, but just as we crested the first hill a patch of silver shone through, tranquil and majestic.

I let Jenny ask the questions. I drove and listened, listened to the resonant, confident way he spoke. He was a man used to being listened to, used to keeping up appearances.

She asked, "You have relatives in Neyash…in McDonnell's Depot? Friends?"

"No." He turned back for another glimpse of the Lake.

"On holiday?"

"Yes, that's right. Just a little holiday."

"Not many people come for holidays, especially this time of year. You have a place to stay?"

He looked at her in surprise. "You know, I haven't even thought about that. I guess I just assumed there'd be some sort of hotel, or boarding-house."

"There isn't," I said, driving.

"Nothing at all? No motel on the highway?"

"Nothing."

"Well, there's Bobby's cabin," Jenny said.

"Cabin? Is it right there? Right in McDonnell's Depot?"

Jenny nodded.

"Might be for rent," I said.

"Could you show it to me?"

"Sure," I said. "It's on our way. How long will you need it?"

He looked at me in surprise. "Why, I don't know."

"No plans?"

He shook his head, looking at me as if I might know the answers to these simple questions. "No plans at all," he said.

"You know who he is?" Jimmy Pagoosie asked out of the darkness. "You know who that sonuvabitch *is*?"

I was on the Council Rock.

When we had dropped the man off, when Bobby Naponse had rented him the cabin, and I had parked the truck and we had climbed the hill to our place, I asked Jenny to go ahead and make a fire in the sauna. I'd be right along, I said. Then I went out and waited. It wouldn't be long; I'd seen Jimmy Pagoosie in Bobby's kitchen having a beer, and I knew he'd be right up, if what I guessed was true. Ten minutes later he came out of the fog like a scrawny ghost, a *jebi*, eyes red with fatigue and beer and outrage. "You know who that man is, Travis?"

"Michael Something."

"Gardner. Michael Gardner. And you know who *that* is?"

"He didn't say."

"Just the president of Aspen, that's all! Just the president of goddam fuckin' Aspen Corporation, that's who you chauffeured over here!"

"He didn't tell me that."

"Well he told Bobby. Gave 'im his card. Little shiny letters—'President and Chief Executive Officer.'" Jimmy

56

squatted down on the Council Rock and rubbed Guaranteed's ears and neck vigorously with both hands. "So what now, Travis? What do we do now? We got the goddam president right here! Jay-*zos*!"

I said to Guaranteed, "Get Cutler." And he was gone into the darkness with a grunt and a clatter of claws across the rock. It took him maybe 45 seconds to cross the bridge and snake up the path to Cutler's house 200 yards away, and it took Cutler only a few minutes more to come back down the same path and across the bridge and out onto the Council rock saying, "No peace! No peace! If it isn't the kids it's Barbara. If it isn't Barbara it's her mother. And if it isn't her mother it's my little brother, Travis, sending his ugly dog to scratch my door when I'm having supper. This had better be good, n'sheemenh. This had better be important."

"We have a visitor."

"*Distinguished* visitor," Jimmy said. "Down in Bobby's cabin. President of Aspen."

Cutler grinned. "Bullshit."

"No. It's true. I brought him from the station."

"You bro..." Cutler came close and looked hard at me from under the brim of his cap. Then he looked hard at Jimmy. "It's true?"

We nodded.

"Then let's go get the fucker!"

"And do what?" I asked.

"Do what? *Get* him! Work him over!"

"Wouldn't help."

"It'd help me, little brother. It would sure as hell help *me*!"

"No it wouldn't. They'd just throw you into the slammer, and we'd all have to look after Barbara and the kids till you got out."

He went to the edge of the Council Rock and stood with his feet braced, staring into the fog. "What, then? You tell me."

57

"We've gotta do *something,*" Jimmy said.

"What *will* you do?" Jenny asked later, in the sauna.

"I don't know yet."

She rolled her head against the wall to look at me. "Anything?"

"I don't know. I don't want to think about him now. I don't want to think about any of it."

"Well," she said tiredly, a woman not wanting any arguments, "looks like now's your chance."

"I know. I know." I inhaled the wet-cedar and spruce-smoke smell of the sauna, and closed my eyes and let the heat work. "You were going to tell me something. In Schreiber. Just before we picked him up."

"Yes, I was."

"You said it was important."

"It was. It *is.*" She smiled and let her head rock from side to side, eyes closed. "But not tonight. Tomorrow's soon enough. When we're clean. When there's just the two of us together."

"In Schreiber it was urgent. It wouldn't keep till we were out of town."

"It'll keep now," she murmured. "Remember what you keep telling me? There's no time in Neyashing."

I grunted. "Yesterday there was no time here. Now there is. It's down in Bobby Naponse's cabin."

"But not in our sweat lodge," Jenny said.

I stood up and dipped water out of the barrel and poured it over my head. It felt like cold breath running down my body and into the cedar boards. I splashed another dipperful across the firestones. Live steam swirled hissing up to the ceiling and back down to enclose us.

"Wonderful," she said. She climbed to a higher bench and linked her fingers across her neck under her hair, and bent until her head came down between her knees. She stayed like that a long time, letting the steam loosen and stretch all the muscles in her back and neck and shoulders. Then she came down and stood feet-apart near the stove reaching up into the steam with her eyes still closed, bending to touch the toes of first one foot and then the other.

I went out and dove into the stream, into the pool at the bottom of the falls. I curled up in it like a fetus. I stretched out on my back and opened my eyes to stars as big as grapes and an orange moon rising.

Jenny came down the path after me, laughing and gasping with the shock of the icy water, and then we ran back to the sauna giggling like kids, and I stoked the fire and got another pail of water from the cabin.

Three times we did this, and then when we were so weak we could hardly move we made love in the last of the steam, just holding each other, just looking at each other and breathing into each other, and at last her eyes grew huge, and I pressed her low on her back and held her neck under her hair, and her love for me swelled, and gathered until at last it moved in gentle waves from her belly into mine, like the waves on the Lake after a storm....

Later that night she spoke out of her sleep, out of her dream. She said, "Oh Travis, keep us, please...."

I waited, but the only sounds were her breathing, and Guaranteed groaning, and the swollen stream tumbling down to the Lake. I held her and kissed her. I didn't ask her who she wanted me to keep, besides herself. I knew she had spoken out of the deepest place in her, the place where she kept her fear.

That was a big place, for a big fear. It was what stopped her from leaving her job and coming to Neyashing, that fear. It was what stopped us from having a baby.

Jenny had read and travelled, and she had seen what was happening in the world. She knew absolutely that what was coming was awful, knew the future would be unfit for any child.

The packsack she carried off the train every Friday night was full of mail, and over the weekend she would read every brochure from her organizations. There were dozens. She belonged to groups concerned about beluga whales and grey whales and fin whales; about seals and dolphins and other sea creatures suffering terrible deaths; about eagles and gyrfalcons; about bears and wolves, rhinoceroses, hippopotami and tigers; about spills and wastes and toxins; about corporate greed and political connivance. They knew about many, many horrors—nuclear fallout and acid rain; lakes lethal with chemicals; dwindling gene banks; rainforests cut away; freaky holes opening in the ozone; blue whales roaming in a futile search for mates.

All these organizations had newsletters and membership drives, fund-raising drives and endless emergencies that required Jenny's attention. She would read everything, drawing up into a fetal position and pulling her big sweater down over her knees. Sometimes she would say, "Awful! Terrible! I don't *believe* it!" But usually she said nothing at all, just read herself into rage or depression.

They were all worthy causes. I knew that. I was fond of Earth too, but I was most concerned about Jenny and Travis, and Neyashing, and whether there'd be enough food for everyone this winter. That sort of thing. Short-sighted, Jenny called me. Maybe, but I didn't like those mail-opening times when I'd learn about all the things it'd take me a thousand lifetimes to fix. Guaranteed didn't like them, either. He'd pick up bad vibrations and start growling and scampering around, trying to cover all sides of the cabin at once.

I knew about these things, but Jenny *felt* them. For her they were personal insults that had to be redressed. At university she was always taking part in marches and demonstrations, always getting both of us in trouble.

Like the peace march in our second year, for example: we were at the end of a long column snaking through the city and bringing all traffic to a standstill. Behind us came a solid phalanx of police motorcycles, and behind them were six officers on chestnut mares, their cloaks flared like cossacks' across the haunches of their mounts. Behind *them* was a crowd whose signs declared that they were in favour of using, right then, whatever was waiting on the launch pads. Some of those people wore hardhats and waved flags. They looked very dark, very earnest. An occasional ursine growl rose from them, as if they were about to tear through the cordon and fall on us.

"Don't look back," I said.

Jenny looked back. "Can you *believe* those signs?"

"They have their point of view."

"I would like to get one of them alone for two minutes! Just *two minutes....*"

She pulled her arm but I hung on. I didn't even want to think about what would happen if Jenny, scarf flying, headed back past that squad of police. All crowds unsettled me because they became mobs too fast. I had seen them, at hockey games, at rallies. So, just being part of that mass made me nervous enough, and having a surly gang of mouth-breathers at my back made me more nervous still.

I held on to her, but a bit farther down the street she got away. We were passing one of the residences when a large, plainly lettered banner fluttered out of the second-storey windows: NUKE THE WHALES. Raucous jeers and cat-calls drifted our way.

"That's it!" Jenny said. "That is bloody well *it!*" And suddenly she was heading across the boulevard and straight for the entrance of that building. A few residents had already spotted her and were beckoning, cheering her on.

I caught her but I couldn't hold her. "Jenny, Jenny! Do we really need this? Let's..."

"Fade? No, I'm not going to fade, Travis. And yes, I really do need this!"

And then she was through the door, up the stairs, down the corridor, and into somebody's bedroom shouting, "Cretin! Troglodyte! Do you think that's funny? *Do* you? Is that your idea of a joke, you ignorant, neckless..."

And there was a huge man, an immense man in a BORN-AGAIN BOOZER T-shirt at the window, holding an end of the banner with one hand and fending off Jenny's jabs to his shoulder with the other, a man whose several friends were cheering him on, saying in a voice like a foghorn, "Hey lady, who the hell, what the hell, who do yuh think..." And then, spotting me, "Hey, buddy, this your broad? You wanna get her off me, do us both a favour?"

"Broad! *Broad*!"

And I was trying to keep my back to a wall and at the same time catch one of Jenny's flailing arms, certain that the least I could expect was to get my nose broken again.

Then, mercifully, the police arrived and we were escorted back down the corridor, back down the stairs toward the sunlight, although Jenny was still very agitated, shouting, "Pigs! Pigs!" up the stairwell, and I was trying to convince those policemen that she did not mean them, but rather the occupants of that building whose banner had personally and profoundly insulted her.

Jenny. I loved her by then, and already I longed for a child of that love, a child in Neyashing, and already she was saying, "Oh Travis, how can you *talk* about that? Look at the mess we're in. Look at the *world*."

Years later, when she came out to Neyashing to be with me on weekends, she was still looking at the world through all those newsletters and grim reports, and after she had read them she'd sit trembling and making sounds of self-disgust, as if she wanted to shiver right out of her skin. She said she felt dirty. "If you know about a crime and you don't do anything, you're an accomplice, right? Until you start to fix it, you're part of the problem."

"There are too many crimes, Jenny. Too many problems."

"But you can at least *start,* can't you?"

And off she'd go, raging, hitting blindly at whatever in herself, in all of us, was allowing these disasters to occur.

And, because she loved me so much, or because I was rooted there, the restless lightning in her came to earth through me. She called me indifferent, smug. She told me to do *something*. She waved brochures, letters, magazines. I should join hands with her around some half-built reactor, or picket the New Zealand consulate against a dam, or write to Queen Elizabeth about the radiation of the Irish Sea, or go to the trial of some company getting its wrist slapped for dumping poisons.

Sometimes I'd just fade when she started up. I'd take my coffee out to the Council Rock with Guaranteed and we'd look at the Lake awhile, feel the rock. I told her once about something I had read, how to imagine the age of Earth: spread your arms wide and clip one fingernail, and you have just snipped away the whole record of human life. "So," I asked her, "does it really matter so much?"

Or at night I'd take my telescope out and escape into space. I'd find a dying star, or a whole solar system blowing away like cotton in a candleflame, and I'd say, "Jenny, I could've worked two million light years and not made the slightest difference to what's happening there."

"But we're *here*," she'd say. "And we have a choice."

Once she really got to me. Once. She made up a list of what was in the Lake and therefore in me: mercury and lead in my brain; nickel and beryllium in my lungs; cadmium in my liver and kidneys; dieldrin and chlordane in my testicles; antimony in my heart. She said I was a hypocrite, that I really didn't care about Neyashing or the Lake. If I did, she said, I'd find ways to fight back.

Little red curtains came down. I pointed at her. "Back off! Don't tell me what I feel, and the next time you come down here leave that shaganash shit behind!"

"Racist! Just remember, Travis, *it's your shit too!*"

That was as far as it went. Guaranteed made growly and disgusted sounds at us both. Later on the Council Rock, when I had drifted far, far out into the Cygnus Loop, she

63

came up behind me in her moccasins and put her arms around my waist. "I love you," she said. "I love you, Travis Niskigwun."

Orbits. Orbiting.

I buried my face in her hair and neck and held her and told her I loved her too. She cried. I longed to say something about a child, but I was afraid. I was afraid she would tell me how dioxin turns fetuses into masses like lasagna, and how, even if the child were born normal...

I've been frightened by lots of things, but what scared me more than anything was the chance that I might listen to her and not want babies anymore, and that other people might be feeling the same way, all over the world, and that *they* might stop having babies too, because things seemed just too much.

What would it be called if mankind gave up? Not suicide. Not even genocide. Anthropocide?

Suicide I knew about. Three people I knew had come to rail lines in personal forests, and lain down on them. Others had smoked or drunk themselves away, or overdosed on chemicals like my friend Maynard McTavish, who I liked to remember laughing at his broken finger that night in Duluth, not the way he looked in the morgue. Other people had just grown so tired and careless that they asked a river or a winter to wrap its white arms around them.

I knew something about genocide, too. Enough to understand that it has many other names.

But the other, the giving-up completely: once I had a job with a wrecker, tearing down old houses in Jackfish. They'd been insulated with newspapers that by then were so old and brown that most of them crumbled into powder when the boards came off. But a few we could still read, and in one of them, I found this:

Remnants of the once-powerful Seri Indians, dancing in barbaric hysteria about the scalp of a white man, renewed tonight their

64

fantastic pact of tribal suicide. In the dim light of the moon, the copper-skinned natives nightly race along the beach and through the desolate wasteland of Tiburon Island, off the shore of Lower California, to re-enact stirring scenes of the days when the tribe numbered thousands. Now numbering less than 100, the Seris, discouraged by disease and poverty, have sworn that the tribe shall die. In the weird dance they don their deerskin armour, pick up long-unused bows and arrows and dance about a pole from which dangles a human scalp. Their "curse of the hated white man" completed, the Indians gather about their venerable Chief, Juan Tomas, and take an oath to remain childless.... Old Chief Tomas said those who do not remain childless may be banished to Mexican villages, where their children eventually would intermarry and the tribe's blood would be lost....

What frightened me was that we, all of us, the whole species might decide to do that without ever discussing it, without even really thinking about it. Maybe we had already *decided* on some level we knew nothing about....

But at other times when Jenny would say, "Oh Travis, look. Look around you. Is this the kind of world you want to bring a child into? *Is* it?" I *would* look around. I'd stand up to do it. I'd look at my canoe in the rafters waiting for spring and open water, and at my paddles on the wall, and at the bed and warm stove, the clean floor and rugs. I'd breath in the smell of cedar and good food. I'd look out at the Lake, and the spit, and Neyashing tucked up behind the beach, and I'd say, "Yes, it *is* the kind of world I want to bring children into. Yes it is, goddamit!"

Two years earlier Jenny persuaded me to go west, to a protest. Afterward I was glad that I had gone, but at the time she had to work hard on me. "Travis, *Travis,*" she pounded her knees the way she did when she was truly upset. "It's the same struggle, don't you see?" She pleaded harder than ever before, and somewhere in the midst of that pleading she called it an act of faith. "Trust me," she said.

"Have faith. Isn't that what you're always telling me? Please, trust me on this one."

"All right," I said. "Okay."

She took a week off school. Afterward they docked her salary and her superintendent told her not to let politics interfere with teaching.

I drove to Thunder Bay and we got on the train there and rode west, watching the Shield and the forest roll by, then the prairies, and finally the canyons and the mountains. We leaned against each other to sleep because we couldn't afford a berth. Vancouver, Prince Rupert, the ferry to the islands—fog and the iodine smell of the sea, and porpoises arcing off the bow, and then trees I couldn't see the tops of.

Jenny wore a big floppy hat from some other protest years before, bright with beads and silver buckles. At some point I took off my cap and tied my red bandanna into a headband.

We waited quietly in the fog, laughing and telling stories, and when we heard the diesels coming we stood up and linked hands with the Haida, across the road. A long line of quiet people, that's what the truckers saw on their way to work that morning. What we saw was a string of truck headlights above a red flasher.

The policemen got out, and settled their caps, and conferred with their hands on their hips. Then the sergeant came up and said good morning, and asked if we would please step aside so the trucks could cross the bridge. When we didn't move he asked again, and when we still didn't move he pulled the court injunction out of his tunic, and read it, and asked again.

Later I laughed at the strangeness of it—that Travis Niskigwun, who had cut his share of pulpwood, should be stopping other guys from making a living doing the same thing, and going nose-to-nose with a Freightliner to do it. But I didn't laugh then. I stood there with those people. They were soft and gentle as grey jays, those Haida, as if they were made of fog and fir-boughs, and I would have

66

stood wherever they asked me to stand. I guess I would have gone under the trucks if it had come to that. But it didn't.

When the policeman finished speaking there was silence for a few minutes, and then one of the elders, a little white-haired woman with bone charms at her throat and a sea-otter pindgigossan at her waist came shuffling down the line flipping her hands as if shooing birds away. "Nobody gets hurt," she said. "Nobody goes to jail today."

We backed off the road, and the policeman said thank you to her and tipped his cap, and the trucks rolled through. Cameramen filmed. They filmed a smiling man from the company and another from the government, both saying economics, economics. They filmed the little white-haired woman watching the trucks go past, tall as half a tire, tall as a tree. And they filmed a fierce Jenny with her arms spread out against the mossy bark of a Western cedar that would soon be bungalows and birdfeeders. She looked like a little frog on the tree; its trunk just kept going up and up and up until it vanished in the mist.

Later we all walked in the rain on the beach at Tanu, and the little old lady told us what had been there once. She described the houses that had stood in the crescent behind the beach with all their doorposts and mortuary posts, and the great poles towering in front of them like dowels holding earth and sea and sky together, every one a proud offering. She recreated them. I don't know how long we stood there; I remember only her voice spiralling down those imaginary poles, slipping soft as drizzle into the cobbles of the beach.

They were right, those people blocking the road. They were right in a way that had nothing to do with law. They were right in the way bedrock is right.

The night we brought Michael Gardner to Neyashing, I dreamed about them. In my dream there were no trucks, no roads or red flashers, no saws screaming. In my dream there was only a village, Village, Neyashing. In my dream the spit rose out of the Lake and pierced the sky through the Pleiades. On top, instead of a bird, sat the little Haida lady, and she came spiralling down around it, laughing and freeing animals and birds and fish from her sea-otter pindgigossan. In my dream the creatures of the pole took life and vanished into the forest as she touched them, and the spit itself vanished, and there was nothing but the Earth and the old woman with her arms raised and her pindgigossan empty, calling my name.

I got up. I wrapped a blanket around myself and went out. I looked at the moon first, and then at the silver plate that was the Lake, and then at the Council Rock.

I knew who I would see there: Aja.

Ajawac was waiting.

Meetings

It had started the summer before, with a blue-and-white surveyors' truck bumping down the hill into Neyashing.

Surveyors are trouble. Always. Their coming means somebody thinks he owns the land. I hate finding their tracks. There's nothing worse in the soft forest than surveyor's orange, so bright you can taste it. You know when you're coming to a splotch of it, because you'll smell it—the sweetish smell of green foliage dying—and there the thing'll be, another imaginary corner, a bright dead place in the living woods.

Cutler would always spit and curse when he saw one of those stakes. We'd put down our rifles and packs and go to work on it, and soon we'd have it out of there. We were in our teens when we started doing that. We called it unsurveying.

68

When the companies figured out they had something more on their hands than casual vandalism, a police car came down the hill into Neyashing, its antenna whipping. Alex Wilkinson was the cop on duty. Alex is as lean and hard as birch. And sensible. And honest. He wears his cap visor straight across, level with his eyes and his mouth. I like Alex.

He was around a lot when Cutler and I were small. Sometimes Mother would get so depressed she would just sit all day on the steps with her hands pushed up into her sleeves, staring at the Lake and often at those times Alex would come around in his bush clothes with his canoe already on his truck, and he and Mother would disappear for a week or so.

She was always better afterwards; she'd be laughing and her eyes would be alive again.

Down came the prowl car and stopped behind the dunes, aerial twitching. Alex got out putting his cap on. Bad sign: for social calls the hat stayed on the seat. He strolled through the dunes and across the beach, one hand in a pocket. Cutler and I were repairing our boat, caulking her, and there was the little *thunk-thunk* of the mallet on the caulking-tool.

"Morning Cutler, Travis."

I said, "Hi, Marshall." We all called him that though nobody remembered why.

"Bojo, Marshall." Cutler kept working.

Alex leaned over the hull and pushed his hat back. He took off his sunglasses and dropped them into his shirt pocket. He waited awhile, squinting across the bay, out to the end of the spit. Back in the car his radio squawked like a raven in a box. He said, "I have a little problem, Cutler. I'd appreciate your help."

Cutler stopped hammering. He put down the mallet and settled his cap to listen properly.

"You boys were hunting last week, Ranger Lake way." It was neither a question nor a statement. Something between.

"That where we were, Travis? Ranger Lake?"

I shrugged. "Maybe."

The Marshall nodded. He kept looking out at the end of the spit and beyond, to the horizon. "You boys know what's going on up there?"

We waited.

He waited.

Cutler cleared his throat. "Lots going on, Marshall. Moose sign all over. Wild rice, too, coming back at the old place in the narrows."

"I mean the development."

"Development?" Cutler frowned. "Oh, you mean all those holes in the bush. All that slash. You mean that fire that got away from them last week, burned out a few square miles. You mean that garbage in the creek. Travis, I think the Marshall means that road going in there, all that crushed gravel. That what you mean, Marshall, development?"

No-one smiled. "Yes," Alex said. "Also stakes. Little orange stakes."

"We've seen those, haven't we Travis?"

"I think so, Cutler."

"Little bright buggers, eh Marshall?" Cutler made a shape with his thumb and forefinger. "Square?"

"Square, yes." Alex pursed his lips. "Those little stakes are very important to some people, boys. Some people, to buy land in that development at Ranger Lake spend more money than you and I could make in twenty years. And then they spend a lot more to have surveyors put in those little orange stakes."

I rolled a tab of oakum between my fingers. I scuffed a piece of driftwood in the sand.

"Strange thing, isn't it Cutler?"

"Strange, Marshall. Sure is."

"But what is even stranger is how serious everyone gets about those little stakes. You wouldn't believe how judges, for example, worry about those stakes. If they lose any of them they frown and ask questions that nobody can answer. Then they tell cops like me to go out and find the answers."

I dug into my pocket for some more jerky and tossed a few pieces on the overturned hull. I took one myself and started chewing it. Alex took one too, and nodded to tell me that it was pretty good jerky.

"So," he said, "then I have to get into my bush clothes and hike back up to where those stakes ought to be."

"Long way, eh Marshall? Ranger Lake."

"Long way. All around Ranger Lake. Up and down those survey lines. And sure enough, I find a lot of places where there ought to be stakes but—" Alex spread his hands "—no stakes!"

"I guess somebody messed up," Cutler said, chewing. "Lost some stakes."

"Somebody did. And if I were to discover that the person who lost those stakes was wearing a pair of size nine Kodiaks with a split across the left heel, like this, do you know what I would not do?"

Cutler stopped chewing. His eyes went glassy, like a statue's. Nobody looked down at the tracks of his boots in the wet sand. "What would you not do, Marshall?"

"I wouldn't tell the judge. If I did, he'd have the information written down and it would cause great trouble. You know how powerful things get when they get written down, Cutler. That evidence about the split heel, it might get somebody sent away from the Lake, from the bush, put someplace where he couldn't do what he wanted when he wanted. Go hunting, say. Go fishing. Caulk a boat. That is very good jerky, Travis. Did you make that jerky?"

"Mom and me."

Alex nodded. He took Cutler's cap gently in his large hands and turned it around and set it on Cutler's head backwards. Then he bent down until his eyes were level with Cutler's, about two inches away. "So, I wouldn't tell that judge. Instead, when I got back from Ranger Lake, tired

71

and sweaty and all chewed up by blackflies, I'd just come down to Neyashing, and find whoever lost those stakes and *kick his ass!*"

Cutler sniffed and pulled a finger across his nose. He looked at the Lake and then he looked at Alex. He took off his cap and shook his long hair out of his eyes. His eyes were black as obsidian. *Okay,* they said. *Close enough.*

Alex took a fresh piece of jerky and walked back through the sand to his parked cruiser. We watched the car turn around and go slowly back up the hill and out of Neyashing.

Later that afternoon, Cutler and I took the boat out to where we had set our gill-net, and hauled it up. We had a good catch—six trout, a perch and a whitefish. It was after dusk when we got them cleaned and reset the net. Cutler didn't say anything, but when he started up the engine he headed west, away from Neyashing, and we went a few miles up the shore to the bay where Alex Wilkinson lived alone. It took just a minute; Cutler went up, I held the boat. When he came back he didn't have the whitefish anymore. It was wrapped in moss inside a plastic milkbag, hanging beside the door where the Marshall would find it when he came home off his shift that night.

We didn't stop pulling up surveyors' stakes. We were just more careful not to embarrass Alex Wilkinson, not to leave evidence that would cause him to lie when he said, "So far, Your Honour, we have nothing to identify these vandals," or whatever it was he said.

Surveyors. They seem so harmless, with their neat little instruments and funny signals, waving to each other. They're usually lean, too. Trim. Smiling boyishly. But they plant evil seeds. They plant numbers. More numbers grow behind them. Behind them people say, "I *own* this." Behind them cities come, and fights.

They came down to Neyashing in a new 4x4, blue, with white pinstripes, and passed me on my way to work that Monday morning. I caught a glimpse of equipment stacked behind the smoked glass, and rolls of surveys piled against the window. COOTES & JACKSON, SURVEYORS, said the sign on the door.

That day they started working out from benchmarks, and over the next two weeks they surveyed all of Neyashing, from the base of the Palisades right out to the end of the spit. Nobody spoke to them; nobody went near them. They were invisible men, waving to each other. I took one close look at them through the scope but I didn't want to watch them. "First surveyors," I said to Cutler, "then lawyers." He nodded. We didn't talk about it; there was nothing to talk about yet.

The problem was that Neyashing did not exist. Not legally. There was no *Neyashing* on any map. There was no sign on the highway. Before the screen of trees grew back after the last logging, tourists would often pull off the road to admire the view of Neyashi Bay. They could see the ends of the beach, and the spit reaching out, and the islands like dark water creatures drawn by the sunset. That was all most tourists wanted to see, that postcard view. They'd snap a picture and drive on to the motel.

Once in a long time a strange car actually drives right down to Neyashing, but most are discouraged by the sheer awfulness of the first quarter-mile, by the potholes and ruts and rocks that make you want to pull your oil-pan and differential up into your belly, and by the signs at the turning place: UNOPENED ROAD. USE AT OWN RISK and JACK'S TOWING AND REPAIRS, 973-8572.

Most cars turn around there and creep out again, leaves brushing their windows and granite scraping their axles; but around the curve past the turning place the road is just fine. We get Isaac Kohotchuk to run the township grader over it twice a year and plough it in winter. Occasionally we fill in the potholes.

At the bottom, at the base of the spit, the road passes the site of the old village, where any child can go anytime and find stone tools just under the turf, dropped when skin lodges stood there. That was where my family came in the spring from their camp on Ningotonjan Lake, and driving past I always like to imagine it the way it was—the lodges open to the breeze, canoes on the bay, kids on the beach. The graveyard's up in behind, in a meadow bright with fireweed and bunchberry, but you wouldn't see it unless someone took you there. Farther on is the old ice-house, all that's left of McDonnell's fish plant, and then our cabins in the dunes, and then the end of the road and the parking-place I share with Cutler and Jimmy Pagoosie.

The map name for Neyashing is McDonnell's Depot, and the spit is McDonnell's Point; but those names are just masks. Neyashing is behind. When people ask, "Where *is* Neyashing?" we answer, "Oh, down the shore a piece."

Down the shore and into our memory. Into our guts. Into our blood.

It's all illegal. It's always been illegal. Indians didn't need anyone's permission to live there for all those hundreds of summers. The first trader didn't have a deed when he built his post up behind the dunes. No lumberman owned that land. McDonnell just squatted there while his boats mined the Lake. No-one ever owned Neyashing.

At least, that's what we thought. But we were wrong. Sometime, someone bought it. Then it was sold again and again, many times. Once owned, it got ownable.

"First surveyors," I said to Cutler, "then lawyers."

So, that fine autumn morning when I saw something glinting, coming slowly down the hill, and fixed the crosshairs of the scope on it, I was not surprised to see one of those foreign cars with four interlocking circles across the grill and tires that always look flat. It stopped at the foot of the hill for a minute, as if the driver was looking for something, and then it came on slowly, rocks nibbling its axles. The next time it stopped there was no reflection off the windshield, and the scope took me right inside.

74

Behind the wheel was a thin-faced fellow about 30, wearing a leather coat and a flat Greek-fisherman hat. He unrolled a big survey, looked at it, bent down to peer up at my cabin and checked the plan again. Then he parked behind our trucks. He took a briefcase out of the back seat, locked the car, and started up the hill.

I carried the telescope inside and came out with my cap on and sat on the Council Rock, thinking *Here it comes*, watching him climb the last of the path with the briefcase in one hand and the roll of surveys in the other.

When he got to the top he paused to catch his breath. He looked at the cabin, at the sauna, at the woodpile, and he didn't see Guaranteed and me on the Council Rock until Guaranteed growled, a throaty sound like bees swarming, and the man looked.

"Well hi! Hello there!" He came out onto the rock, shifting the briefcase into his left hand.

Guaranteed growled again, and showed teeth. He lay poised and bright-eyed in the shadows at the edge of the Council Rock.

The man stopped and laughed a nervous, treble laugh. "Some dog you've got there! What sort of dog you call that? Kinda flat, isn't he?"

I saw a flash like dark lightning in Guaranteed's right eye, and I knew he was about to take a mouthful of silk stocking and ankle. "N'dai." I said in Ojibwe, "Get Cutler. Get Jimmy."

And he was gone.

"Eric Morrow."

I took his hand. I didn't shake it, or squeeze it. I took it. Held it. Firm handclasps are very important to businessmen as a sign of sincerity and decency—which means that the harder a stranger grips your hand the more wary you ought to be. But I have found few men prepared for this handshake I use when I am genuinely interested. I held Eric Morrow while I looked at him hard, in the eyes. His eyes were like

75

clear pools, like big sunlit rooms, like empty vaults. I saw no horizons. Only verticals and diagonals. Only climbing lines.

"Travis Niskigwun," I said, and let him go. "Can I help you?"

He laughed that high laugh again and gave me a business card with letters that glinted in the sun and told me he was a lawyer. "Other way around, I think, Mr. Niskigwun. I'm here to help *you*." He waved his arm over the village. "Help all you folks here in McDonnell's Depot."

I laid his card on the Council Rock beside me and placed a stone on top of it. "Do we have a problem?"

"I'm afraid you do. Yes. *Not* insoluble, mind you," he spread a hand to prevent my jumping to disagreeable conclusions, "but a problem. Very definitely a problem."

"Take a seat. Open that map. Explain this problem to me."

He glanced at the Council Rock and saw that it was damp, strewn with chunks of moss and bug, so he didn't sit. He pulled up his beige slacks and squatted with his back to the Lake, unfurling the survey and holding down the edges with the shiny tips of his shoes. I laid stones on the other corners, and there it was, an eagle-eye view of Neyashing as I had seen it many times, flying home with the Krautlet. It was a very expensive and powerful map. It smelled of surveyor-time and lawyer-time.

"This is not a problem," I said. "This is Neyashing."

"Neyashing, yes." He rubbed his nose. "I understand you call it that. But the name isn't a problem. The real problem is here. And here. And here." He pointed to the little rectangles that were our homes. "These are the real problem, I'm afraid."

"Don't be afraid. Tell me why."

"Because, you see, you're squatting. You have no right to be where you are. Nothing in law..."

He stopped abruptly and began to straighten up, laugh-

76

ing that treble laugh and staring wide-eyed past the west side of my cabin to the path leading down from the bridge. Cutler and Jimmy were coming, with Guaranteed in the lead.

"Those are just two parties interested in this problem," I said, but I saw why Morrow was nervous. Cutler had on his black high-crowned fedora with the beaded band and the eagle feather an Arizona girlfriend had given him years ago. It was a ridiculous hat but it emphasized the way my brother walked—smooth, one foot flat in front of the other, so that the brim of that hat cut a knifeline across the pale trunks of the aspens. He was carrying his 30 / 30 Winchester in one hand and an open twelve-pack of Blue in the other. He swung the beer high when he saw us. "N'doo neezaniz kina gego n'dayan!" he shouted.

"*What?*" Morrow leaned down to me.

"He says he is well armed and dangerous," I said.

Behind Cutler, Jimmy Pagoosie danced through the shadows like a crazy ghost, a *jebi*. He'd been in his shop welding some part for the *Bad Loon* when Guaranteed found him, and he hadn't bothered to wash. His arms and face were smeared with sweat and grime from the torch and the scrap steel, and he was still wearing his floppy grey coveralls and welding glasses that bulged like weird eyes out of his forehead. His black cap was turned backwards, so that in the shadows he looked headless above the glasses. He was cackling and swatting loose-wristed at his ears, brushing away phantom bugs.

I knew what was coming. Usually episodes that began like this ended with Jimmy twitching and drooling and making obscene sounds while Cutler leaned close to some victim and said, "Look, look, you'd better just do what I'm asking because I don't know how long I can keep this crazy bastard *off* you!"

I tried to signal that the whole routine wasn't really necessary because all we had here was a poor fractured lawyer from

Thunder Bay, but it was too late. They were into it.

"Eric," I said, "meet my brother Cutler. And Jimmy Pagoosie, Cutler's friend."

Cutler set the wet twelve-pack on the survey and reached over to grab Eric Morrow in a double-handed, elbow-snapping handshake, saying, "Any friend of the kid's!" And Jimmy crowded in from the side, slapping him on the back. "How ya doin', Eric? How ya doin'?"

Morrow glanced behind him but there was nothing but cliff—a hundred feet straight down to Neyashing. "Fine," he said. "Just fine."

I said, "Eric tells me we have a problem."

"Piss on it!" Cutler shouted. "Problems, a day like this, we don't need. What we're gonna do, Eric my friend, is have a few beer, go back into the woods, and blow the shit out of some living things!"

"Yeah!" Jimmy said happily, swatting imaginary bugs.

Morrow made little no-no gestures with both hands. "Thanks. I'd like to. I really would. But I didn't bring any clothes."

"What's wrong with them clothes?"

"Well, they're not exactly..."

"You don't have to dress up to go with us, Eric."

"Also, I have appointments."

Cutler shrugged. "More time to drink, then. When we run outta this you can drive us over to Nattie's for more, okay Eric?" He popped caps off and handed bottles around. He downed a beer in one gulp, making a straight pipe from mouth to stomach, howled, yelped, did a quick-step dance in his black hat.

It cost him, that performance. It cost him. Cutler hated beer. He never drank it anymore. In fact, he had given up drinking completely as the kids came along and finally there were four of them to feed and clothe and make dentist appointments for. Any alcohol made him sick now, especially beer.

"Drink up!" Jimmy Pagoosie shouted, waving his bottle at Morrow and sloshing beer froth across the map.

Morrow sipped, glanced at his watch, and squatted again, pointing to the survey. "What I want to show you..."

"Get drunk, blow the shit outta something!" Jimmy shouted, one foot in the air. "Gotta get my gun, Cutler!"

"Right!"

"The old twelve-gauge!"

"Right!"

"Wrap some more wire around her, blow the hell outta anything!"

Morrow laughed nervously. "If one of you..." he pointed to the carton of beer in the middle of his survey, and then lifted it off himself. "Could I show you something? Could I explain this?"

"Cutler," I said. "Jimmy. Take a look at Eric's problem."

We hunkered down in a little semi-circle.

"It's very simple," Morrow began.

"Good! So're we!" Jimmy cackled wildly and elbowed Cutler.

"I represent certain principals..."

"That's good too, Eric." Cutler nodded soberly. "Good to have principles."

"No, no. Not that kind of principle. I mean, I work for a company, a branch of a company..."

"You *don't* have principles?"

"No. I mean, of course I have principles. Standards. I'm a lawyer, Everything I do is legal."

"Good," Cutler said. "Continue."

But Jimmy looked perplexed and annoyed, as if someone were playing a trick that he did not understand. He frowned and twitched. He slapped at phantom flies nipping his neck. Flecks of beer froth sailed off his chin.

"The fact is, the people I work for own this land. They've asked me to come down here to negotiate with you folks, to..."

"Own?" Cutler asked.

Morrow nodded.

"This rock?"

"Rock, slope, beach, promontory, everything."

"House?"

"All of them." Morrow indicated the blue rectangles on his survey plan. "All these buildings are illegal. None has any right to be there. No right at all."

A sudden frenzy of swatting sloshed the contents of Jimmy's bottle across the plan. Beer frothed on Morrow's polished shoes.

"Jeez! Sorry, lawyer! Spilled zhingobabo all over your map! Let me wipe it up." Jimmy whipped a grimy rag out of his coveralls and smeared large greasy circles into the paper. "Lookit that! Not a damn bit better, is it?"

Morrow stood up, not smiling anymore. "All right. Okay. You know, this isn't easy for me."

"I sure as hell hope not," Cutler said quietly.

"Do *you* think this is easy?"

I shook my head. "Just keeps on getting harder, doesn't it Eric."

"You think this is my idea of fun, telling people they're going to be dispossessed? Relocated? Some of you have been here a long time, I know that. But you're squatters. All of you. And you're going to have to move, that's all." He started patting his shoes with a folded handkerchief.

I asked, "Why *is* that, Eric?"

"Development. *Big* development." He waved toward the bay. "Two years from now you won't recognize this place. And if you're smart you can be part of it." He rubbed his thumb and forefinger together and smiled. "There's going to be a lot of money made here, and just because you have no claim to the land..."

Jimmy took off his black welding goggles. He took off his cap and swatted it across his forearm, loosing a cloud of grit on the soggy document. Then he put it on his head the

80

right way around and said: "Hey, lawyer..." pointing to a little box above the brim:

If I want to hear
from an ASSHOLE
I'll FART

Morrow's mouth worked like a worm on a hook. He said, "That sort of thing doesn't help much, you know."

"Helps me," Jimmy said.

"So. I assume you're not interested in hearing my principals' offer. Any of you."

"You assume right," Cutler said. "Have a nice day, now."

"'Bye," Jimmy said.

"You can't possibly win this. Sensible compromise is your only..."

"Let me help you pack," Cutler said. He opened Eric Morrow's leather attache case. It was suede-lined and very thin, and contained a few blue file folders with plastic tabs on the edges. Cutler crumpled up the filthy, sodden mass that had been the survey plan and stuffed it inside. Then he closed the lid and clicked the combination latches shut. "Ready to go."

"You'll regret this."

"I regret it already. You've spoiled my whole day, Eric."

"It's no wonder you people..."

Cutler's eyes went black. Jimmy Pagoosie put his beer down very slowly on the rock. "Oooh," he said. "Matchi magwud. Bad smell here."

I handed Morrow his briefcase. "Goodbye," I said.

"Think it over. If you change..."

"Goodbye," I said.

He headed back down the road toward his car. Jimmy signalled *come* to Guaranteed, and when the dog was beside him, bright-eyed and ready, he pointed at Eric Morrow's left ankle. But I signalled *sit,* and he sat. Jimmy rubbed his

81

ears. "Sorry, anim. Another time we eat lawyer bones."

Cutler dumped out the rest of his beer and dropped the bottle into its case. He looked sad, and worried, and sick. "Jimmy we're too old for this," he said.

"Squatters' rights, that's what we've got! To hell with him! We'll be all right."

Cutler pursed his lips dubiously.

"We will be. Come on, Cutler, we've been here before. Lots of times. We wait it out, that's all."

"This smells different," Cutler said. "This time, Jimmy, I think we are for the high jump."

We watched Morrow's car make its way back along the road and up the hill. Jimmy sighed. "And I have to take Maynard and Tega into town for shoes. We're hunting tomorrow, right n'sheemenh? Right."

I watched them go back across the bridge and up the trail toward their houses. They looked smaller and tireder. Cutler's hat wasn't quite square anymore, and Jimmy's fists were plunged in his pockets. His welding glasses drooped around his neck.

Cutler was right; this time it *was* different.

A week later a new office opened in Schreiber. It had beige vertical blinds, and a secretary, and a sign on the door that said, BRIGHTSANDS VILLAGE DEVELOPMENTS.

No-one ever saw anyone go in or out except the secretary, but the rumour was that it would soon be used for hiring. A stretch-cab ¾-ton pickup with the same sign on its door also appeared, with four strangers who stayed down at Meg Johnston's motel during the week and disappeared on week-ends. Some said they were from Toronto, some said Vancouver. They didn't do much but drive around, so far as I could see, often showing up on Neyashing beach in the afternoon, holding site plans like sails against the wind and pointing here and there.

Two weeks after his first visit Eric Morrow called a public meeting in Neyashing. He put notices in the papers in

Thunder Bay and Schreiber, and had letters delivered by a courier in a little blue Chev. They got most of our names right too, even Aja's.

The meeting was held in the old ice-house that had been part of McDonnell's fish plant. Crews came to clean it out and prop it up, and trucks came with enough folding chairs for twice as many people as there were in Neyashing. A television crew arrived. Electricians worked two days wiring that old hulk of a building, hanging fluorescents and spotlights, fixing outlets, and rigging a PA system. On the afternoon of the meeting they brought in a big generator and started it up.

The noise of that machine drowned all sound. We couldn't hear gulls or loons anymore, or the wind in the grass. We couldn't hear each other doing things around our places, living our lives. Worst, we couldn't hear the Lake. It was as if the adhesive that held us together had already begun to weaken under the hammering of that machine.

We all went to the meeting. Jenny rented a car and drove out from Thunder Bay, and she and I walked down the hill with Cutler and Barbara and the kids. All the way Maynard kept asking me questions. He was getting tall for fourteen—up to my shoulder.

"Uncle Travis, is it true they're gonna cover up the beach?"

"I don't think so, Maynard. Why would they do that?"

"Is it true they're gonna take down our houses?"

"They might try to."

"Greg said it was true. He said the government was gonna move us all into the city."

"He doesn't know that."

"But what if he's right? What'll we do, Uncle Travis?"

"Maynard, we'll just have to deal with that when the time comes."

"Yeah. We'll deal with that when the time comes."

"First, Maynard, we listen. We listen to what these men

have to say."

Jimmy Pagoosie and Karen and their kids had arrived before us and were sitting right in the centre of the hall, a solid little island, with TV technicians eddying around them. The Josephs were there too, and the Shawbonoquets, all staring skeptically at the lectern and the big screen beside it. Mary and Weass Faille were there with the two little girls they had adopted after their own kids had grown up and moved away. And Julie Cat was there in the front row with her arms folded and her bandanna pulled forward into a kind of cowl.

At the front, Eric Morrow sipped coffee with two coiffed and sleek men in dark suits, smiling and checking his watch often. We were fifteen or twenty minutes late, but others were still arriving—Moses Chab, and Archie and Ellen Misabi, and Meg Sugedub with all her kids, even the baby, and Abner Bagg IV, and Amable Dubois on his crutches, and Sandy and Emma Mackenzie, and Custom Penassie with Albert, his retarded brother, and Simon Littlewolf and Sarah Foster, and all the Naponses, and Agnus and Bella Mamakeesik, and Richard Gwinguish, who drove all the way from Sault Ste. Marie where he'd taken a job just the week before, and Jonas Manitouwaba. A steady, casual stream of latecomers kept arriving, ignoring the big friendly urn of coffee and the stacks of white cups and saucers. Every time Eric Morrow tried to call the meeting to order he was interrupted by fresh arrivals and hearty greetings called across the room.

Finally, half an hour late, Harry and Ethel Trowbridge arrived with their tweeds and white hair and canes, and Harry called across to Morrow, having interrupted him in mid-sentence, "Sorry, old chap. When you're retired, you know, you lose all track of time. Carry on! Carry on! Pay no attention to us."

Aja was there too. I felt her there, although her body was not inside that place; her body was out in the dunes, close to the Lake, waiting.

84

Finally Morrow got started. He pulled down the cuffs of his jacket, adjusted the microphone, and said, "Good evening. Hear me at the back okay?"

No-one answered.

"On behalf of Aspen Corporation, welcome and thank you for coming. My name is Morrow, and it's my pleasure to introduce these gentlemen, who will be making a very important announcement. On my left is Mr. Leonard Marx, chief planner for Aspen. On my right, Mr. Bert Weir, vice-president of Aspen and Chairman of the Resort Division. I'll call on Mr. Weir first. Sir."

Weir came to the microphone with only the clatter of the generator to welcome him. He was tall, grey, affable, suave. He looked like a kindly grandfather. He said: "Thank you, Mr. Morrow. And thank you, ladies and gentlemen, for coming here this evening for the unveiling of this important project. In a moment I'll ask my associate, Mr. Marx, to describe it to you in detail, but before I do that I want to say two things. First, we at Aspen are very proud, not only of our chain of fine resort hotels, but also of their effects on local economies. Wherever they have been built the region has benefitted immediately and substantially, and I'm sure that will be true of the hotel that with rise here in McDonnell's Depot. Secondly, I want to emphasize that Aspen is equally proud of its social conscience. We understand that progress and development may bring change and some dislocation. We want you to know that we are prepared to retrain anyone who is inconvenienced by the project we're announcing tonight, to re-establish them, and to reimburse them. Of course, rumours have been flying, and we understand why you might be apprehensive. But I am here to assure you, to *assure* you, that there is not one person sitting in this room who in the long run will not be better off because Aspen selected McDonnell's Depot, this beautiful location, as the site for its newest hotel. Thank you. Mr. Marx, over to you."

No-one applauded except Eric Morrow. Behind me, Abner Bagg belched and said, "Gas."

Leonard Marx got to his feet smiling, nodding to the projectionist who stood ready beside two carousel machines. "Lights, please," he said. Gentle music played. The beam of his tiny flashlight floated and soared in intricate little patterns, picking out various details before sweeping on.

"Here, ladies and gentlemen, you see the concept, Brightsands Village, a holiday resort for the twenty-first century. Phase One, here, will include the core hotel of three hundred and fifty units, lounge, disco, dining-room and, of course, indoor and outdoor pools with gym, saunas, and various other amenities—everything necessary for the convenience and enjoyment of our guests. Phases Two and Three will add the time-sharing condominiums, here, and the retirement village, here. Ultimately, as you see, the development will include parks and greenbelts that will come up almost to the highway at the foot of this line of cliffs, here."

He swept a cross of light over the Palisades as if they could be eliminated by the stroke of a corporate pen. The music purred.

"Hillside, beach and bay are the three elements in this natural resort-recreational continuum, of which the bay itself is the most important element."

Marx paused and turned to face us in the semi-darkness.

"But, you are asking yourselves, isn't the water too cold? Isn't the lake too rough, too unpredictable? Isn't the location too exposed for the safe mooring of pleasure boats? Aren't those the reasons why there hasn't been any significant hotel development along this shore?

"Of course, you're right. But here is what makes McDonnell's Depot different. Here's what makes this bay different." His little spotlight glided out along the spit. "This. This curved promontory on the southeastern side of the bay is the key element in our concept."

86

New slide. Same music.

"All that will be necessary is to extend this point for less than half a mile, 727 metres, to be exact, almost to this point on the west, and what do we have? We have protection. We have a perfect yacht basin." The slide was an artist's sketch of a breakwall, a gleaming concrete mass. Under it the spit had vanished.

The next picture showed Neyashi Bay as it might appear from the end of this new wall. There was the hotel tower with its glimmering wings. There were the terraces and swimming pools. There was the beach, dotted with romping bathers. And there at anchor were many luxurious boats.

"As you know, this bay is relatively shallow. It's mean depth is just under four metres, ideal for our purposes. As you can see, the new breakwater is designed to curve slightly here, tucked in behind this west point, so the prevailing winds and the cold water churned up by storms will roll past the entrance to the harbour. Some groin work might be necessary here, but very little. So, the other thing we have is a large, sun-warmed, recreational body of water."

Next slide: Neyashing—the river flowing past the site of the ancient village site of my people; the stream tumbling down to the Lake halfway between my house and Cutler's.

"Dams here and here, on this river and this creek will create large pools, lagoons really, which will also be sun-warmed and will further warm the bay. We calculate an overall increase in the summer temperature of the water to 15 or 19 degrees Celsius, very comfortable for swimming. Almost sub-tropical, in fact. And, given the area of the bay, we expect that the yacht basin and the swimming area can co-exist very nicely with the usual water sports—windsurfing, waterskiing, parasailing and so forth."

The final slide presented Brightsands Village as it might be seen from high over the Lake, by a group of revellers helicoptering in for the weekend. It was a travel-agent's delight. I heard little gasps and groans and whispers all around me in

87

the darkness. My palms were damp and cold.

"Access," Leonard Marx concluded. "Of course we've projected for that as well. Clients will naturally come by yacht, but we're also discussing with government officials the possibility of passenger vessels running regularly from both Thunder Bay and Duluth. Highway access will be improved. Long-range plans include the construction of a private airport here, behind the highway, contingent on the Phase Four ski facilities, which I will not describe now. Lights, please."

The nightmare visions vanished. The audience uttered a little sigh of horror and relief.

"Let me conclude by saying that through the good offices of your Member of Parliament, Aspen has secured sufficient financial backing to guarantee construction through Phase Two. So, ladies and gentlemen, there you have it. Are there questions?"

Eric Morrow was up immediately, giving no time for silence. "Unfortunately, Mr. Weir and Mr. Marx have another commitment this evening in Thunder Bay, but are there questions before they leave? No? None? Well then, thank you very much, gentlemen."

There was a moment while Weir spoke close to Morrow's ear and the lawyer put his hand over the microphone and nodded, saying "Yes, sir. I will sir." And then the executives were gone with their retinue, through the side door and out to the road where a black Chrysler waited.

"We know," Morrow said, spreading his arms and smiling understandingly, "that the Brightsands development is going to mean some upheaval and dislocation, as Mr. Weir said, and he has asked me to assure you again, before I outline Brightsands' offer, that as special needs arise we'll do everything we can to accommodate them. I hope that's clear.

"As you know, the land you have been living on is owned by a subsidiary of Aspen Corporation, Brightsands Village Developments. Some of you, because you have lived here for many years, or because your ancestors lived here, may feel that you have a legal right to be here, effectively a claim against Brightsands, on the grounds of adverse possession, sometimes called 'squatters' rights.' Of course, you're entitled to make such a claim in court, but I assure you that you will fail. You have no grounds, and the process would be long, and difficult, and expensive. Also," Morrow paused and rolled his notes into a little tube, "—and this is just a statement of fact, something to keep in mind—big projects like Brightsands Village enjoy broad support in areas of high unemployment, like this one, and any court challenges that delay them are likely to be seen as nuisances by the man on the street, the man who could be earning a paycheque.

"Now then, the offer Brightsands has authorized me to make is simple but extremely generous. It extends to all present residents of McDonnell's Depot, with only two or three exceptions where there are special difficulties. Each nuclear family will receive $5000 from Aspen for assistance in relocation. Also, the jobs in construction, maintenance and service that this project will create will be offered *first* to you and members of your families. This brochure..." Morrow raised a blue pamphlet and paused.

People were getting up.

"This brochure," he said louder, "describes the offer in detail. It also contains an application form. To apply..."

More people got up. Everyone was getting up. Leaving. Jimmy Pagoosie and his family left first. Then Julie Cat. Then the Trowbridges with a clattering of canes. Then Jenny, going straight down the aisle and across in front of Eric Morrow as if he did not exist. Then everyone was up and leaving.

Morrow was flushed and his smile was not pleasant. He held up a thick package of blue pamphlets. "We'll send them," he said into his microphone over feet shuffling, and coughs, and chairs banging. "*Think* about this!"

Next day at work I learned that TV news that evening

carried footage of a dignified group leaving the ice-house in McDonnell's Depot ("a quaint relic of the great days of fishing on Lake Superior..."), while the commentator outlined the Aspen offer and described the splendour of the Brightstands project. But the people filing out of that building—grandparents, parents and kids—were not in McDonnell's Depot. They were in Neyashing. They were contained by Neyashing as by the fluid of a warm womb, oblivious to reporters, and to bright lights, and to cameras zooming. They did not hear the rattling generator anymore. They were listening to the heartbeat of the Lake, the Lake tumbling across a beach and a spit that would never be owned by anyone.

And they were not quite finished with Eric Morrow. He and his partners left the ice-house behind Cutler and me, in a laughing, tight little group. I heard Morrow say, "Stupid..." and "a bailiff and a bulldozer..." And then, in the sudden stillness that followed the dying of the generator, I heard him say, "What the hell is *this*?"

Aja was there, down out of the dunes. Her hair shone white in the darkness and the light in her eyes was the pale green of the lake over quartzite shoals. She hobbled close to him leaning on her stick, close enough to peer into him, see through him. Her gaze went around him, wrapped him up and held him for a long time. Then she sighed and shook her head and backed away a step or two from Eric Morrow, profoundly saddened by what she had seen in him, by what the spirits had in store. She uttered a soft and mournful sentence: "Gega ogee n'sigoon aamooyan..."

"*What?*" Grinning, Morrow bent toward her, reached out a hand that did not quite touch her. "What did you say, old girl?"

Aja repeated what she had said in a whisper, a hiss, backing toward the shadows, her hair full of light.

Morrow spread his arms wide, shrugging. He turned to me. "Can *you* tell what she's saying?"

I nodded.

"Well, what?"

"She says bees will eat your meat."

Shadow Man

Jenny and I parted after university. We needed different things, separate things. I had to come back to Neyashing; she wanted to travel, become a teacher. So a time came when I stood in the vestibule between railway cars and saw her waving goodbye and crying, a knuckle pressed against her lips. "You know where I am," I called, and she nodded, yes. I watched her until a curve in the track moved the train between us, and then I was going out of the station and the railyards, out of the suburbs and the plazas, out of the labyrinth of the city. I was going home.

I wrote to keep her mindful of how I felt about her, and what the Lake was like, and she wrote often, too. I missed her. Sometimes after work, tired and dirty, I'd go to the pub with friends and have a beer, and it was good to sit in that cool twilight listening to the music and watching the girls. A lot of them were young and pretty, and even the older ones were lovely when they smiled, with a fragile and fleeting beauty like an autumn day. I was friends with them; we'd talk and share jokes, but when I left I'd go alone. I'd get into my truck and drive out to the Neyashing turn, and then down the hill and along between the dunes. I'd park and walk up to my place, and Guaranteed would come to meet me, shaking all over. We'd eat supper together, looking at the Lake. And then, if the night was clear I'd take my telescope onto the Council Rock and begin my journeys.

One night I heard someone coming softly up the path,

sitting down behind me on the Council Rock, wheezing like a little breeze in aspens. I heard Guaranteed's nails click across the rock, but he did not bark.

"Bojo, Aja."

"Bojo, Travis."

We drifted through silences together. I voyaged in other galaxies; she rubbed the ears of the dog who lay contentedly beside her. At last she said, "I have come because there is loneliness here. Emptiness."

More silences, long silences.

"It is an emptiness that this old woman might help to fill. Shall I go, or stay."

"Stay."

"Is it deep, what you feel for this woman?"

"Deep as the Lake, Aja."

"She is a good woman, but she is not here in Neyashing with you."

"She needs time."

"Time to come out of time."

"Yes."

She laughed softly. "Anim, flat dog, shall we help? Shall we?"

And, indeed, as the months passed and I traced Jenny's sweeping journeys around the globe during her breaks from teaching—to India, Australia and California; to Europe, Russia, Japan and Alaska—I saw that she was drawing closer in a slow and ever-narrowing spiral, and I began to wait for the letter that said, when it finally came, "I've taken a job in Thunder Bay...."

I met her on a cool and gusty evening. I waited outside the terminal so I could see her as soon as she got off the plane, and she ran to me, letting her packsack fall as her arms went up around my neck. We stood while the other passengers filed past us. The wind swept Jenny's hair around our faces.

Later that night a tremendous storm rolled across the Lake

and hit Neyashing. It was a *zhawanibines,* one of those late winds from the south that sweep away the highest summer driftwood and reach almost into the black timber from the gales of the thirties and forties. It howled up the hillside, and tore at the eaves of my cabin, and pummelled on the roof. It was an exultant storm, and twice during that night as I held Jenny in the warmth between the fires, I was sure I heard soft laughter in the wind, Aja's laughter....

After the Brightsands meeting, after Aja told Eric Morrow what would happen to him, I knew it was only a matter of time, and I was not surprised one Sunday morning in October, to hear Jenny say, "Oh! That's awful!" She was on the porch reading her newspaper and mail. "I mean, the man is a toad, but that is really *awful!*"

"What?"

She read, *"Lawyer Badly Stung."*

"I like it," I said. "Tell me more."

Last Wednesday afternoon, Eric G. Morrow, a prominent attorney with the local firm of Breslin, Swerny & Haines, narrowly escaped death when he was attacked by ground wasps while helping a friend clear brush near the Kam River.

"So," I said quietly.

Mr Morrow apparently stood directly on the nest for several seconds unaware, because of his thick socks, that the insects were swarming inside his trousers.

Jenny shivered. "Aaaw! Awful!"

"Terrible," I said. "Think of it."

Doctors at St. Joseph's Hospital confirmed that this was the worst such case in hospital records. Mr Morrow sustained 27 bites on one leg and 30 on the other, as well as numerous stings on the buttocks and in the groin and lower abdomen.

"Oh, Travis! The poor man!"

"Yes," I said. "Imagine..."

That was the only good thing that happened that fall.

Autumn is the best of seasons. I love its frosts and its sudden storms that trail long fingers of rain through the forests. I love the layers of smoke hanging above Neyashi Bay at dawn, and the flocks gathering in the evening off the end of the spit. I love the plaintive calls of the young loons left to fish and grow strong for the journey south. I love the way the sun slants on still afternoons, and the golden farewells of the aspen leaves, and birch, and tamarack, brilliant on dark hills. I love the first frail terraces of ice at the Lake's edge. I love the way bears lift their snouts to smell the coming of the cold, and the way they grow slow and fat. I love the grunting of moose in the night, and the elegant conversations of the wolves. I love the way all things draw in, gather up and welcome the coming cold.

But there was no beauty in the autumn of that year, none of the sense of everything-in-its-place necessary for beauty. Not that year. Not in Neyashing.

For a few days after the Brightsands meeting, things seemed normal. It was as if everyone had the same nightmare and agreed not to talk about it. No-one said anything about the meeting. No-one mentioned the brochures and application forms when the courier delivered them in his blue-and-white Chev. People talked about other things, but their eyes were full of hurt and questions. They looked at me as if they expected answers, magic words that would keep Neyashing as it had always been. But I did not have the answers, or the magic. I could not return those stares. So, for a time Neyashing staggered on like a man who has received a mortal wound, and knows it, but must keep up appearances for a few final steps.

One morning on my way to work Weass Faille flagged me down, carrying his steaming mug, hunched against the first serious frost. His white hair flared over his ears like small wings, and a white stubble covered his creased face. Weass has a harelip that stiffens in the cold, and that morning he smelled of Scotch, but if his speech was muddled his mind was not.

"Travis, this Aspen thing. I hate to say it, but it looks like they're right—legally right, I mean. I drove up to the Lakehead and had a talk with my lawyer. Know what he told me?"

I reached out through the window and relieved him of his Dewar's-and-coffee and had a sip. "What?"

"He talked about the Land Titles Act, and how we have no claim against Aspen or the government. Said he's known for years something like this might happen. Said I'd've been better off retired in Florida. Gave me a little lecture—you know. 'And now,' he told me, 'you and that place are gone. Not a thing I can do for you. Nothing anyone can do. You are history, Weass.'"

"Is that what he said? *History?*"

"That's what he said."

I laughed, but Weass didn't.

"Thing is, Travis, what now?"

I spread my hands and shrugged. "They won't start construction this year. It's too late. We'll have the winter to think it over."

"Sure, but meantime..." The thought died there, in the empty place where our gazes met. But I knew what he meant: meantime things would begin to come apart. People would begin to die small deaths.

He was right. Two nights later Guaranteed whined at the door, and when we went out we found Albert Penassie hugging his knees on the Council Rock and rocking back and forth, making his low sound that was part hum and part groan. His face was wet. I talked to him, got him on his feet, took him back down the hill to his brother's place. He couldn't understand what had happened at that meeting, but he knew. Albert knew. He could feel something horribly wrong, and even after I got him home he kept looking at me. Looking at *me*.

And then late one afternoon out on the very point of the spit I met Meg Sugedub, who had always feared that place and had never gone there in all the years I'd known her. There she was wearing only her jeans and a thin shirt and denim jacket, shivering in the wind. When I put my coat over her shoulders she asked, "Travis, what *are* we going to do?"

"I don't know, Meg."

She kept shaking. "I won't take them to the city. I won't take my children there. I won't."

"We'll have the winter," I said.

"Sure." She was looking down at the place where the slope plummeted into the dark body of the Lake.

I put my arm around her. "Don't even think about that, Meg. Don't. It'll work out. You'll see."

"How?"

"I don't know, but it will. Come on, now. Let's go back. Kids alone?"

She nodded.

"Let's get them. We'll all go up to Cutler's and Barbara's for supper. Sound good?"

"Yeah," she said, with the little flickering smile that had made her so beautiful once. "Sounds good."

And later that fall, when the poplar leaves had turned from gold to brown to black and begun to scuttle across the sand like swarms of little crabs, I came upon the Trowbridges in the Old Place, the campsite near the river's mouth. They were sitting on a log with a blanket around the two of them, and Harry waved his cane when he saw me coming down the beach.

I went up through the grass and sat down with them.

"So, what are we going to do, Travis?" The old man looked at me in the same way he might have looked at officers in Italy 40 years ago, except that his eyes were red now, and watery in the wind.

"I don't know yet, Harry."

He swept his cane back and forth, tracing an arc in the sand, part of an unfinished circle that enclosed us all. "Ethel and I have discussed this. Twenty years ago we would have fought these people a different way, but now..."

"I know," I said, and I did. For him: cataracts, and shrapnel, and both kinds of arthritis, and a love for his wife so deep it was a fatal disease. For her: cancer that had worn her skin thin as rice paper, and Alzheimer's that had left only fragments of her days. "Oh Travis," she had said once, holding my hand in both of hers and smiling, "I have such wonderful memories, if only I could remember them...."

But I remember. I remember for her. I remember her laughing in the wilderness, lifting her arms to the sun and the wind, "Oh, the wonder! The wonder of it!"

"Ethel and I have discussed this," Harry was saying. "We have a little money...don't interrupt, Travis...a little money. Not a lot but we want it used however you decide. We've made provisions. So if we're not here in the spring, Travis, the money will go to you. It's all arranged. Do you understand? Do you promise?"

"Yes."

"Good. Look. See what we've found!" He held out Ethel's hand, and she opened it to reveal a perfect spear point of white chert, the size of a small corncob, chipped so finely it was almost smooth. I took it and pressed it between my hands and felt the age of it while the two Trowbridges watched, radiant as children. "Old, old," Ethel Trowbridge said.

Old, old. Yes. From a time before time. When the Lake was higher. When creatures forever gone drank at the edges of its coves....

I gave it back to her. I closed her hand and held it with both of mine and looked into her eyes, innocent as space. Then I went on down the beach to the river mouth and up the trail beside the bank. They were gone when I came back, but I knew the spear point would still be there, reburied. They would have taken only the pleasure and the memory, and in the end they would give back even those.

There was craziness, too. One night coming home from work I saw human shadows in the doorway of the old ice-house. Not children. I stopped the truck and walked over. There was a lot of shouting inside, and banging. It was almost dark, but light enough to see two bottles and three drunks: Moses Chab, Amable Dubois and Abner Bagg IV. They were all hoarse with rum and cursing, but they had enough co-ordination to keep smashing at the fragments of the lectern the Aspen executives had used. Abner and Moses were reeling around with axes and Amable was sitting on the ground, swinging one of his crutches.

I pulled the axes away from them and went for Bobby Naponse, and we got them home one by one and into bed. What made the incident grim and sad was that Abner had been on the waggon so long that no-one could remember his last drink; and, so far as we knew, Moses Chab had never had a drink in all his life. Half a century before he'd signed some Methodist pledge, and he'd stuck to it.

So there was that craziness, and this: Barbara running down the path at dawn one morning when Cutler had gone with Jimmy on the *Bad Loon,* screaming my name, bursting in even before I had my trousers on, saying, "Travis! Travis, Maynard's gone! He's *gone!*" and showing me the kind of confused and pathetic note fourteen-year-old runaways leave.

I got dressed and Guaranteed and I ran down to the truck and drove up to the highway. It was cold and deserted, and there was wet snow falling. Maynard was half a mile east, on his way to Toronto if there'd been any cars to pick him up. When he saw my truck he dropped his pack and headed for the bush, but we had him before he got too far. Guaranteed tripped him and I fell on top of him in the wet leaves, and when he came up his face was smeared with mud and tears and he had to spit before he could start cursing me.

"Big man! You're gonna let 'em screw us, aren't you! You're not gonna do one goddam thing, you and the old man! Big fighters! Shit!"

I grabbed a handful of shirt and jacket and held him against a tree so that his toes were just scuffing the leaves, and said, "Big enough not to run." I held him there until he looked away, and then I let him down. He cleared his throat and pulled a sleeve across his nose, and I gave him my bandanna to clean up. "There'll be time to talk about it," I said. "Not now. There'll be all winter to talk about it. Now, are you going to walk back to the truck or do I carry you?"

He came. He calmed down and I took him home and Barbara held him and cried. Maynard cried too. So that episode had a happy ending, except that it was part of something larger, something still circling out there in time, beyond the winter.

"Big enough not to run," I'd said to him. But I wasn't sure of that. I wasn't sure at all. I wasn't even sure I knew the difference between running away and drawing back; the truth was that I was already thinking about leaving for other places, places north.

And then, when all the gold of the fall had gone and the first snow squalls swirled in off the Lake, just when I thought we were safely into winter, I had the meeting that bothered me most of all.

They came in the night, young men that I remembered playing on the beach, except that they were no longer children: Richard Gwinguish, Simon Littlewolf and Jonas Manitouwaba. Guaranteed growled, staring at the door, and when I looked they were waiting on the Council Rock. I put on my cap and jacket and went out.

"Thought you were in the Soo, Richard."

"I came up for this. We've had a meeting."

"A meeting. I see. Must be important."

"We think so," Simon Littlewolf said quietly, hands in hip pockets. "We want to find out if you think so too."

Jonas waved an angry arm towards Schreiber and the highway. "You know, Travis, we don't have to take this *shit*!

99

This Brightsands Village shit!"

"I know, Jonas. There are alternatives."

"Well, that's part of our problem," Simon said. "We've been waiting for those alternatives to get talked about, Travis. We sort of thought maybe you, and Cutler, and Jimmy..."

"We have the winter," I said.

"Unh uh." Richard shook his head, spat over the edge of the rock, and turned back. "No way. We're not waiting that long."

"This is important," I said. "It needs to be thought about. It takes time."

"We don't think we have the time. We've asked for help," Jonas said.

"What sort of help?"

"Experienced. There are people who help you fight back. You know that, Travis."

Red haze flickered, and little claws of fear tugged inside my belly. I nodded. "I also know that there are ways and ways of fighting."

"We like this way," Richard Gwinguish said.

"Do you Richard? Do you like this way or do you just like the sound of it? Do you like the sound of something blowing up? People getting hurt, maybe? Does that make you feel big and powerful, back at your desk in Sault Ste. Marie?"

"I don't need that, Travis."

"You don't know what the hell you need!"

"We know we need help," Simon said. "No accusations, okay? Nobody's fault. We just need help."

"It has to stop somewhere, Travis," Jonas said. "You know it does. They're ruining everything, killing everything."

"No," I said. "I *don't* know it has to stop. Maybe it'll keep on till there's no Earth left! Maybe there's nothing you can *do* to stop it! Have you thought of that? Nothing anybody can do! Maybe it doesn't even matter!"

"Take it easy," Jonas said.

"*You* take it easy! You've got a whole winter to think this thing out."

"Look, we just wanted you to know," Simon said. "We've already asked. Somebody'll be coming."

"Don't do this."

"We haven't made any commitments," Richard said. "We've just asked them to send somebody. For information, okay? An information session, they called it."

"Grow up, for God's sake! You think you'll sign a contract? Is that what you think? You'll have a nice little conversation with these people and then sign a contract?"

"We didn't come to argue, Travis. We just wanted you to know. Somebody's coming."

"We'll keep in touch."

"Do that, Jonas. Keep in touch. Let me know when you're ready to start hurting people. N'dai!" I said to Guaranteed, and we walked away from the three of them.

"Giga wabamin," Simon Littlewolf said quietly, wishing me good evening, but I didn't answer him. Guaranteed and I went up the steps and I shut the door.

I didn't sleep well that night. My dreams were all full of gulfs and endings. I got up with a headache and a sick feeling in my stomach. I lit the fires and had some breakfast and then went out into a cold, clear morning to split some wood in my chopping place beside the Council Rock.

Everything is good about splitting wood—the rhythm, and the smell, and the promise. I had chosen the chopping place carefully, so that while I worked I could look down over Neyashing, down over the spit and across the Lake. But that morning I did not see Neyashing when I looked down; instead I saw that white concrete mass in the architect's drawing, all balconies and sealed windows and air conditioning. And instead of the shimmering and magical light on Neyashi Bay I saw pleasure boats huddling at their piers like pigs at feeding time; and instead of the spit there was only the seawall curving to the western point, severing us from the Lake.

Something let go inside me. Everything went red. I walked away from the chopping block swinging my axe and shouting warnings in Ojibwe. I remember Guaranteed barking, tangling up my feet, and I remember kicking him out of the way and going down that hill into Neyashing, and other dogs barking a long way off, like ghost dogs in the fog, and the ghosts of people coming to the doors of cabins that were not there anymore, and calling my name mournfully and pleadingly, raising beseeching arms. I remember swinging my axe again and again at that white building but not hitting it, not connecting because the whole vast structure swirled away into a red mist and I was walking into it and through it, shouting and hitting at something that wasn't there until I came out the other side on the road beside the Old Place, beside the cemetery. I went up through the blurred meadow and stopped at the wooden marker on Mother's grave and when I reached out to touch the spirit bird Cutler had carved for her it lifted away from me as gently as a grey jay fading into the snow and the firs, and for a moment I heard Mother's voice, her storytelling voice, before it too drew away from me, and faded.

After that I don't remember anything until Cutler was slamming me against the door of my truck. I must have walked back through Neyashing to the parking-place. I must have thrown the axe into the front seat and started the engine before Guaranteed and Cutler got there, because Cutler was holding me against the open door with his left hand and reaching into the cab for the keys with his right, saying, "What're you *doing,* you crazy sonuvabitch! What're you *doing*!" And I told him I was going into Schreiber to smash that Brightsands office to ratshit.

Cutler slammed me against the door two or three more times, and the red blurry haze drained away under the pain in my head and the pressure of the door handle in my back, and I pulled my wrist across my nose and said, "Okay. Okay, put me down."

"N'sheemenh, n'sheemenh," Cutler was saying, "little brother," holding me but not hurting me anymore.

"I'm okay. I'm okay, Cutler."

"You sure?"

"Yes."

"No attack on Schreiber?"

I shook my head. He let go of me and I bent down and picked up my cap and dusted it off and put it on again.

"So. Now what?"

"I'm going to work."

"Oh no. Oh no, no, no. *I'm* going to work, not you. And on my way I'm going to tell your foreman you won't be in for a few days because you're ill, right? You *are* sick, aren't you, n'sheemenh?"

"Okay," I said. "But Jenny..."

"I'll explain to Jenny. You're no damn good to her the way you are. No good to anybody."

And so Guaranteed and I went back into the bush. I didn't hunt; didn't even carry a gun. I took my tent, my sleeping-bag, some food. We found a quiet place and just waited. I let the wildness work. I watched the lake open to the stars and moon, heard spirits and animals moving home to Earth in November evenings, listened to songs older than all sanity. I kept still, watching and listening, taking health from Earth. I don't know how long we were gone—perhaps two weeks, perhaps longer, until there was no hatred and no anger anymore.

We returned to Neyashing in the first real blizzard of that year. By the time we reached the mouth of the river, the Old Place and the graveyard were snow-covered and safe....

The Shadow Man came in the middle of January. Richard Gwinguish brought him from the Soo.

He was not what I imagined.

The man Richard introduced looked as innocuous as a fifth grade teacher. He had on a clean sports shirt and slacks and Wallabees. His black hair was washed and trimmed, and he smiled genially and often. Besides being Indian, only one thing would have distinguished him from any commuter on a morning train, from any citizen lined up for a movie: when you looked closely you saw, flickering across his eyes, a light as cold and hard as the flame of a welding torch. It was there and gone, there and gone, just long enough for each of us to see it and know this small, bland man would kill.

There were six of us. Cutler was the oldest, Jonas the youngest. We sat with mugs of tea in a circle in Richard's big kitchen, parkas on the backs of our chairs.

"I'm here because Neyashing has a problem," the visitor began, "and when you have a problem we all have a problem. I'm here because some of you have invited me. You want to know about the Shadow Man Society—who we are and what we stand for. You want to know if we can help you, and how. Good."

He spoke softly and smiled so gently that he might have been a pastor in Sunday School; but he let each of us see that hard light, and his smile was like a distance.

"For those of us in the Society there are no tribes anymore, no nations. We recognize only one division: between First Peoples and all others; between those who still live near to Earth and those who have turned their backs and built another world, an artificial world. We live in the shadow of that artificial world. We know that it is a huge and terrifying world, that it has almost ruined our people, and that it is devastating Earth. We know that it must be destroyed if our children are to live with dignity, and if the earth is to flourish again. Each of us..."

"Excuse me," Jimmy Pagoosie said, frowning, waving his hand like a kid in school, "excuse me. Bit of a problem there."

"Let him finish, Jimmy," Jonas Manitouwaba said. "There'll be time for questions later."

"Lots of time," the visitor nodded, looking steadily at Jimmy. "As much time as you want, okay?" And when Jimmy leaned back he went on. "Each of us in the Society has taken the name of a leader of our people. So we are their shadow-spirits. So their work is carried on in us. My name is Red Cloud."

"That what your kids call you?" Jimmy asked, grinning.

"Look," Jonas leaned forward and pointed. "This is serious, all right? If you don't think this is serious, Jimmy, then maybe you should..."

But the Shadow Man was also leaning forward, the hard little flame in his eyes boring into Jimmy Pagoosie. "No kids," he said softly, shaking his head. "There never will be. As for my name, use it or not, as you like. Nothing you do will change what I am." He waited until he was sure Jimmy had nothing else to say. "The Society has many forms, many branches. All you need to know now is that we are close to you here in Neyashing and understand what you're going through. Listen. See if we don't understand..."

His voice grew even softer and took on the cadences of an elder telling an old, old story, the rhythms that every man in Richard Gwinguish's kitchen remembered from infancy. We held our breath, listening.

"You live where your people have lived for thousands of years, needing little, taking little. You know where you belong. Your being here does not damage the land, or the mystery of other creatures, or the mystery of spirits. But, all your lives you have watched the whiteman abuse Earth. Here on the Lake. Everywhere. You have watched him damage Life, and sometimes, because you have wanted to live in harmony with the whiteman, you have helped him. You have been respectful to him as you would be to a guest, gone along with his laws and his civilization. You have been taken in by his smiles, by his gifts and promises. You have tried to speak to him, although he has no ears to hear; you have tried to show him, although he has no eyes to see. You have been insulted and have ignored the insults; you have been humiliated and have endured the humiliations."

The Shadow Man shook his head sadly. He leaned forward with his elbows on his knees.

"So you too have become shadow men. You have been pushed into the shadow world, out of the sun, by the white-man. So you have suffered. So Earth has suffered because you have been collaborators, accomplices. You know this, don't you." He said it like a statement, not a question, and I saw nods when I looked around.

"*I* don't know that," Cutler said, suddenly. "Do you know that, Travis?"

I shook my head.

"Do *you* know that, Jimmy?"

"Hell no!"

"Sorry to interrupt," Cutler said. "Continue. We're learning quite a lot here."

"Listen to the man, Cutler." Simon Littlewolf spoke without moving, his arms folded and his gaze steady.

"Cutler," Richard Gwinguish said, "in social work I see a lot of denial, a lot of rationalization, a lot of what this man is talking about. I understand how repression can be internalized. And you know what I think? I think that's what's happening right now," he pointed, "with the three of you."

"Oooo, those big words!" Jimmy Pagoosie said, shivering. "They are so *sexy*, Richard!"

"Give the man a chance," Simon Littlewolf said quietly, still not moving anything but his lips. "What are you afraid of?"

The Shadow Man laughed without humour. "And now the problem is right here, isn't it. In Neyashing. What will you do if you don't face it? What will you do if you give in again, are polite again? Where will you go? To the cities?"

"North," I said.

106

His gaze settled on me, and he nodded agreement, not smiling anymore. He did not look now like a citizen in a commuter train or a movie lineup; he looked like a man bereaved, and for the first time I saw something I liked. "North, yes," he said. "Always we carry that promise in our hearts. Always we've told ourselves, 'Well, it's not so bad yet. When things get *really* bad we can always move on, move north, back into the wilderness.' But where *is* north now? Where's the lake that's not already poisoned?"

"They're still there," I said.

The cold light froze his eyes, froze all his face into a hard mask. "Oh? Are they? Then why not defend them?"

"Question! Question!" Jimmy Pagoosie's hand went up, fingers snapping. "What do you mean, *defend*? Defend how, exactly?"

"With power, my friend. Power is the one thing that whiteman understands, and until you use it, he'll pay no attention. He won't even notice you."

"Use it how?" Richard asked.

"Three steps: First, claim Neyashing. *Take* this place! Don't waste more time talking to the whiteman about sharing, or how no-one should own the land. He'll laugh at you. He'll tell you that's romantic nonsense that won't work in the modern world. He'll show you treaties, deeds. So, don't talk, act! Claim Neyashing. You know you have a moral right; assert it!

"Second, announce what you're doing. Let everybody know. You'll get sympathy from many places, sympathy from people who want to use you for their own ends, sympathy from people who have no idea what the real issues are. Use it! Use that sympathy. If you do it right there'll be editorials about injustice, questions in Parliament about people trapped in bureaucratic red tape, maybe even hints of scandal—some Member or Minister on the take from private business, that sort of thing. The Society can help you do that.

"But, finally, it will all come down to you here in Neyashing, and you men in this room must have no illusions. None. You must plan for a time when you will confront your enemies and enforce your claim." The Shadow Man's voice had grown lower and softer as he spoke, and now it was barely audible. "You must be prepared to fight," he said, "as we are. As the Society is prepared to fight for you and for the rights of others like you, all over Earth."

"Maybe we won't need to," Simon Littlewolf said in the silence.

"Perhaps, but you must be prepared nonetheless. From the start, in everything you do, your enemies must see that you're prepared. If not, you're just playing political games."

Cutler said, "Tell me more about this fighting, friend."

"It can take many forms."

"Oh, I know that. I know that. Just tell me what forms you folks have in mind."

"First, sabotage."

"Sabotage."

"Yes."

"Sand in gas tanks? Slashed tires? Leaky boats? That sort of thing?"

"To start with, yes. Even children can..."

"To start with. And where does it end, this method of asserting our rights?"

"We're talking about extreme measures. You realize that."

"Measures that you say we have to be prepared for. So tell."

"Guns. Explosives."

Cutler's black eyes narrowed. "Always did make me nervous, guns. How about you, Jimmy?"

"Bad things. Very bad."

"As for explosives, you never know when they might hurt somebody. Even somebody on our side, wherever that is."

"There could be martyrs," the Shadow Man said, eyes

bright. "There often are, in any cause. You have to be prepared."

"Well," Cutler said, standing up slowly and stretching.
"I think I've heard enough of this horseshit. You coming,
n'sheemenh, or you feel like a little martyrdom tonight?"

"Wait, I want to be sure I've got this right." I pointed at
the man. "Enemies. You said enemies. Who, exactly?"

"Whites."

"That's one whole lot of enemies."

"You can't make distinctions. If you..."

"Can't I? You're telling me Abner Bagg is my enemy?
Harry Trowbridge is my enemy? The Marshall is my enemy?
You're telling me *the woman I love is my enemy?*"

"Yes," he said. "If they're white, I *am* telling you that.
Exactly."

Jimmy Pagoosie was on his feet too. "You know what you
are, friend? You're a goddam racist!"

"That's your word," Red Cloud said. "Mine is soldier."

I'll give him credit. He was honest and blunt, and if he
was afraid he didn't show it. He held his ground. In the end
it was we who retreated, Jimmy and Cutler and I. He was
still there, and the others were there with him, listening.

Next morning on my way to work I saw that someone had
tramped a big clear message in the snow along the beach:
THIS IS INDIAN LAND.

Most of that winter Aja slept.

She wrapped herself in the huge bearskin that was her
only blanket and went to bed. Weass Faille shook his head
and said he thought she had decided not to be here in the
spring. He said he guessed she wanted to go with Neyashing.

I went to see her twice a day. I took food and fed the fire
in her little stove and spoke with her if she was not sleeping
or talking to beings I could not see.

I said, "Eat, Aja. Live."

And she took the food I offered.

I said, "Keep warm, Aja. Feed the fire."

And sometimes she did and sometimes she forgot.

Guaranteed kept in touch. One morning just before dawn he leapt out of a sound sleep, whined and scratched at the door. I let him out into 50 degrees of frost and he hightailed down the road, only to come back a few minutes later, barking. I dressed and strapped on my snowshoes and followed him down to Aja's. Her fire was out; it was almost as cold inside that cabin as outside, and when I saw her opened eyes in the dark I thought she was gone. But she was not; she was warm inside that bearskin, laughing softly.

"Aja, Aja, why have you let this fire go out?" I relit it, and when it was blazing I rapped a stick on the ice in the bucket. "Hear that? That's what you'll sound like if you let the fire go out. A frozen old woman."

"No. Not yet. I have friends who look after me."

"Some friends, if they let you freeze."

"But they have not let me freeze. They have brought the flat dog, and you. N'dai," she said to Guaranteed, her thin arm finding its way around his neck. "You see? We have fire. We have a warm place again."

Perhaps it was that time, or perhaps another of the many times when I split wood for her, cooked for her, sat in silence with her while the little stove crackled and snapped, and smoke curled through the cracks in the pipes when I asked, "Aja, what shall we do?"

"Do nothing yet."

"I'm afraid, Aja."

"Life will live itself."

"I'm afraid that we shall go down a wrong path, and there will be no turning back."

"Which path?"

"To bitterness and blood, blood and bitterness."

"Yes. But you are also thinking of another path."

"North."

"Do not take that path either, Travis."

"But Aja..."

"Promise me. Not yet."

"All right. I promise. Not yet. But I see no other path. Do you, Aja?"

"Not clearly."

"What shall we do, then?"

"Wait. In spring the path will open."

"By spring it will be too late."

"No."

"In spring people will get hurt."

Painfully she turned over in the bearskin and peered at me, her eyes small and shrewd. "It is winter, Travis. Everything stops now. Wait. Listen. Save strength. Do what the Old Ones did."

"Aja, the Old Ones stayed close to the fire. They told stories."

"Yes," she said. "Yes."

Given by the Winds

"What does that mean?"

We'd been hunting, Maynard, Guaranteed and I. We snared three rabbits and shot three more. It started snowing at dusk as we were coming home along the river, and by the time we took four of the rabbits to people who needed them, the wind had built into a howling blizzard.

"You clean the guns," I told Maynard when we got to my place. "I'll cook."

He had started coming over a little more in the evenings. He didn't talk much. If he had a problem with schoolwork he'd put his book down in front of me, and point to the troublesome spot, and I'd help him through it. Sometimes he'd just take the cribbage board from its place on the shelf, and we'd play. Sometimes we'd hunt as we had that afternoon, going for miles up the river and into the hills beyond the Palisades, only the creak of our snowshoes breaking the silence. Sometimes he'd ask about the old people and the old ways.

"What does...eye, nadj, moom-igak..."

"Ae naadj moomigak bi gamaan imok," I said.

"What's it mean?"

"Stories the winds tell."

I kept stirring the rabbit stew. I knew what he'd found on the shelf with the other books, beside the gun oil. A child's scribbler.

"Empty." He brought it over to the stove, flicking his thumb across the pages. "That's written on the first page. Nothing else."

I nodded. "It was something I was going to write."

"What?"

"Stories your grandmother told me."

He put the scribbler back and broke down the guns beside the fire and started cleaning them. We ate in silence, and afterwards, when we were drinking tea between the two fires, while he finished the guns and I fixed a split snowshoe, he said, "Travis, do you remember those stories?"

"I think so."

"Will you tell them to me?"

"They're little legends, Maynard. Myths. Tales for children. You sure you want to hear them?"

He squinted at the fire through one of the oiled barrels, long enough to remind me that he had turned fifteen the week before, and that childhood was no longer a threat. Then he clicked the barrel back into its stock. "Yeah," he said.

"Okay." I worked at the snowshoe, wrapping wet rawhide around the broken place. I could hear my mother's voice again, and I could hear both winds, the cold wind of the gale piling snow against my cabin and that other wind, the summer wind of the third-last day of her life, blowing through the pines of the spit and across the bay. For a minute I listened to that other wind, and the story came.

"The first story is from Wabaninodin," I said. "The East Wind."

"Why?"

"Why what?"

"Why east?"

"Because, Maynard, everything begins in the east. Obviously. The sun rises there. You ready now?"

He nodded.

"Okay. Here we go."

Long ago the world was very different. For one thing, there were some very large animals around. The reason for that was that any animal could grow to whatever size it wanted. That was the rule. Nothing had to stop growing. So, if you were paddling, you might see a frog's eye as big across as your canoe was long, staring at you out of the marsh, or you might hear branches breaking off all around in the woods because bear-sized sparrows were landing on them. It was a very strange world.

"No order," Maynard said.

Exactly. Just chaos. Burgeoning chaos. Of course, humans could also grow as large as they wanted. The important thing was in knowing when to stop, because if you stayed too small you got stepped on or rolled on or brushed off or eaten by the big things. But, if you got too large then you couldn't move very fast or see very well behind, and sometimes quicker and smaller animals sprang on you in groups and ate you.

Having to make a choice about size gave everyone problems. There were housing problems, and marital problems and dietary problems, and many sanitary problems, as you can imagine. There were also problems caused by competition. All through the forest you would come across the skeletons of animals that had growing competitions until they collapsed under their own weight. It was awful, but the worst thing was no-one could imagine anything different. You see, it had just always *been that way.*

Maynard asked, "What if they tried growing some parts of themselves but not others?"

"They tried that but soon gave it up. Didn't work at all."

"Why not?"

"Too much impulse growing. Too many fantasies being fulfilled on the spur of the moment. No, it was a disaster for anybody who had the talent for it."

"But why didn't..."

"Maynard, don't interrupt."

"Sorry."

Now one day a man walking on a beach was swallowed by a huge fish. This man's name was Narrow Eyes. He was an ordinary man about the size of men today, and he was married to an ordinary wife and he had ordinary children.

The fish that swallowed him, however, was not an ordinary fish. It was a sturgeon that had decided to grow as large as a whale. Almost immediately, of course, it regretted making that decision, because the lake it lived in was not large enough to provide all the good food that sturgeons love to eat, browsing along the bottom like vacuum cleaners. However, there was no going back. Very quickly this sturgeon ate up everything normal, and it therefore had to change its diet. It began to lurk in the shallows and to leap out at deer or moose or whatever else came down to the beach in the evening. In one gulp it would swallow its prey and then sink to the bottom to digest the enormous meal. All the meat and bone was hard on the sturgeon's stomach and it belched a great deal, its burps erupting to the surface in huge explosions that kept everyone awake at night.

The sturgeon's name was Nahma. All sturgeons were called Nahma then.

Now when Nahma went for Narrow Eyes he almost missed him. It was a near thing. He miscalculated his angle in the glare of the setting sun and plopped out onto the beach four feet short of his target. He had to scoop Narrow Eyes up with some very quick fin action. By that time, however, Narrow Eyes had enough warning to go stiff and stick out his arms and legs, so that he made the fish very uncomfortable going down his gullet. He also cursed a lot. Sinking, Nahma looked mournful, as if he wished he were as small as other sturgeons once again, browsing contentedly along the bottom.

Inside, Narrow Eyes kept up the struggle. He said, "Lemme out, you slimy sonuvabitch!" And, "Who do you think you are?" And, "I'll get you for this!" His shouts echoed around in there, and his blows on the inside of Nahma's stomach sounded like a drum. He was a lusty chap, and he had no intention of being caressed and absorbed by the translucent lengths of Nahma's digestive tract that he could see stretching ahead.

But it was no good. Drowsily there on the bottom of the lake, Nahma had already begun to squeeze him, to digest him. All Narrow Eyes' vital juices were about to be sucked out to feed the great fish. He would end up as a little cloud puffed into the clear lake. He was about to be recycled.

In panic when he realized this, Narrow Eyes decided to grow. It was not a thoughtful decision. He had always resisted this temptation, although many of his friends had given in and become lumbering monsters who strode about mashing hills and forests. Narrow Eyes had wanted to stay light and quick, and he had never regretted his decision until this moment. Now he changed his mind. He exercised his option. He willed himself to grow. Instantly he grew like a balloon being blown up inside Nahma's stomach. Soon the fish began to feel very uncomfortable, and he peered down his gullet and asked, "What's going on? What are you doing down there?"

"I'm...getting...big!" Narrow Eyes said. Puffing up rapidly the way he was, talking was difficult.

"Don't do that!" Nahma said. "Co-operate. Be digested. Enzymes and acids are already at work on you."

But Narrow Eyes just got bigger, and at last he was so huge that Nahma bulged out like a blow-fish, like a huge soccer ball with quivering little fins. His eyes stuck out. His voice got squeaky. "All right!" he cried at last. "I give up!"

Narrow Eyes' voice was now a huge, echoing sound, like thunder in a cave. "Let...me...out!"

So Nahma did. He struggled to the surface and onto the beach. He opened his mouth.

Narrow Eyes clambered out, stretching Nahma very badly as he did so, and he strode around the beach waving his huge arms and beating his huge chest. The sound was like mighty drumbeats, and all the animals cowered in the trees to hear it. Even the trees quivered. "Let that be a lesson to you!" Narrow Eyes said to the dazed and exhausted fish, who had begun to slide back into the depths. "Don't meddle with me again!"

Then he strode off to find his wife and children. But when they saw him they screamed and ran away and hid in the woods, for he had become more monstrous even than the great fish. "I'm your husband!" he shouted. "I'm your father!" But they clamped their hands over their ears and refused to listen.

"It's true I'm big, but I had to do it! I had to do it or die! You believe that, don't you? I had to survive, don't you see?"

But everyone stayed in hiding, and after a while Narrow Eyes had no choice but to go off in search of other people his own size, weeping for what he'd lost.

After a few minutes Maynard said, "That's it?"

"That's it."

"So what happened to him?"

"He's still roaming around out there, a big survivor."

Maynard replaced the two clean guns in the rack across the room. "That's the first story?"

"Right. Given by what wind? You didn't know there'd be a test, did you."

"Wabaninodin." He came back and sat down. He looked at me, looked at the fire. He nodded. "You're right. It's a story for children. Little children."

"Maynard, would I lie to you?"

"So, maybe I should bring Tega when you tell the next one."

"Sure."

"Maybe Joe Pagoosie."

"Why not?"

"When you think that might be?"

"From the sound of this storm, maybe tomorrow afternoon. Beats school."

He nodded. "Thanks. See you."

"Giga wabamin."

"Yeah," Maynard said.

The storm raged all that night and all the next day. By midnight the highway was closed. By first light the snow had drifted over my porch. I shovelled out and Guaranteed and I took rabbit stew down to Aja. She was sleeping soundly, a small, shrivelled figure in the great bearskin, so I fed the stove and carried in more wood, and left without disturbing her.

By mid-afternoon the drifts had covered the porch again. I had trouble getting the door open when the children knocked. There they were, the three of them—Maynard, his sister Tega and Joe Pagoosie, who was just about up to my waist. They were all muffled in scarves and toques, and they were very white. They'd already taken off their snowshoes and stood them up in the drift.

"Come on in. You want some tea?"

Tega and Joe shook their heads. Maynard said, "Miigwetch," and when I poured him a mug he took it in both hands and sipped. "I told them." He raised his chin toward Tega and Joe, who had already sat down between the fires.

Tega took a little notebook and a ballpoint pen from the back pocket of her jeans. "Our teacher says that when the elders speak we should always listen," she said, looking at me very sternly. "It's oral history."

I pulled over a stool and sat down beside her. "Tega, I'm not exactly an elder. Not yet. Also, what I'm going to tell you is not history. It's a story."

"But our teacher says…"

"Tega, here is the difference: stories live. Stories have souls. Will you explain that to your teacher if you have a chance?"

She nodded.

"And will you put away that notebook? Because I am going to give you a story with a soul, and you will not be able to hear it if you're busy writing it down."

She laid the pad and the pen on the floor beside her and wrapped her arms around her knees.

Joe Pagoosie sat wide-eyed and silent, like a small owl. I winked at him. "Ready?"

He nodded.

"Here we go, then. This is a story given by Shawaninodin, South Wind."

In those days, not far from Neyashing, lived the greediest person anyone has ever heard of. No-one remembers his real name; everyone called him Many Arms.

Even when he was a child Many Arms grew very fat very quickly because he ate his brothers' and sisters' food. "I'll take that!" he would say. "That's mine!" And with both hands he would reach over and grab whatever food he wanted and stuff it into his mouth. All the other children made fun of him behind his back. "I'll take that!" one of them would say in a fat and grumbly voice. "That's mine!" And he would reach over and grab a stone, or stick, or whatever anyone else was playing with and stuff it into his mouth and make his eyes bulge out, and all the other children would shriek with laughter.

But although they laughed at him behind his back, no-one dared to laugh at Many Arms to his face, because he had grown so large. If he caught you he would roll on you and squash you flat.

As Many Arms grew older he grew greedier, and he began to take more than just food and toys. He began to take things that he could not possibly use. Canoes, for example. Whenever he caught anyone finishing a new canoe, he would reach over the man's shoul-

118

*der and say, "I'll take that! That's mine!" And off he would go,
carrying the canoe by its thwart, until he had 165 new canoes piled
up around his lodge. Or, if he saw women finishing new pots or baskets he would grab those things and carry them off, until he had
more pots and makaks than you could count. And very soon he began
to take other peoples'* houses, *even, just to store all the things he
had, and before long he had his own village, the village of Many
Arms, in the best place on the whole meadow, and all the other
people were squeezed out to the edges, where the ground was rocky
and uneven.*

*At that point, the villagers called a council to discuss what
should be done. Many people spoke at length. Everyone had suffered
as a result of Many Arms' greed, and everyone had an opinion.
Some were even in favour of killing him, but they soon decided
against that, because life is precious. Some were in favour of
imprisoning him, building a high pointy fence around him while he
was asleep, but they decided against that because not even the greediest people should be shut away from the forests, from the lakes and
rivers and the four winds. Some recommended banishing him forever
to some distant place. But they decided against that because they did
not want to send Many Arms among their friends, or even among
their enemies. Some suggested just abandoning him, going away
and leaving him alone. But they decided against that because they
could not bear to imagine the great loneliness that would descend on
Many Arms.*

*At last, at daybreak, they decided that some of the old people of
the village would go to Many Arms and attempt to reason with
him. So the little group of chosen elders set off down the hill to the
centre of the village where Many Arms lived, and as they
approached they could hear his grumbly voice saying, "That's mine!
I'll take that!" and the sounds as he grabbed fish out of the lake or
seized passing deer, or reached over to snatch someone else's breakfast. So they knew he was awake.*

*"Well," he asked as they approached, "what have you brought
me? What have to got for* me?" *He sat there like a large, round
hill of flesh.*

"We've come to talk to you," said their spokesman, whose name was Nokomis. All wise old women were called Nokomis.

"Excuse me, excuse me," Tega said, hand straight up. "Shouldn't that be *spokesperson?*"

"No, Tega, it should not."

"Our teacher says that words like that, *chairman, airman* and so on are all sexist and should be done away with."

"Your teacher and I hold different views on that. It is an unresolved matter. When you tell the story of Many Arms, Tega, you will tell it in your way. When your teacher tells it, she will tell it in hers."

"My teacher is a man. Mr. Montgomery."

"Well, Mr. Montgomery will tell it in his way. Meantime, I am telling it, and I am fond of the word *spokesman.* So, for now, that's what Nokomis was. Okay?"

She nodded, looking doubtful.

Nokomis told Many Arms, "We've come to talk to you."

"Talk? Talk? What good is talk to me? I'll take that*!" And Many Arms reached over and snatched off a shell necklace Nokomis was wearing, an heirloom from her grandmother.*

"You will not*!" Nokomis said, and she grabbed the necklace back again and gave Many Arms a slap across the face for good measure. "Now straighten up! We've come to talk to you because you are a major problem for us. You are* bad *news, Many Arms!"*

"Yeah," said all the other elders, nodding. "Yeah, yeah!"

"Look at you!" Nokomis went on. "You're so big and fat you can hardly move anymore, and you have more canoes, and lodges, and pots and baskets than you'll ever know what to do with. You're a disgrace, Many Arms, and the fact is we're at our wits' end. We don't know what to do with you."

"Yeah!" said the other elders, nodding sternly.

"I can't help it," Many Arms said, pouting a little and rubbing his bruised cheek. "It's the way I'm made. It's in my blood. Can a fish change its fishness? Can a hawk change..."

"Rubbish!" Nokomis said. "Knock it off! You know as well as I do we're talking adaptation here. Either you adapt or you're

finished, Many Arms. It's out of our hands."

"*Yeah,*" *said the other elders.*

"*But I'm an* individual," *Many Arms pleaded.* "*I'm just expressing my individuality. You expect me to* conform? *To be like everyone else?*"

"*Yeah,*" *said the elders.* "*That's the way we're thinking, all right.*"

"*How dull! I can't do it! Impossible! I'll take those.*" *And Many Arms sneaked a hand over and ripped off a nice pair of moosehide moccasins lined with rabbit fur that one of the elders was wearing.*

Nokomis stood up. "*Enough! Too much! We warn you, Many Arms, this situation is out of control. Totally!*"

"*And that!*" *Many Arms cried, making a grab for a coat that one old man was wearing, but missing, because the old fellow tottered backwards in time, swatting at Many Arms with his cane.*

Dejected, despairing, the elders wound back up the hill and brought the bad news to the rest of the village: Many Arms would not listen to reason. And so, sadly, a second council that night decided that Many Arms must be left to his fate, and that the village must move elsewhere for its own survival.

"*More for me! More for me!*" *Many Arms cried, when he realized that everyone had gone away and deserted him, and he began to ransack the forests and lakes of everything edible or useful.*

Now, you know that there are spirits whose task it is to keep the world in order. They were here in those days, too. They travelled around correcting mistakes, balancing imbalances, boosting energies where required. Some of these spirits were small and fast, darting here and there like dragonflies, and some were even smaller and quicker, so quick that you would never even notice them. But some were very, very large. These big ones spent most of the time sleeping, conserving their strength, but when they were needed they woke up and went into action. You could tell when they were waking up. Earth shook. Tidal waves rose like walls of water and rushed at the shore. Hurricanes and cyclones roared in the air.

These spirits, you see, were part of Earth. They hovered in the warm breath of Earth, or slumbered in mountains and caverns, or lay in the depths of seas and great lakes. They felt Earth like a body, and just as you know when something is not right in your body, they knew when something was wrong in Earth.

The villagers knew that one of these spirits would be coming sooner or later to correct things, since they had failed to do it themselves. They knew that Many Arms was a threat and a menace, a one-man disaster area, creating a kind of vacuum all around him. They didn't know which spirit would come, or when, but they knew it would happen and they didn't want to be around.

They left.

And the other animals left, too.

Misshipeshu was the spirit who came. Misshipeshu lived deep, deep in the Lake, so deep that everything about her was green— teeth, claws, horns, long body—all pale green, the colour of new forest in the spring. Soon, Misshipeshu began to feel the irksome presence of Many Arms. She began to smell the noisome greed of Many Arms.

Misshipeshu rose.

Now, I can't tell you how big Misshipeshu was. Very, very big. I can't tell you exactly what she looked like, either. Many people had seen parts of her, but only parts. For some, Misshipeshu was the yellow light of eyes fixed upon them, like two suns behind a shifting bank of fog. For others, she was white horns rising out of the Lake, casting long reflections at their canoe. For others she was claws reaching like knives in the rapids, and for still others, Misshipeshu was an enormous back and tail sliding into the depths of the Lake, so smoothly that she could be mistaken in the distance for just another promontory.

Imagine Many Arms now, big, fat Many Arms, shouting "All mine! All mine!" Alone on the dry shore.

And imagine Misshipeshu, slow and green, rising through the layers of the Lake. Imagine Misshipeshu's horns breaking the surface, Misshipeshu's eyes, like twin suns, finding Many Arms; Misshipeshu's throat stretching in a roar like ten terrible storms; Misshipeshu's tail lashing the Lake into huge waves that crashed against the beach where Many Arms sat.

When Many Arms saw Misshipeshu in the Lake, when he heard that roar and felt those cold winds, he stopped saying, "That's mine! I'll take that!" He gulped. He tried to make himself invisible. He reached underneath himself and dug his fingers into a deep crevasse. He wiggled his fat toes under thick tree roots. He hung on to a tiny patch of Earth and he said, "Please, please *let me stay here for a little while."*

But Misshipeshu ignored his pleas. Misshipeshu had not risen all the way from the bottom of the Lake for nothing. Something wrong sat there on the shore of the Lake. It needed to be scattered. It needed to be dispersed into tiny bits. So, Misshipeshu rose step by step out of the Lake and came ashore. Spray and sand flew everywhere. Lightning flashed wherever her claws struck rock. Whirlwinds lifted all the lodges and all the possessions of Many Arms and smashed them to bits and sent them spinning far into the forest, far out into the Lake. Boulders snapped and splintered under the lashing tail of Misshipeshu. For miles around trees were ripped out of the ground in the breath of Misshipeshu and the hills behind the shore were shaken flat by her roaring.

Many Arms clung desperately to his bit of rock while chaos swirled around him. All his clothes were blown off. All his hair was blown out. The Lake surged over him. He was a bald, bare, fat man in the middle of a disaster. It took so much energy just to hold on that Many Arms got thin right on the spot, so thin he looked just like a skin-covered skeleton. So thin you could see his knobby backbone on both sides of him.

And as his body changed, Many Arms changed inside too, and all this happened very fast.

Still growling, still striking flashes of lightning off the cliffs with her claws, Misshipeshu slid back into the depths and vanished, first her snout, then her horns, then her front legs, and then her long body and spiny tail. She looked just like a slender promontory, sliding into the Lake. Gradually the Lake grew calm above her. Gradually the whirlwinds dwindled to little spinning places in the dust. Gradually the clouds lifted and the sun returned, very pale.

Slowly, Many Arms opened one eye and looked at himself. He saw a bald, bare, thin man sitting on a rock in the midst of devastation. "Help!" said Many Arms. "This is awful! This is terrible! There is no-one! There is nothing!" And, indeed, as far as he could see, there was no other living thing.

But then, when he opened the other eye, he saw another animal. This was a turkey vulture, which appeared first as a tiny winged speck, and then drifted closer and closer until at last it settled on a rock a short distance away. "Isn't this terrible?" Many Arms asked it. "What shall we do?"

"Alll miiine!" the turkey vulture said, watching him with beady eyes.

Many Arms scampered away to the top of the bare hill. Up there he discovered that something else was alive. This was a tiny blueberry bush. Perhaps it had survived because it was growing in a crevasse, or perhaps because it was so small. It had only four leaves and two berries.

Many Arms sat gazing at those two berries for a long time. He was terribly hungry, but when he finally reached out he did so very cautiously, saying to the bush, "Do you think... I mean, would it be all right if... I mean, may I..." And then he picked one of the berries.

He cringed, but all was still. There were no howling whirlwinds, no lightning flashing like giant claws.

Very slowly, Many Arms ate that blueberry. Nothing had ever tasted so good.

And then, to his astonishment, he saw other berry bushes close by, as if they had sprung up at that moment. He got up. He began to move. Cautiously he crossed the bare rock to those other bushes, taking only a berry or two from each before passing on to others. Soon he had reached the crest of another hill, and when he looked back he saw that the slope was already green with life behind him.

On the other side of the ridge, however, the next valley was still a smoking ruin, and when he looked down into that desert he saw a small boy wandering there, hungry, and dirty, and tired, and weeping. "Hey!" Many Arms shouted. "Come on over here. There's food! Lots for everybody!"

And to his astonishment, that valley also began to fill with life before his eyes. The child began to laugh with delight at the magical thing that was happening around him, and Many Arms laughed with him.

Then, as he looked out over the Lake, he saw canoes coming, first two, then two more, then several in a group, coming on the sparkling water around the point where Misshipeshu had re-entered the Lake. They were his people returning. Joyfully, Many Arms raced down to the shore to greet them. "In here!" he called. "There's plenty for everyone."

One of the first to step ashore was old Nokomis, followed by two or three of the elders. "Many Arms?" she asked, edging close. "Many Arms?"

"Yes. It's me."

"You've changed." Cautiously Nokomis leaned forward and dangled the end of her necklace in front of him, the one made of shells given to her by her grandmother.

Many Arms laughed and waved it away. "Give it to someone who needs it," he said.

One of the elders, leaning on his cane, wiggled a very fine moosehide and rabbit-fur moccasin under Many Arms' nose, and Many Arms laughed again. "Give it to someone who needs it," he said.

Nokomis grunted. She looked around at the results of Misshipeshu's visit—the levelled hills, the altered river-courses, the frail new life just beginning to spring up again amidst the devastation. "Well," she said, "it certainly took a lot of nonsense, didn't it, to teach you that simple thing?"

I got up and went over to the stove to pour tea. The storm howled over us. I lit the lamps.

"What's the next one?" Joe asked.

"A story from West Wind, Gwabeeung-nodin."

"Can we hear it now?"

I shook my head. "One day, one story."

Tega picked up her pad and pen and returned them to her hip pocket. "Thank you," she said, offering her hand. "It was a very nice story. Mr. Montgomery says folklore..."

I took her twelve-year-old hand in both of mine and held it. "Tega, give my regards to Mr. Montgomery. Please invite him out to see me. Tell him I know lots of folklore."

"When's the next story?" Joe Pagoosie asked, pulling his toque on. "Tomorrow?"

"Same time, same place." I opened the door and they filed out into the storm. "Take care, Maynard."

"See you," he said, giving me a small wave. "Thanks."

The next day was a Friday. During the night the storm passed to the east and the sun rose on a glittering world. At dawn I put on my snowshoes and took a shovel down past the buried trucks to Aja's place. She was awake, and warm. I helped her make breakfast; I brought in some wood. I cleared her entrance, dug out her woodpile, shovelled a path to her outhouse.

The rest of the morning I spent digging out my own porch and windows, stopping often to look across the bay and the spit, out over the black Lake. Far to the east, storm clouds billowed like quilts tossed by children.

They came down the trail on their snowshoes after lunch, the three of them, ready for their story. But when we were all inside between the two fires, I had trouble getting started. I listened for the wind but there was no wind, only the vast silence with the tiny sounds of the fire in its centre. Then I listened for Mother's voice telling the last story, and after a little while I heard it—soft, the way it was at the end, like a ripple at a bend in a dark river before the currents reach up for it, and take it down....

"Okay," I said. "Ready? This is the story given by the west wind, Gwabeeung-nodin."

One of the most fortunate hunters in those days was Wabimakwa,

126

White Bear. He earned his name from the vision he was given on his journey from boyhood to manhood, a vision of a gigantic bear rising in the north, his arms spread wide to embrace the Lake.

White Bear was a good man who lived at peace with himself, and took no more than he needed from the land. If the needs of others were greater, he gave what he had to them. He watched the signs and observed all the warnings of the spirits, so that if he needed their help one day he would have it. He knew if he saw a white animal on a summer hunt he must stop hunting immediately, or some misfortune would befall him or his family. He knew to preserve the tips of birds' wings, and the skulls of bear and deer, so that the animals might find them and use them again. He knew how to make snow by casting rabbits' fur into the rising smoke, and how to summon rain by killing a blue-bottle fly, or wind by spinning a bone disk. He knew where maymaygwayshi lived in the rock faces, and where Nanabush had brought fire from the heavens for man.

You might say that he was a very superstitious and ignorant fellow, this White Bear, with no proper scientific sense at all. Still, he was happy , and he was very lucky, so he believed he must be doing something right. He continued to respect the spirits and to teach his children about them.

One day disaster struck him. Pajak stole his wife. Now Pajak was a large skeleton who wandered through the woods stealing people whenever he could. He was very noisy. He clattered. If you take some stones and toss them in your hands you will know how Pajak clattered. On still days and nights you could hear him clattering, trying to creep up, and you could shout out to your friends, "Hey! Watch out! Pajak's coming!" And you could all run off laughing in many directions, and Pajak would go back into the wilderness wringing his bony hands and saying "Oh darn, darn!"

However, on windy and rainy days you had to be very careful, because you could be playing a game of hide-and-seek, say, and suddenly you'd turn around and there would be Pajak's bony knee-caps right in front of you, and Pajak's bony hands would clamp down on your shoulders. "Gotcha!" and off you'd go to that place where Pajak took everyone he stole. Some said it was just a large cave. Some said it was a hole in Earth that went down forever. Nobody knew for sure, because nobody had ever come back. Nobody was quite sure, either, why Pajak spent so much time kidnapping people. It was just his peculiar, natural, monstrosity.

White Bear's wife was picking blueberries on a windy hill when Pajak stole her. When people looked for her later, they found only her basket tipped over with berries spilling out, and Pajak's bony footprints leading away.

White Bear was devastated. He loved his wife dearly and could not imagine life without her. For several months he hardly moved from his wigwam. Others brought him food. Others looked after his children. They waited patiently for White Bear to come out of his terrible grief and begin to live again, and, at last, when the first storms of winter struck and his children complained of hunger and the cold, White Bear left his lodge and began to hunt again, finding warm rabbit fur for their beds and warm beaverskins and deerskins for their clothing. "I shall look after my children first," he said, "and then go in search of my wife."

But before he had completed his preparations for winter, a second calamity struck. This time all the village was affected, not just White Bear. Snow got deeper, winter colder, game scarcer. Wolverines ravished the caches of smoked fish and dried meat and berries. People starved. One day White Bear returned from a long hunting trip to find that Wendigo had visited his village and carried off everyone who was still alive.

Wendigo is the most fearsome of monsters. He is as tall as a tree and his teeth are gleaming points of copper, his eyes raging suns. The nails of his huge feet and hands are like curved knives. His breath is the wind. Where he walks Earth quivers and breaks. Rock shatters. He is voracious, insatiable. He snatches up a whole village, and stalks on to the next, and then another. Usually, when the ice of the lakes begins to turn soft and dark under spring sun, Wendigo sleeps. But when the first frosts come again he grows restless, and bellows in his sleep, and roams abroad.

Nothing was left of White Bear's village after Wendigo had gone. White Bear sank down into a snow bank and asked the empty *sky and the bleak land, "What is the use of living? I have lost my love, I have lost my children and my people. What is left to lose?" And he folded his arms and bent his head against the storm and prepared to die.*

But he could not die. And, when he could not die he got angry and began to lash out blindly, tearing the limbs off trees and kicking up great clouds of snow, and shooting arrows at the sky, as if all of these were enemies that had conspired against him. "I'll show you!" he shouted. "I'll show you!" But exactly who or what he was showing he did not know.

Spring came. The days grew longer and warmer, the river mouths opened, the scent of Earth drifted in the breeze. By then White Bear was very thin. His ribs and pelvis stuck out at sharp angles. So tight was the skin on his face that it drew his lips back in a weird smile. In fact, White Bear looked like a Wendigo himself.

Then, just when things should have improved, just when the breezes should have filled with life and promise, White Bear received the cruellest blow of all. For the Earth that emerged from beneath the snows was not the green world he had always known, but a black, silent and sterile place.

Fear, Segisiwin, had altered everything in the eyes of White Bear.

What does Segisiwin look like? Its eyes are wide, with pupils like empty sockets. It had no nose, only round holes for nostrils, and its mouth gapes wide, stretched for a scream that never comes. Fear is silent. It moves in white silence. It clasps its victims with cold and silent fingers and glides worm-like on the surface of the skin and underneath, glides into the belly and upward, downward. Fear twists and distorts. Fear changes.

So, now. Segisiwin changed all that White Bear saw and made it monstrous. Where once he had drawn sweet sap from the birch trees, now he heard the rushing of that sap like rapids tumbling upon him from all sides. Where once he had found joy in the calling of the long wedges of geese, now he heard these only as shrill, laughing mockeries. Where once he had welcomed new shoots thrusting out of the damp earth, now he saw only ghastly tendrils reaching to entrap him. And the waters, those waters upon which he had once paddled with such joy, into which he had plunged in the heat of summer, from which he had drawn an abundance of trout and sturgeon and whitefish—these waters were now dark and oily, filled with the menacing shapes of death.

White Bear screamed and screamed. He buried his face in his knees and drew his arms over his head, and screamed to blot out the rushing of his own blood, the sound of his own poisoned life.

Others heard his screaming. Far off, Pajak heard it and approached, his bones clattering across the last of the ice. Far off, Wendigo heard it and strode toward it, his huge mouth open and his greedy arms outstretched. And nearer, Segisiwin heard and turned back, gibbering and shrieking, waving his fleshy fingers.

Now, in spite of everything, deep in the heart of White Bear there lingered a little core of courage and manhood. If you were to draw a picture of this core it would be like a tiny sun, here in his breast, and if you were to trace a spirit line from it, that line would wind down deep, deep into the true heart of Earth, deep beneath all that White Bear was imagining in his terror, for all that lives is connected to that same place in the heart of Earth, and each spirit line sings its own song, and blends with the song of Earth.

Passing among the firs, Weesakayjac heard the howling of this pitiful man, this White Bear who had once been so proud and confident, and he heard also the faint humming of the spirit line, frail as the smallest insect, the tiniest sandfly struggling to land on your arm, a brown dot that could be swept away by a breath.

Weesakayjac is the grey jay, softest of birds. Like a shadow he flutters among the evergreens. Like a ghost. Yet he is a staunch friend to man, and some say that he is one of the disguises of Nanabush himself.

Down Weesakayjac came, alighting on a melting snowbank near the man. He asked, "What's wrong? It's spring, Why aren't you rejoicing, as we are? Look around you! Look at the beauty and the wonder!"

"Beauty?" White Bear wailed. "I see nothing of that. Segisiwin *has stolen all of that away, just as Pajak has taken love out of my life, and Wendigo has taken the joy of children and of friends. Even now they're coming back, all three! Don't you hear them?"* And White Bear continued his howling.

"Quiet, fool!" Weesakayjac said. "What's the use of crying? You must act!"

"Act? With what?" White Bear flourished his empty bow. "I have shot all my arrows at the sky. I have nothing to defend myself against these monsters!"

"Wait and be quiet, then!" Weesakayjac commanded, and flew away as swiftly and silently as a ghost among the tangled branches, only to reappear a short time later with a single gleaming arrow clenched in his beak. "Take this! It is a magic arrow. It will kill whatever you aim it at."

"But there are three of them," wailed White Bear, "and only one arrow!"

"Fool!" Weesakayjac said again. "Be a man! Think!"

And so White Bear thought as he strung this magical arrow into his bow, watching his three enemies circle closer through the forest, through the clearings. So he was ready when the moment came, when good fortune offered him a perfect shot, an instant when his enemies were all in line—Segisiwin, the closest, his slack fingers already reaching for his prey, and then Wendigo, a little behind him, and then Pajak.

In that moment White Bear ceased his whimpering and acted like a man. He loosed the magic arrow. Swoosh, it went, through Segisiwin. Swoosh! Swoosh! through Wendigo and Pajak, and on through the clouds far away to a place known only to Weesakay-jac.

All three monsters froze. Then each uttered his exclamation of surprise—Ugh! Ough! Awk!—and crumpled silently, and vanished. White Bear had not killed them, for they never die, but he had defeated them for a little time. He had made room for life.

And then the true miracle occurred. Everything he had lost was given back: first, the greenness and freshness of his world; then all his people, just as they had been; and finally, most wonderful, his *wife and children running toward him with their arms outstretched.*

"*Miigwetch! Miigwetch!*" *White Bear said.* "*Thank you!*" *But Weesakayjac was only a small shadow, fading among the trees.*

Joe Pagoosie wrinkled his nose. "I thought Nanabush was gonna be in that one."

"Maybe he was," I said. "He has a lot of disguises."

All three started to pull on their hats and coats, looking out at the sun on slopes perfect for tobogganing.

"I'll bet the North Wind story is the best," Joe said. "I'll bet it is."

I helped him with his coat zipper. "There isn't a North Wind story. The one I just told you is the last."

"But there were only three," Tega said. "Why aren't there four? Are you *sure* there isn't one from Keewaydin?"

"Yes."

"Why not?"

"Because, Tega, your grandmother was very sick when she told these stories, and she died before the fourth."

She looked at me very solemnly for a moment, and then she stretched on tiptoe and gave me a small kiss on the cheek. "Come for supper," she said. "Bring Jenny if she gets here."

"Sure."

Maynard paused in the doorway. "Miigwetch," he said.

"You're welcome, Maynard."

He nodded. "About that last story, you know what I think?"

"What?"

"It's waiting, I think. Waiting for you to tell it."

There was a rumbling in the east, a roar with a whine in the centre. Isaac Kohotchuk had swung the snowblower off the highway. He was coming down into Neyashing, and soon a feather of snow would rise above the trees and the dunes, and we would have our road again.

Neither Maynard nor I looked toward the sound.

"Maybe you're right," I said. "Maybe by spring I'll have that story for you."

We had one more meeting with the Shadow Man.

It was supposed to produce a strategy. It was supposed to involve only a few men, this meeting—"community leaders," Red Cloud called them—who would decide what the rest of us would do when the road dried up and the first flatbed truck came down into Neyashing.

I didn't let it happen that way. I went to every house and invited everybody—men, women and kids. There were so many people that Richard Gwinguish did not have room for them in his kitchen, and we moved to a sheltered place in the dunes and built a big fire. It turned out to be a long meeting. Many people spoke, and they said the same thing in many ways. They said that they would not hurt anyone, that they would rather give up Neyashing, and that Red Cloud should leave now and let them find their own way. When everyone finished speaking, they voted on whether he should stay or go. He went bitterly, telling us we were weak fools, but he went.

I stayed a long time by the fire after that meeting, looking sometimes at the embers, sometimes at the stars. I thought I was the last to leave, but Simon Littlewolf was still there, watching from the shadows. "So, what now?" he asked.

I had no answer for him. And by that spring morning when Aja moved out to the end of the spit and sent swans soaring like a beacon, I still did not have an answer. Even after Michael Gardner arrived I had no answer.

Considering the Client

I dreamed that night, after we brought Gardner from Schreiber station. In my dream the spit became a great tree rising out of Earth and through the Lake, a pole like the totems at Tanu, reaching into the sky through the Pleiades. High upon it Aja laughed, spiralling down and freeing its creatures as she came. But she was not the Aja I had always known. She was young; her hair was black, the black of final space, and the light in her eyes was no light of Earth....

When she called me I woke, wrapped a blanket around myself, and went out into the darkness. An old woman waited on the Council Rock. Her hair gleamed like snow in the moonlight; her eyes shone with the living light of the Lake where it moves cross quartzite shoals.

"Aniin, Aja."

"Aniin, Travis."

"It is a long climb from the beach."

"There are things to be decided, now that the man is here. The tiredness of an old woman is not important." She motioned to me, and I sat opposite her.

"We have come to a place that you must cross for me."

"Aja..."

"Hear me. You believe you have failed. You are thinking you will leave Neyashing and go north and live in the old way, close to the spirits."

I nodded.

"So we have always thought. That is why the space for spirits grows small. But you must stay, Travis. You must act, now."

"Tell me what to do."

"I cannot. You must tell yourself."

"Help me."

She laughed a soft and hissing laugh like an otter's. "I have done what I can do. *I have brought him to you.*" She leaned forward with her eyes wide, head swaying slightly, her gaze going through me and around me as it had with Eric Morrow the night of the meeting. "Now *you* must act."

I trembled inside the blanket. "You see…"

"I see only a man walking alone on the beach, seeking."

"But he is only one man, Aja."

"One is enough. *You* are enough."

"It's too late."

"No, it is not too late. It is too late when something has died. Neyashing lives. There."

I looked down at the village, and when I turned back, Aja was gone.

I have been frightened by many things. Bears have frightened me, coming fast with their snouts down and their shoulders rolling. Moose have chased me up trees. Four years in the city frightened me almost to death. Brutal faces have frightened me, and ugly books and photographs and movies, not for themselves but for the lurking meanness in the lives that made them. But I have not been so frightened as I was then. I stayed a long time on the Council Rock, inside my blanket, shaking. I gazed down at the roofs of Neyashing, so small in the pale light that when I held out my hands I could cup the whole village into them. I stared a long time at Jupiter, and at Antares blazing in the southwest, and at Vega straight overhead, like the point of a hot needle pinning me to Earth.

Finally, when the first grey streaks appeared on the horizon, I went in and put on my moccasins and got my telescope, quietly so as not to waken Jenny. Guaranteed came back out with me, his nails clicking like insects on the rock.

I went out into deep space then, and grew still and calm.

Cutler has no interest in what lies beyond Earth. For a time after I came back from university I told him things that I had read about the planets and the stars. He listened, but then one night he said, "N'sheemenh, it's all interesting, it's another way of knowing them. But I'm going to stay with the old way. I want to keep the old stories about the Bears, and the Fisher, and the Hole-in-the-Sky that other people call the Pleiades. I like those stories Mother told about the falling stars. I like the idea that the Northern Lights are the souls of warriors dancing. So please, don't tell me more about space and time so huge that they are meaningless."

But for me there is comfort in viewing the stupendous accidents of those distant, manless worlds, beyond all responsibility. So that night I escaped out of time. I gazed at bodies gone for a million years, gazed at ghosts. I found M-68, and then moved through Hydra and out to M-83 and hung in the ether of that constellation, 15 million light-years away. And then, just before dawn, I moved out, out again, to M-104, across 40 million years of light. And so clear was the night, so pure the emptiness between that galaxy and me, that I caught glimpses of the dust it left behind.

And then, time returned.... Time was morning, sunlight, space going flat. Time was misty breath on my hands and neck, and grey jays fluttering in the firs beneath the Council Rock. Time was a shifting horizon, and a winged boat sliding through phantoms between Lake and sky, and a serpent lifting its crested head toward the dawn. Time became a cloud of insects swirling out of the warming forest, and Guaranteed's groan as he stretched stiff muscles. Time became a flurry of mergansers breaking away from the western point and into the new light.

Time became a hazy beach, and a man.

A man watching the sunrise.

Gardner.

I have brought him, Travis, to you.

Jenny embraced me from behind, rumpled and half asleep, holding one of my shirts around her, saying, "What are you doing here? It's cold! You're trembling, Travis! Come in. Come to bed."

"I'm frightened."

She turned me to face her. "Oh, so am I," she whispered, arms around my neck. "I'm frightened too, but I want us to have a baby anyway. That's my news, Travis. That's what I wanted to tell you, last night in Schreiber."

Cold and fear drop away from me. Morning, and day, and all of time fall away. In our bed her body is beneath my own, her lips beneath my lips, her breasts and hair and hips beneath my hands. And all of life is with us in the moment when we say each other's names, in the whitehot point where we cry our love, in the place where the names and the love become the salt of tears flowing away, and the point grows and shatters into galaxies....

We drift in space, drift across the mighty body of the Lake, our craft the frailest act of faith, and I am watching the muscles ripple in her brown back as she paddles, the wind move through her hair. I watch the curve of her breast when she half-turns to speak, the softness of her smile when she says my name, and lost in that mystery we are not afraid, Jenny and I. We know where we belong, and what we are part of, and what living spirits we will make refuge for, forever, as long as we live....

We drowse and wake, grow aware of strands of moisture brushing across the windows of the afternoon, of spruce smoke curling off the roof, of the shifting grunt of an indifferent dog beside the stove. We become aware of each other again, and her hair drifts across me, her lips and teeth close urgently on me, and soon we are crying and clasping each other again, sure in that embrace that preserves us on this spinning and perilous Earth....

Out, out, out. Far out beyond the western point. Far enough so that the brooding shore becomes only shadows of blue and purple, and the hills fold up like soft pelts under the fog. Far enough to know that the gathering and ambivalent wind could sweep us out to die, shifting, bringing on the southern fog until the sun is a bleak disk, until loose skeins of wool snag on the promontories and tumble

137

into the bays, and Neyashing fades and blurs like an ageing photograph—hillside, houses and beach. Smoke plumes blend with the fog, and thicken, and then vanish altogether with the buildings and the beach. Like a slender island the crest of the Palisades floats above time and space, and then grey arms reach out to enfold it also, and we are alone....

Jenny is laughing. Naked in the firelight, she is pouring tea, bending to scratch Guaranteed's ears and nose, and we are sitting on the bed with steaming mugs watching the fog move, watching the reflections blend and hover on the walls, on my snowshoes, and guns, on the drum of my grandfather, watching them dance in the rafters, making love, making life, borne with us beyond time and certainties. There, in that other realm the spit lies in fog, a troubled man groping toward the spirits at its end, and there suddenly, in a vision above sanity and reason, small as a star and absolute as light itself, I know what should be done with Michael Gardner. I know exactly what I should do....

A little hook, a melancholy and relentless little hook of time draws me up to dusk, to embers in the hearth, to Guaranteed's cold nose pressed into my bicep, and Guaranteed's unblinking, dinnerless stare.

"N'dai," I say to him, getting out of bed and pulling on my trousers and boots. "Get Jimmy. Get Cutler."

Jimmy arrived first. He came so quietly down the path and across the Council Rock to the edge where I was standing that I didn't know he was there until I saw his hand waving slowly across my face. He grinned. "Nice day, Travis?"

Cutler came a hundred yards behind, just as silently, wearing his big hat with the eagle feather.

"I have a plan for Gardner," I said.

"So have I. I plan to re-organize his fingers."

Jimmy frowned. "Cutler, that's the same unco-operative attitude that got you expelled from kindergarten."

"I can't help it. I've been listening to Barbara. She's

taking assertiveness training."

"Assertiveness training." Jimmy lifted a finger, rolling his eyes and frowning. "Is that the same as affirmative action?"

"Jimmy, you should go to those sessions. Every Thursday night at the school in Schreiber. They'd do you a lot of good. Help overcome your painful shyness. Nice little group. Take your leotards."

"Gardner," I said. "Here's what we do." And there on the Council Rock I told them my idea.

When I finished they looked at me in silence. They looked at each other.

"You're not serious." Cutler laid his hand on my head and shook me gently. "Tell me you're not serious."

"It'll work," I said.

"Oh sure," Jimmy grunted, rubbing the back of his neck. "It'll work fine. It'll work well enough to get you about eight years!"

"That's a chance I'll take."

"Like hell!" Cutler said. He turned in a little circle, arms raised to the stars. "What you have got here is a white man, a *businessman*!"

"I've seen him, talked to him a bit. I think he's different."

"Different how?"

"Well, he's here, for one thing. He's here alone. Came on the train. No luggage, just a pack. No place to stay. Why *here*? Why Neyashing?"

"Makes no sense," Jimmy said.

"Exactly. So, maybe all we do is help."

"It's not a plan, it's an impulse. Even if you're right, he's only one man."

"He's right, n'sheemenh. You haven't thought it through."

"Sure I have. I've told you what'll happen tonight. And tomorrow."

"And the next day? And the next? And the next?"

"Cutler, I can't plan that. You know I can't."

He walked to the edge of the Council Rock and stared down at the dim lights of Neyashing, shaking his head.

"Too much faith," Jimmy said. "Too much trust. To much Aja."

"Maybe." I waited. After a minute I asked, "Do we go for it?"

Jimmy took off his cap and put it on again. "What the hell," he said, "it's all we've got."

"Cutler?"

My bother turned his back on Neyashing and looked at me steadily. He looked doubtful, frightened, amused. He asked, "You sure about this, n'sheemenh?"

"I'm sure."

"All right," Cutler said. "We go."

By the time we agreed on details and headed down the hill, wind was gusting around the Palisades and the western point, whipping sand off the dunes. When we got to the road, Jimmy headed right and Cutler and I swung left, to Bobby Naponse's cabin.

Bobby's guest cabin stood alone in the dunes, kept apart for occasional fishermen and hunters, and for the many visiting relatives of Ellen Naponse. It had three rooms, and a porch, and a stove big enough to heat it year-round. It also had bright yellow curtains sewn by Ellen herself, but when we approached that night we saw that the curtains were open, like an invitation. Light spilled through the windows from an oil lamp on the table, and sitting at that table was Michael Gardner. He leaned on his folded arms, watching the lamp flame, listening to the wind.

Cutler touched my arm and we stopped and took a hard look at him. His square jaw was freshly shaved. His hair was brushed and his blue eyes were alert, expectant. He reminded me of a heron poised in the shallows.

"Smug sonuvabitch!" Cutler said. "*Look* at him!"

"Stick to the plan," I said.

140

We went up onto the porch.

Gardner heard us coming and met us at the door before we knocked. "Gentlemen," he said quietly, with no trace of sarcasm but only a benign and ironic little smile.

I introduced us and Gardner nodded, shaking hands. "Glad you're here. Come in."

I began the lies even before we were inside: "We just came to see how you're getting on. See if you needed anything."

He laughed, motioning to chairs at the table where he'd been sitting. "To tell the truth, I don't know what I need. I haven't really taken stock. I know there's a little tea here. Like some?"

"Maybe later," I said. "We just want to check..."

Gardner laughed again and touched me lightly on the arm. "Sit down. I know why you've come."

"You do?"

"Brightsands," he said.

Cutler had sat and folded his arms. Now he took off his tall hat and placed it carefully on the corner of the table. The feather stood like an exclamation point. He leaned forward. "I'll start. You know why *we're* here. We live here. This is our place. But why are *you* here?"

I held my breath. I caught a fleeting glimpse of that wreckage in his eyes and I feared that it might overwhelm him now and he would lie or lose sight of the thing we might do together. But then the clutter vanished, and the gaze he turned on my brother was surprised but clear. "I don't know," he said. "I don't know why I'm here."

Wind shook the little cabin. Sand hissed across the stovepipes and the windowpanes, and waves roared, and broke, and swept up to cleanse the beach of scraps and corpses. There inside, the lamp burned with a pure and hard-edged flame.

I have met people who claim that truth is elusive, evasive, elastic. Truth is relative, they say, depending on points of view and on factors that shift like quicksand. I've met people who argue that truth is altered by the very act of stating it, like Heisenberg's particles, and I've met others who say it is like that elephant with the blind man groping for various parts, and still others who think that since no-one can ever know everything, you can never be sure of anything.

They may be right, some of them, or all of them; but, for me truth is a deep river flowing forever. You can dip into it and drink anytime you want. Sometimes you use words, sometimes other things. You never take it all, but you get enough to stay alive. You get enough to keep laughing.

And at that moment when Michael Gardner told the ridiculous truth—"I don't know why I'm here"—*he laughed.* "I don't," he said, and opened his hands, still laughing.

Cutler leaned back and linked his hands behind his head. His look said, *You may be right, n'sheemenh. There may be hope for this shaganash.* "Your turn," Cutler said to me.

I said, "I want to ask you about your company, about your place in it."

"Sure. Go ahead."

"You're president of Aspen Corporation. Head honcho."

He nodded.

"So you're the man who approves projects like Brightsands Village. Finally."

"Finally, yes. With a board of directors. A very strong board of directors."

"Now here's a scenario: suppose, just suppose for a minute, that the three of us sat here tonight and re-examined that whole project."

"And you gave me your side of the story..."

"No, not exactly. If we did that we'd likely get into an argument or a debate. No, let's say we just showed you that there were many factors you had not considered in your original decision. Human factors. Environmental factors."

"Spiritual factors," Gardner said, watching me.

"Spiritual factors, yes. Suppose we talked about those things, and we persuaded you that Brightsands should not go ahead. Could you stop it?"

"I don't know." Gardner rubbed his chin. "I think so, but I'm not sure.",

"You have...power," Cutler said softly, smiling.

"I have power and power has me."

"What's that mean?"

"It means I can't always do what I think should be done, just like you."

"Don't patronize me, mister."

"I'm not. I'm stating a fact. Look, we're all human. I probably like the same things you like. I've spent all day walking around here—along the beach, and out to the end of the peninsula, and a few miles down that trail at the foot of the cliffs. I can see the beauty just as you can, and I know you can't quantify it, can't weigh it or measure it, can't bottle it. And I know you've got a community here. I can see that too. So, to come back to your scenario, Travis, you and I could talk here tonight and you might—you probably could—convince me that Brightsands should be stopped. Then what?"

"You tell us," Cutler said.

"Then I go back to a problem. No, that's not quite right. Then I take a problem with me. It's this: the person who goes back to that other world, that world of calculations and studies and plans and money, that world where beauty and emotion *are* quantified, is not quite the same person who was so moved, here, by your persuasive arguments."

"Why not?"

Gardner spread his arms. "Because of old habits. Because of other people's expectations. Because of masks. Because of *momentum*. Because of an environment that will absorb him again like an amoeba and carry him with it."

Cutler sniffed and rubbed his earlobe. "Horseshit. Do what you want. If you want out of something, punch a hole. Walk away."

"It's that easy, is it?"

143

"Damn right."

"And where will you walk *to?*" Gardner laughed sadly. "No, that's an orphan attitude, Cutler. The world that formed it just doesn't exist anymore."

"That so?"

"I'm afraid it is."

Cutler leaned forward. He pointed down through the floor of the cabin and down toward the sands of the dunes and the bedrock beneath. "As long as I'm here, my friend, that world exists."

And there was a rap on the door then, and Jimmy Pagoosie walked in looking sore and sullen and bringing a big gust of wind with him. He was wearing one of the caps that he had made for all his family, with *Matchi Maung* and a crest of an evil-looking loon in sunglasses. He pushed it back on his head and introduced himself to Gardner.

Cutler stared darkly at him as he sat down. "Who the hell invited you?"

"Free country, ain't it?" Jimmy pulled a finger across his nose. "Blowin' like a bitch out there!"

Gardner got to his feet, smiling. "Let's see if I can find that tea."

"Push off," Cutler hissed, glowering at Jimmy.

"You should know the situation here, Mr. Gardner," Jimmy said, looking very aggrieved, very bitter. "You're entitled to know. The fact is that these two men don't want me to speak to you. They don't want you to hear what I have to say."

Gardner turned from the sink where he was filling a kettle. "Oh? Why's that?"

"Well, like yourself I'm a businessman. An independent businessman. I'm in favour of development, free enterprise. I want us to get ahead in this region. And this Brightsands plan, why it's the best thing that's happened to us. The best thing *ever.* Some of us here respect Aspen Corporation and appreciate what you're doing for our community. We just

144

want you to know that." Jimmy waved his arms and jumped up. "Stagnant! That's what this place is. Anybody with sense can see that, for godsake! This whole region's depressed. You think I want my kids growing up here, living this life? No sir! I want something better for my kids."

"You want them in little uniforms, that it? Little waiters and waitresses saying yes sir?"

"So what do they have to look forward to now, Cutler? A life on that cold bloody lake up to their buns in fish guts! No sir! Brightsands gets in here, at least they'll have a chance."

"A chance at what?"

"Times change," Gardner said gently, sitting down. "People have to change with them. Everybody makes compromises."

"Compromise, sure!" Jimmy stretched his arms wide. "Makes the world go round. You and me, Mr. Gardner we understand that. And you and the others, Cutler, would be one hell of a lot happier if you'd recognize that too, instead of living in some other goddam century." Jimmy took the kettle off the stove and poured boiling water into the teapot. "And your *kids'*d be a lot happier too, believe me."

"Servants!"

"Why not? What's their choice? You want them to be free spirits like their old man? Just do what they want, whenever they want?"

"That thought had crossed my mind," Cutler said.

"So they can be poor and ignorant like their old man too, eh?"

Cutler stood up. "Don't mess with me, you little chickenshit!"

"Threats! See that? See that? Typical! Just like what your kids are gonna be, dumb fucking rednecks!"

Cutler seized Jimmy and lifted him so his heels drummed on the cupboard doors. They snarled and shouted. Jimmy pounded at Cutler's head and shoulders.

"Good God!" Gardner said.

145

I jumped up and grabbed them. "Cutler, sit down. Please. Jimmy, make the tea, will you? Just make the goddam tea!"

"*You couldn't say progress if it crawled up your ass!*"

"*You are unglued, Pagoosie! Unstuck! You're a goddamn flake!*"

I got between them and pushed Jimmy over to the counter. Cutler paced around near the door like a rooster all puffed up.

"Sorry," I said to Gardner.

"That's all right."

"No it's not all right. It's very embarrassing. We invade your privacy, start behaving like primitives. Like savages."

"He's right," Jimmy said. "I'm sorry, Mr. Gardner. I just worry about the kids a lot, know what I mean? I worry."

"Sure."

"Sorry, Cutler."

"Forget it." Cutler took the mug of tea Jimmy handed to him. "What's a redneck?"

"Emotions get involved," Gardner said, "and people just don't think clearly, don't think rationally."

We sat quietly, sipping tea, watching him.

"But compromise is the key, isn't it. Reason."

We nodded.

And then Gardner laughed a short laugh that did not belong in any office or boardroom. It belonged in the crazy wind howling across the dunes; it belonged with the breakers roaring on the spit. "But then, then *everything* gets compromised, doesn't it. Betrayed." He stared blankly at the door. "And then, what's left...what's left that isn't...-can't be..."

"It's all right," I said. "You'll be all right."

He looked old and tired. His gaze wavered, glazed. He lurched to his feet and shuffled toward the door, groping for the knob when he was still six feet away from it, toppling, "Martha..."

I watched this unfold like a movie I had already seen, and behind it, in double exposure, I was seeing something else: Aja returning with her basket full of delicate herbs and tubers, humming and talking to herself, coming home from those places where strange plants swell in the dripping shadows of the Palisades. I was watching Aja hang the products of her foraging on the low rafters of her cabin, and then in the dry fullness of time, begin to crush and blend them. I was seeing again the furtive gleam of birchbark in Jimmy's hand, and the little cascade of dark powder into Michael Gardner's mug of tea.

"Martha," Gardner said again, and his knees buckled.

Jimmy and Cutler caught him before he hit the floor, and Cutler's big arms went around him, cradling his head. "Okay, friend. We've got you."

We carried him to the bed and laid him down and covered him. We didn't talk; no-one was very proud of this. It was, after all, a violation.

Jimmy sighed. "Okay. Let me make sure I've got it from here on." He held up fingers. "One, I pack everything he owns. No traces."

I nodded.

"Two, I pour a little rum on him."

"Yes."

"Three, I fill Bobby in on what's happening. Everything."

"Good. And stay here, Jimmy."

He nodded.

"Cutler, get the Krautlet."

He jerked his head sideways, toward the storm. "No way he'll get in with this wind."

"Then we'll think of something else. For now, just tell him to come."

The wind dropped and the Krautlet got in at dawn.

We waited for him on the beach, sipping the coffee and

eating the scones that Barbara had sent down with Maynard.

He came exactly where and when we expected him—over the tip of the western point at first light. He crossed Neyashing at three hundred feet, banking the old Beaver to have a look at the bay, and then crossing the spit, banking again, starting the landing run behind the trees to the east where we couldn't see him.

He was a good flier, the Krautlet. You felt safe going out with him, or seeing him come in to get you. Some claimed that he was not as good as his father, the Kraut, and discussions about their abilities went on for many hours. But the bottom line for me was that the Krautlet was alive and his father wasn't.

His father, the Kraut, had come to the Lake during World War Two. "Hitler's War," Jenny's students called it. He was a prisoner. He came by train with other prisoners to a camp at the mouth of the Little Pic, and he stayed there for three years, cutting pulpwood, smoking in the evenings at the mouth of the river. When the war ended they returned him to Germany, but he was back in a few months. He said he liked the Lake.

He was still young, in his mid-twenties, but in the pictures I've seen he looks to be some ghostly age between very young and very old, his face fading in the yellowing emulsions. His hair grew at crazy angles, in spiky contrast to that blond silk we see under the caps of German fliers in most old photos, and he had awful burn scars on his face and hands from having rolled around too long in a flaming Messerschmitt before he could free the canopy and fall clear. They were mainly what had stopped him from ageing, those scars. They had smoothed out his face and yet distorted it so that you could never be sure if he was smiling, or even if he could smile. His eyes were full of the ghosts of flames, someone had said of him, and I saw that was true when I looked at the pictures; but in there, behind the fire and the smoke, I saw horizons, too.

148

I used to try to imagine what he might have seen. But I couldn't. Not till a lot later, when I began to go to movies and to read. I could imagine, though, how that cold air at 3000 feet must have felt when it washed across the burns; it must have soothed like the Lake.

People said the Kraut could have had a job flying with the government, or even with one of the airlines, making big money. But he didn't want that. Organization was the last thing he wanted after he came back to the Lake. Somebody else telling him what to do, that was the last thing he wanted. He started to fly for Delaneys' Bush Service, which in the late forties consisted of one Noorduyn Norseman held together by tape and baling wire. In a few years he owned the company, and a new Beaver, too. He was a hell of a flier, no doubt about it. He was one of those legendary bush pilots who have stories told and retold about them so often they get polished as smooth as agate pebbles on a beach.

For twelve years he lived on the very edge of life. He lived and flew like a man going into a long and misty rapid that he has not bothered to scout out. Always he emerged, and his clients with him, although some who climbed out of his Beaver gave a new meaning to the word *paleface*. He flew in fog. He flew in thunderstorms. He flew into lakes that were too small for anyone to fly into, and he came out. He put down in huge seas to snatch people from the Lake who would have been dead of exposure long before the boats or the rescue chopper got to them. He walked away from many minor crashes and from two major ones—once with a crushed arm and collarbone, and once hopping with a makeshift crutch, his leg snapped in two spots below the knee. Then there came the crash that he did not walk away from, the one that did not take searchers long to find because he had carved his own runway through a quarter-mile of mature black spruce. The Beaver lay at the end—a crumpled-up ball of yellow papier-mâché.

Some said engine failure. Some said he just got tired.

But he had lived long enough to create with the woman who had loved him in spite of his face and the ghosts in his eyes, a son, the Krautlet, who was now feathering his engine and gentling his own Beaver across the base of the spit and down into the bay, a hundred yards off the beach, where there was protection from the wind behind the Western Point.

Cutler and Jimmy waded out under the propwash to hold the floats, and the Krautlet came down from the cockpit in his toque and arrow-sash, and caught the end of the canoe when I pushed it out to him. Together we lashed it onto the struts of the left float. Then we loaded the paddles and the packs.

Then he said, "Morning, Travis."

"Krautlet."

He rubbed his red beard. "Travis, seems to be an item of baggage still on the beach, there."

"I'll need some help with him," I said.

"Travis, is that your client, unconscious in that sleeping-bag?"

"It is, yes. He asked me to load him gently and not waken him. He doesn't like to fly."

We nodded at each other, sharing this interesting fact, and then the Krautlet climbed up into the cockpit and moved the co-pilot's seat behind the pilot's, making room on the right side for the stretcher, which he carried out. Together we rolled Michael Gardner onto this and, with Cutler's help, loaded him into the aircraft.

"He's fermenting," the Krautlet said. "He smells like a man who could use a time of dryness in the bush."

"He's relaxed and on holiday," I said.

He grunted and took a pinch of snuff, looking up and down the beach. "That it? No more unconscious clients in sleeping-bags?"

"He's it."

"Let's go then, before my rudders get chewed to ratshit in

150

the swells on this miserable beach. Allons, mes amis!"

Cutler and Jimmy pushed us off, labouring out until the cold swells were up to their waists, and then swinging the Beaver around into the breeze. The Krautlet flicked switches and the engine whined like a kid who has just skinned a knee, and then choked and roared, and we began to move, rocking in the swells. We taxied downwind toward the spit, with the Krautlet humming "En Roulant Ma Boule" and testing his rudders and flaps. Ahead lay a sandwich of horizons—grey-green lake on the bottom, pewter-grey sky on top, and in between the blue spit and a roseate line of sunrise.

Close to the spit he swung the plane around, made his final check, began to sing "A La Claire Fontaine" and pressed the throttle forward. The Beaver roared and shuddered as it gained speed. It lurched up to the wave crests and then scampered across them like fingers across a washboard, and then we were airborne, rising over the western point and banking south.

The Krautlet was rhapsodically into a bass rendition of the second verse of "A La Claire Fontaine."

He was a voyageur freak, the Krautlet. He knew everything there was to know about the fur trade of 200 years ago, and about the men on whose backs it rode. He owned a fibreglass replica of a *canot du maître,* 36 feet long. Sometimes he closed down the flying business for a week or two so he could stern this monster, and he and like-minded friends paddled off on the old routes. He also had a smaller *canot du nord* that he and his buddies took west sometimes, into what he called *le pays d'en haut,* munching pemmican and roaring songs and blasting a lot of black powder through their muzzle-loaders. They grew big beards and wore long stocking-toques and *ceintures fléchées* and luxurious moosehide moccasins that would have made the little bandy buggers of the eighteenth-century drool with envy. They also took snuff out of little oblong rosewood boxes, drank a lot of high-wine and bellowed at each other in French.

They were quite a show. I watched them a few times. It was all harmless fantasy, not a bad response to the twentieth-century—better than getting drunk, or swallowing pharmaceutical cocktails, or taking weekend commando training. It was silly, yes, but sometimes magic too.

The first time I saw a brigade I was very small, maybe seven, playing on the beach at Neyashing. We were making a lot of noise as kids do when they're having fun, when suddenly everything went quiet. My friends were standing still, some open-mouthed, looking out at the Lake. I turned around. Two big canoes were gliding past the end of the spit. *Big* canoes. They had bright circles on the bows with a wavy pattern inside. Large flags hung in the sterns. Each had ten or twelve paddlers, besides bowman and sternsman, all swinging long paddles in time to a beautiful sad song that I had never heard before, a song that drifted like an invitation across the bay.

As I watched, a third canoe appeared out of the mist at the end of the spit, and the sternsman cupped his hands and called to the others, and they rested. Drifted. All three hung in the shimmering reflections off the Lake. Then the gouvernail of that last canoe lifted a musket and fired a single shot to announce their arrival. It made a small, clear *pop* in the distance. It echoed down the spit, and around the beach, and rebounded off the western point, back to everyone in Neyashing.

Then I was a child of Neyashing 200 years earlier. Traders had arrived. There would be much laughter and bartering with these windblown men who spoke French, and in return for furs we would be offered miraculous goods—pots of iron, and thick blankets, and firearms, and bright glass beads for necklaces, and wonderful steel needles that gleamed in the sun, and much more besides. Much more. And that night there would be large fires down the beach where the bearded visitors slept under their canoes....

Voyageurs. Travellers.

So, although a part of me was amused by the silliness of the Krautlet's stocking-toque and red sash, another part thanked him and his friends for that moment out of time, and for the strong clear voice with which he sang "A La Claire Fontaine," that most haunting of their old melodies, lifting it above the roar of the engine as we banked and came back across the bay, climbing toward the sun.

I saw Jimmy and Cutler there on the beach with their arms raised, and Neyashing still asleep in the new dawn, and my own cabin with Jenny on the Council Rock, waving her white handkerchief. Then we rose above valleys brimming with night, and all North lay ahead.

When he finished the song the Krautlet turned and shouted over the engine, "Where to?"

"Ningotonjan Lake."

He glanced at me. "Maybe, maybe not. We'll see if the ice is out. When does he want to be picked up?"

"He doesn't. He's a canoeist. He wants to paddle out."

The Krautlet held the plane on course with his knee and took another pinch of snuff out of his little rosewood box. "You said Ningotonjan Lake?"

"Yes."

"You said paddle out?"

"Yes."

He reached back and offered me his hand. "Zhawendago-ziwin, Travis. Good luck!"

We flew on for a while without speaking, deep into that labyrinth of lakes and rivers.

Jenny had wished me good luck too, finally, waving that white handkerchief in the shadows before the dawn. She had not done it earlier, when we last talked; she had not been happy then. "You're *what?*" she asked.

"Kidnapping him."

She sat down abruptly on the bed, frowning and holding her belly as if someone had struck her there. "No," she said.

"Yes. The Krautlet's coming. I'm taking him back to Ningotonjan Lake."

"But *why?*"

I stopped packing. "Am I hearing properly? Is this the same woman who has been urging me to act?"

"But why *this?*"

I laid down my map case and went over and took her hands and sat beside her. I told her I loved her. I talked about the many trips she and I had taken and would take, and about the healing of the wilderness. I talked about Gardner and my feeling that I knew the man and knew which side he was on, deep down. I talked about Neyashing, and although I did not say "spirits" or speak Aja's name, I let my explanation come out of the place I loved, and wrap around it like a spider's strand many times before winding away into the wilderness, into the heart of mystery. I told her I loved her and asked her to trust me in this, to have faith in me.

She listened uhappily. "The fact is," she said when I finished, "there isn't a logical reason, is there? You just have a hunch. You have a feeling, an *impulse.*"

"Jenny, I'm sure about this in my own way."

"You'll lose your job. You know that."

"There'll be other jobs, not another chance with Gardner. Remember what you said when we went to Haida Guaii? You told me it was big. It wasn't just personal, you said."

"That was civil disobedience; this is criminal. Besides..."

"Jenny, don't cry."

"Oh. All right. All right. Anything else you'd like? Let's live together, Jenny! Let's have a baby, Jenny! Stop crying, Jenny! Anything else? Maybe you want me to wait till you get out of jail, do you? Is that your idea of being together?"

"Jenny..."

"No." She pulled away from me and went to the window, holding herself tight, looking out across the Council Rock and the Lake. "I know. I do understand. I think I do. I'm just frightened, that's all. I just need a little time. Can you give me a little time and not touch me, please?"

I finished packing quickly because there was already light in the east, and hauled the packs out onto the porch. "So long," I said to Guaranteed. "Say goodbye to that woman for me."

Jenny came to me and kissed me before I left. "G'doo za zaagiin," she said. "I love you."

Cutler and I drove down through the dunes in his truck, down to the place where the Krautlet would come in. "Barbara was very angry. She told me not to let you do this damn fool thing. She swore at me. She swore at me all the time she was packing food." He laughed. He leaned over and cuffed the back of my head. "Zhawendagoziwin, n'sheemenh. Damn, I wish I could come with you!"

Zhdwendagoziwin. Good luck from Cutler. Good luck from Barbara—the coffee and scones sent down with Maynard in the darkness. Good luck from Jenny—the dot of white handkerchief. And good luck from the Krautlet.

I looked down at that melting labyrinth, all purple and orange in the new sun, and I leaned back and pushed my hands deep into the pockets of my jacket. There, in the left pocket, was something that had not been there the night before. I pulled it out: a walnut-sized knot of buckskin. I loosened the tie and the little bundle fell open. A necklace lay coiled inside, woven strings of seed-beads, dark brown with flashes of red and blue, and a single strand of yellow.

I knew what it was; it was one of the old, old charms.

Good luck against the snakes in Sioux country. Good luck against the Sioux. Good luck against all perils, all false turnings in the path, all that would lure spirits elsewhere.

We have come to a place you must cross alone.

I dropped it around my neck, inside my shirt.

Good luck from Aja.

Considering the Guide

Cutler could be right; the man could be too far gone....

I have taken my share of unhappy people into the bush, people so burnt-out and bitter that nothing I could do would help them. I have guided people who wanted only to be taken as fast as possible to where they could kill as much as possible. Pigs, Cutler called them. Fishing pigs, hunting pigs. Anyone who's done any guiding has met people like that. From the beginning I hated taking their money. I felt dirty. I felt like a pimp, and it wasn't long before I stopped accepting every job that came along. I started to discriminate. I'd go down to the outfitter's and size up the clients from a distance. Sometimes I didn't even get out of the truck—just had a look and drove away.

I had some run-ins before I reached that point. I dropped fishing-rods into a few lakes, lost some rifles in rapids. Once I left four drunks on an island. They had built a fire so big it scorched the pine boughs above. They hacked trees, drove nails into them. The trampled everything, fouled everything. They swore at each other, cursed and roared at me.

I stood it as long as I could, but when they started smashing their bottles on the rocks, I went down to their boat and freed it into the wind and the darkness on that big lake. Then I packed my gear, took my canoe and faded. When I got back to Neyashing two days later I told the Krautlet where they were, and after a while he went in and got them. I caught hell from Alex Wilkinson. The Ministry threatened to cancel my guide's licence, and two weeks afterward I got a letter from some lawyer in the south threatening "action." I went back and took pictures of what those four people had done to that little island, and sent them to the lawyer with a note asking if he didn't think we had enough action, and I never heard anything more.

Another time one of my clients intentionally gut-shot a

sow bear, and when the animal bawled and clawed the ground in its agony, tangling itself in its intestines, he laughed. I shot the bear through the head, and when I turned around to face that man everything was bright red— sky, forest, fat man. I dropped my rifle and went at him as the bear would have, low and fast, snarling, and before his friends could get me off I had hurt him badly. I broke his nose, and his jaw, and something in his chest too, because he was on his knees, coughing blood.

When he fined me the judge said I was very lucky the man didn't die, and I guess he was right. The bear died, though.

People like that were closed up tight against everything, closed to all chance, to all mystery and spirit. Guiding them in the bush was like trying to drive a truck in a garden without hurting anything. And it wasn't just the damage they did that made me sick and sad; it was what made them do it—the emptiness, and the dread.

But there is another kind of guiding, a good kind. It happens when you take people into the wilderness who are alive and vulnerable, who sense the mystery, know that spirits are moving in the winds and currents, watching from the shadows. Sometimes such people keep silent to listen, and sometimes they brim over with questions. But when they ask these questions it is not to dispel the mystery but to reaffirm it, feeling it stretch to infinity beyond them and in them.

Harry and Ethel Trowbridge were like that when they first came to Neyashing from England, and they still are, even after all the cataracts and cancer, the Alzheimer's and arthritis. They are like little children, and the wild world is full of wonders for them.

Such people I would take anywhere, for any length of time. I would let them take *me* anywhere. And when I remembered that look I had seen deep in Michael Gardner's eyes when we first met in Schreiber, and again in Bobby Naponse's cabin, a blurred and brooding line like the far edge of the Lake, I thought that here was a man who was less certain than he appeared to be about definitions and edges, about the places where he stopped and nature began; and when I heard him say, "I don't *know* why I'm here," I was pretty sure he'd be a client of that second sort.

The engine pitch changed. We nosed down. Ningotonjan Lake came up under the horizon, a big, round lake with a sandspit curving like a beckoning finger from its east shore. A winding river entered from the south and left to the north, meandering past a row of cliffs and draining into the endless marshes of the James Bay Lowlands.

The Krautlet made one circuit at 500 feet. He put on his amber glasses, squinted down, and then pointed to the lifejacket on the floor beside me. I got up and opened the little hatch in the belly of the plane, and on the next pass, when the Krautlet shouted "Now!" I dropped the jacket out, watching it grow small as it tumbled, until finally it was only a tiny bright-orange seed on the surface of Ningotonjan Lake.

We circled again, climbing to the southeast and then banking and settling into the glide path for landing. The lake was so transparent and so calm that windless day that it was surfaceless, except for the speck of orange. We touched a hundred yards away from the jacket, swept past it, settled and swung back to pick it up. I handed it up to the cockpit and stayed on the float while we taxied to the sandspit. The Krautlet gunned the engine a bit, just enough to nudge the floats into the sand, then he cut the power.

The first sound in the sudden silence was our wash against the shore; the second was the crystal welcome of a whitethroat sparrow.

We unloaded. We left the canoe on the beach, but the packs and Gardner we hauled up into the shade of the pines. When we finished, the Krautlet folded the stretcher and stowed it back in the cabin. He secured the doors. He came out on the nose of the left pontoon, one hand on the engine cowling, and he looked slowly all around the shore of that tranquil lake until he was looking right at me.

"Cutler will pay the bill," I said.

"The bill doesn't worry me. That unconscious man worries me. The fact that he doesn't want to be picked up worries me a lot."

"He insisted," I said. "He's an adventurer, I guess."

We gazed up at the pine grove where Gardner lay asleep.

"Maybe," the Krautlet said. "But what if he and you are still adventuring a month from now, and what if other people less venturesome—his wife, say—want him back? What if maybe they don't even know where he is?"

"Don't worry, I'll look after those things."

"But I do worry." He took out the rosewood snuffbox. "What worries me more than anything is that this gentleman might be very angry when he wakes up. He might not like the place where we have brought him. He might hire lawyers in blue suits to sue you." The Krautlet sniffed his pinch of snuff, closed and opened his eyes, and returned the box to his pocket. "Worse, they might sue *me*! They might even put me and my airplane in separate places, far away from the Lake. That worries me very much."

I took off my cap and scratched my head. "Krautlet, I'll make sure he knows you have lived a pure and blameless life."

"Miigwetch." He pulled a paddle out of its bracket and leaned on it, pushing off. "Au revoir, mon ami. Bonne chance."

"So long, Krautlet." I raised my hand. I watched him taxi across the lake and take off, and then I went up into the shade of the pines to set up the tent and wait.

"What *is* this?"

Gardner surprised me. I expected him to wake up like a drunk, looking as if demons were busy with pins inside his eyeballs; but I underestimated Aja. When I came back from gathering driftwood, he was standing under the pines with his hands on his hips, wide awake and curious, just as he had been the night before in Bobby Naponse's cabin.

"Where am I? What's going on here?"

"You're at Ningotonjan Lake. We drugged you, had you flown here." I dropped the wood beside the fireplace.

"Why? What *is* this?" He stepped closer to me, looked hard into the shadows under the brim of my cap.

Again he surprised me. I expected some show of anger. I was braced for a fair amount of posturing and ranting, for some shouting and arm-swinging, maybe even a struggle. I expected at least a few demands and threats, until he understood that the only alternatives were the ones we shared. I was ready for all of that, but I was not prepared for *interest*. It unnerved me a little to see the man's calm and inquiring face close to my own, asking, "What's this all about?"

"Many things," I said, turning away. "Mostly Neyashing." I tore some birchbark, lit it and placed a few twigs on top. "Let's have something to eat, then we'll talk."

He peered through the smoke, smiling incredulously. "You expect that we can just...*have a meal*? Just like that? As if this were a perfectly normal situation?"

"Well, Michael, what are your options?"

He waved a hand in exasperation, brushing this away. "Where are the others?"

"There are no others."

"Just you?"

"You, me and one canoe."

He squatted down on the opposite side of the fireplace, level with me. "Look, why don't you just tell me what's going on?"

"I have told you."

"But *why*? What's it all about, ransom?"

I shook my head. "You haven't got enough money to buy what we want. Neither does your company."

"Then what? Why can't you give me a straight answer?" He was not smiling anymore. "That's what makes dealing with you people so difficult, you know, that sort of evasion."

You People. Evasion. I turned away from the fire toward the lake, everything suddenly pink and hazy. I didn't want to look at Michael Gardner. I wanted him to back away from me across a clearing, back away so that when I broke cover, running, he would see clearly the glint of my axe, and the angry stripes on my face, and the war-feathers in my hair. I wanted him far enough back that when I screamed he would hear it well.

Not that way, Aja hissed, the whisper of an owl's wing.

Not that way, the old ones said, out of the flames.

I waited, grew calmer. The haze cleared a little.

What do we want? I'll tell you. We want you to give life to the buffalo, to give them their plains again. We want you to restore the forests and their creatures. We want you to heal all the wounds you have made in Earth, to suck your poisons out of the lakes and rivers. We want you to create clean and living air. We want you to fold your cities like infected blankets, and burn them, with all your greed and fear.

No, no, Travis Niskigwun. Not even that way.

I fed twigs carefully into the hot little fire. "What we want is for Aspen Corporation to take its plans for Brightsands Village and put them away until they crumble to brown powder. We want you to leave us alone. We want you to let Neyashing be."

Gardner sat down heavily, away from the smoke. He rested his elbows on his knees. He shook his head. "I've already told you why that's unlikely. You didn't believe me?"

"Well, let's say I thought we could use more time to... consider alternatives."

"You think *this* is the way to change my mind. Change Aspen's plans. You think you can *force* us?"

"I'm not forcing you to do anything. Not even to have supper."

161

"Then why am I here?"

"A good question. Why *are* you here, Michael? What brought you to Neyashing?"

He looked at the fire, at the setting sun, back to the fire again.

"Now who's being evasive. Why not tell the truth? You did last night, in the cabin. The truth is, you don't know *why* you came, do you."

"That's personal. That's a private matter. It's…it's got nothing to do with Aspen or Brightsands."

"You're sure?"

Michael Gardner stood up suddenly, staring at me. "If there's some connection," he said, "I certainly don't know what it is," and he turned away and walked out to the very end of the sandspit, as far away from me as he could get.

I lifted the pot of stew off the fire and set it to keep warm. I waited, waited while the sun set, listening to the first loon cries of the spring drifting over Ningotonjan Lake, watching the troubled man on the end of the spit.

He came back in the dusk, and we ate in silence.

When we finished I took the pot and bowls down to the shore to wash them. A crayfish waited for the scraps, his tail in the shadows of the lake, his feelers brushing the surface. "Bojo, zhagesheenh. Aniishezhi b'maadizi yin?" I touched him and he scuttled backwards into the darkness.

"Crayfish," I said when I returned to the fire. "Nice to see them. They die at pH6, you know that? He says he's feeling fine, so it must still be pretty healthy, this lake."

"Very comforting," Gardner said, staring at me.

I built up the fire. The lake beyond the pines was a glass tray full of stars, with a little aurora shimmering in the centre. A beaver whacked the surface near the cliffs at the north end, and two moose splashed and grunted in the darkness just down the shore. "Lots of people out,' I said.

"Look, can we talk rationally about what's happening here?"

162

"Where do you want to start?"

"With your plans."

"Very simple. I have no plans except that you and I will paddle back to Neyashing."

"That's *all*?"

"That's all."

"No demands? No ransom?"

"No. Just the journey."

"How long will it take?"

"Eight days. Maybe ten."

Gardner smiled and shook his head. "This doesn't make sense."

"Not yet, but..." I opened my hands.

"And why start here? Why *this* lake? Ninga..."

"Ningotonjan. I'll tell you. It's because this lake is a centre. It's where my ancestors came for the winter. My grandfather told me the name means "All the Children in the Family." He remembered coming as a very small child. He remembered the warm fires in the lodge in winter, and the stories, and the paintings at the north end of the lake."

"So," Gardner said. "It's personal. You've brought me to a place that's important to you. Personally."

I nodded.

"Is this where they stayed, on this point?"

"Yes. And up in the trees, where there was protection from the wind."

"You mentioned paintings. What sort of paintings?"

"Small ones. On the cliffs. There at the north end."

Gardner looked up the lake, into the darkness.

"Would you like to see them?"

"Yes," he said, "I would."

I stood up. "Let's go then."

"Now?"

"Why not? Nice night."

We walked down to the beach and launched my canoe. Stepping into the craft, paddling around the point and out into the starlit lake, Gardner looked like a man at home, a man beginning to relax. His stroke was strong and steady.

"You've done this before."

"Many times."

"Where?"

"Oh, in the south. When I was younger. My family had a cottage. Later, my wife and I took some trips. For a while."

He was silent for a few moments. Then, "May I ask you a question, a personal question?"

"Go ahead."

"You're an educated man. You could be doing well for yourself somewhere."

"You mean making money?"

"Yes. Why not?"

"Because I belong here."

Gardner stopped paddling. "How do you *know* that?"

I said nothing.

"Please," he turned around to look at me. "Tell me how you can be so sure of that."

"All right. It's because I can't tell the difference between me and this lake, those sounds, that moon. It's because I don't know where I end and the wilderness begins." *Now we'll see,* I thought. *If he laughs...*

But he did not laugh. He started paddling again and there was only the soft splashing of the blades, and the frolicking of the shrieking loons, half-running, half-flying across the lake.

"I don't understand why you think bringing me here might stop Brightsands. I don't see the connection. You think there is one. So there's something you're not telling me. There's a..."

"Shh. Listen. Listen..."

We heard the cliffs—meltwater trickling off high ledges and splashing into the lake with a sound like soft laughter. We slid close to the face, slapping into the darkness behind the thin veil of spray until we came to the place of the paint-

164

ings, the place where, many years before, Grandfather had brought Cutler and me.

They were there still, just as I remembered them, dozens of little figures on the smooth rock. Even in the starlight we could see them, some clear and bright against the fawn-grey gneiss; some faded, almost indistinguishable from veins in the mother rock; some nearly obscured by washes of calcite. One by one I found the few I remembered vividly—the little shaman dancing to celebrate that life which lifted his phallus; the caribou heads with their sweeping antlers; the magic turtle scattering eggs through space; the snakes and meandering spirit-lines; and finally, three pale, frail canoes bearing tiny occupants on endless journeys.

Gardner reached up silently and touched one.

In university I spent hours in the libraries with pictures of other sites—Altamira and Lascaux, Altxerri and Monpazier, Lespugue and Pech-Merle—spellbound by the swirling power of those paintings, those caverns where the record of Earth and Man were one. I loved the spindly, elegant African pictographs too, and the tubular Scandinavian glyphs, and the strange pecked anthropomorphs of Arizona. I wanted to visit these other places then. I wanted to see them all. Back then, I had a different idea of travelling.

I had no pigment, but I dipped my finger into Ningotonjan Lake and drew a small crescent above one of the crevasses—a fourth canoe precariously airborne, bearing two small passengers at the mercy of the wild, as we are, all of us, in our dreams of sleep and waking.

So, our strange journey began.

It continued with Gardner's story in the darkness, among the stars in Ningotonjan Lake, when he stopped paddling and said, "You asked me earlier why I came here. I didn't answer you. I want to tell you now. At least, I want to tell you what happened to me..."

And it continued beside the fire late into that night while

I waited, and listened to the man's words, and watched everything unfold as he told it.

The man wakes up alone in his large bed and rises immediately. He dresses and eats breakfast alone, begins his drive to the commuter station alone. So far there has been nothing unusual about the day, the Thursday before Good Friday. Driving, he decides to accept the invitation of friends to spend the long weekend in Vermont, perhaps stay into the following week. He will call them that morning, he decides, and depart that evening.

He leaves his house in the hills and proceeds down through a rolling countryside of farms and woodlots, his window open and his tires crackling through brittle white ice that has no water underneath. The odour of spring frost sweeps in, mingling with the scent of leather seats, and the black coffee he sips as he drives. He arrives a few minutes earlier than usual at the station, and because the morning is so radiant and promising he leaves the car and strolls down the platform toward the rising sun. Other commuters with attaché cases nod as he passes. He knows that this idle walk to the end of the platform will seem capricious to them, but he is long past caring about the opinions of others. Those who know him know also that he has nothing to prove anymore in the world of business; those who do not know him can draw their own conclusions from his costly automobile, his tailored clothes, his deportment.

He walks away from that human world of signs and assumptions. He walks toward the sun and watches its rising above the glittering fields, receives like a benediction its warmth on his face and closed eyes. And then, with the train's whistle, he returns among the little groups of fellow-commuters and exchanges pleasantries until the Dayliner glides to a halt beside them and they greet the conductor as usual, climb aboard as usual.

So far, except for that stroll down the platform and a peculiar feeling of lightness, of insubstantiality, the day has unfolded normally. He settles in a customary seat on the north side, crosses his legs, watches as the train rolls through the level crossing and picks up speed, rounding the bend that will take them through the worn hills of the moraine, along the gravel shore of an ancient lake. He is aware of the conductor approaching as usual, the same gold watchchain across his vest, the same five gold service bars on his sleeve. He opens his wallet and finds a ticket, as usual.

And then the routine breaks.

For instead of the predictable exchanges, the conductor is speaking urgently to each passenger, his eyes dancing. "Never seen anything... Thirty-one of them... Just ahead..."

As he takes the ticket: "You haven't been with us for a couple of days, Mr. Gardner."

"I've been in Seattle, George. Got back yesterday afternoon."

"Well sir, we have a treat for you. We have a real treat for you this morning!"

"That so?"

"I want you to watch right up here, right around this curve, and you'll see 'em, sir. Swans. Whistling swans. Thirty-one of 'em! They've been there for two days in a little pond in the hills. Just waiting, I guess. Just resting up. I asked my wife if she'd ever heard of such a thing, a migrating flock like that in one place for so long, and she never had, in all her years of birdwatching. Watch now, folks! They're coming up! They're... Yessir! There they are! Isn't that one beautiful sight, now?"

There is an appreciative murmur in the car, an exclamation or two, even a little ripple of applause for George, conductor and magician.

There they are indeed, gleaming white in that dark meltwater pond cradled in the hills, their soft bodies blending into a single body, their heads turning toward the train, their long necks stretching like the stalks of exotic flowers. Even as Michael Gardner stares in awe the 62 wings surge together and the flock is airborne and rising in the new sun. Effortlessly for half a mile they keep pace with the train, and then gradually the space between machine and creatures widens as they swing north.

The man beside the window rises with them, reaches toward them. "No!" he says. "Wait!" He strikes the glass, waves his arms, looks wildly up at the encaging ceiling and at the uniformed

167

man hurrying toward him.

"Mr. Gardner…"

"All right," he says, waving him off. "Just a little dizziness. Just a touch of claustro…" And he gropes toward the washroom through a thicket of astonished glances.

But it is not just claustrophobia, that visceral surge that has lifted him to his feet and which, even now, as he stares at the strange ashen face in the mirror, possesses him so completely that he must obey it. He will not reach his office that morning; he will not return to his empty house that evening; he will not drive south to spend Easter weekend with friends.

He will go north.

He struggles to restore some semblance of control. He splashes water on his face, his wrists. He knows the words: manifestation, satori, epiphany, revelation. But these are surely the stuff of tales, the perils of the overtired, the unwary and the vulnerable. They do not occur early in the morning, to well rested executives aboard commuter trains. "No," he says to the image in the cloudy glass. "No!"

But the smiling man in the mirror nods.

Yes, they do.

"Do you believe that?"

"Yes."

"Do you? Do you really?"

The face I saw through the smoke was not that of a confident man. It was all uncertainty and doubt, all frailty and confusion and misgiving. At that moment I liked Michael Gardner very much. "Go on, my friend," I said. "I'm with you."

On his arrival in the city he makes the phone call that will free him indefinitely from business commitments, purchases a few clothes and toiletries, and boards another train, northbound.

He will not journey all the way to Neyashing in one trip. He is not even thinking about McDonnell's Depot, or Brightsands Village, or the affairs of Aspen. He is responding only to that inchoate summons of the birds, that summons to the North; and so he returns first to that place which for half a century has been North to him.

168

This is a region in the maple forests where the Shield begins, of old cottages more sumptuous than hotels, of summer resorts and little villages set on tranquil waters plied by steamboats. Indeed, in Gardner's childhood the steamboats were there still, huffing and hooting their passages around the lakes, up the rivers and through the locks constructed for them. They went laden with supplies and tourists, nourishing the sprawling Edwardian hotels that once, before fires claimed them, gazed drowsily down over terraced lawns to their covered wharves.

That was a white and domesticated world in which Michael Gardner spent the summers of his youth; and yet there were pockets of mystery still—islands uninhabited, wild stretches of shoreline, even some smaller lakes reachable only by portages, where loons might nest without fearing for their eggs. Gardner dwells on these wild places as he speaks. He recreates them, and when he has recreated them, his story touches them like talismans.

That evening of the swans, the Thursday before Good Friday, he gets off the train at the small town of his childhood and hires a taxi to take him, a few groceries and his plastic bag of clothes and toiletries, the three miles to the lake. He finds the ice still thick enough to walk on, and he starts off alone, out to his family's island. In fact, making the crossing in the dusk, he notes that there is still a congregation of ice-fishermen's huts a mile or so up the channel.

On his arrival he lights the fire and the lamps, removes a few storm windows, and begins to warm that big, cold space.

"The Cottage" he calls it, although it is more than that. It is a summer house, a small mansion built by his grandfather at the turn of the century, shortly after the lumber barons had left that land stripped and stark. Somehow the island on which the cottage stands escaped timbering. Lofty red and white pines give it the look of a flowerpot, or of a high feathered head-dress, in all weathers except utter calm; then, with its reflection, the island becomes an egg.

Low cliffs ring the western and northern shores, but on the east and the south, out of the prevailing winds, are two small coves with crescent beaches. Between these, on the island's spine, Michael

Gardner's grandfather had built his house. It is hip-roofed, ringed on three sides by a broad verandah. It is all pine and cedar, and as it aged its interior darkened, so that Michael Gardner remembers it glowing red-brown in sunlight reflected off the lake and filtered through the pines, the colour of tanned skin. On the hottest days it is still cool inside, for this is a house of cross-drafts and lofty ceilings, of gauze curtains moving even when there is not enough breeze to ruffle the lake.

North, to this place, Michael Gardner naturally returns. It has been reliable and adequate through all the years, through many turmoils. It is the place where bedrock is.

Here he warms and nourishes himself, and sleeps on a high-back couch in front of the fire, under a mantel holding his grandmother's collection of birchbark boxes, fragrant with sweetgrass even now, and one of his first toys—a tiny birchbark canoe.

The next morning, wondering at his inexplicable presence here, not yet knowing what is to be discovered, he begins to search through the stacks of old albums in the glass-doored bookcases under the stairs.

In yellow Kodak snapshots, postcard size, he inspects frozen moments from the building of the cottage. Workmen in overalls and cloth caps look up from the surveyor's cord in a glade full of violets and trilliums, look up amidst sawhorses and stacks of lumber. An architect points to something in a plan with the stem of his pipe. A small stream-launch waits primly at the new dock, her driver obscured by her awning. Labourers bear chairs, tables and rolled rugs from the after-deck of a stout, white workboat. Behind, the lake is full of clouds.

Gardner searches in these pictures before passing them by.

There is a photograph of the newly raised flagpole taken from low on the shore to show the Union Jack and the red ball on top. Around the base is the whole family: grandmother stern in puffed shoulders and mannish straw hat; grandfather offering a solemn wave, as if in greeting to some visiting chieftain; Uncle Roger, who was to die at Ypres, mugging a music-hall shuffle; and Michael Gardner's mother, aged eight, demure in taffeta.

Later, a boathouse rises in the cove on the east side of the island, complete with an airy apartment on the second storey, a huge room with pine floor and exposed rafters. Underneath are slips for two boats. One is a beamy and wide-decked sailboat with a retractable mast, designed for lazy afternoons. The other is an inboard runabout (a "launch," his family called it) all mahogany, spar varnish and gleaming brass. The twin hatches above the engine are always kept open in the boathouse to release the fumes, and the launch is never started inside but is guided out with careful boathooks. It has a forward cockpit, just large enough for two....

And now, as he stares at a photograph of himself and his mother in this small compartment, an image flickers deep in Michael Gardner's memory, an image that he suppresses immediately, although he feels at once that it is vitally important, crucial to this strange quest on which he has embarked.

He breathes deeply. He lays down the album and retreats from it, leaving it open at the photograph of the smiling young woman and her child in the bow of the gleaming boat. He knows he will return to it, must return to it, but he now goes in search of the camera that took the picture. It has suddenly become vitally important to reach across and touch some object from that other world, that lost world brimming with such confidence and optimism, such surety. He finds the camera upstairs in the bottom drawer of an oak bureau, among woollen bathing suits, and he carries it in both hands down to the warmth of the fire. There he releases the little catch on the cracked leather case, draws the camera out, and opens it. The supple bellows unfolds with a tiny gasp. He places it on the table beside him, its front supported by a small, hinged leg. KODAMATIC. NO. 3A AUTOGRAPH KODAK SPECIAL. 1909.

Gleaming black and silver, the instrument evokes Edwardian amplitude. The lens mount and focusing devices glitter with mirrors and rigorous little dials and levers. Set and released, the shutter snaps precisely. In the cruciform viewfinger, Gardner sees his own face reflected back in fire. He touches the camera, turns it, examines it from many angles, and peering close to one of its enamelled surfaces discovers a blemish, a fingerprint etched by the sweat of a far-off summer day. Perhaps his father's.

Still holding the camera, still keeping that turbulent, clamouring memory deep in his recollection, he looks again at the photograph of the launch and the two people in its forward cockpit, concentrating on the details of the print—the chrome stem-plate curving up to meet flared bows, chrome cleats and lights, bent and brass-capped mahogany mast with its little pennant, expanse of flawless mahogany deck, a little two-paned windshield protecting the smiling young woman who has tied her sun hat with a scarf and is embracing a child in a cloth cap, himself....

Gardner broke off his story there, leaving it to eddy behind some dam of memory or of will. "So," he said, slapping his knees, "that's why I came. Pure impulse. A flock of birds."

I urged him further, "The boat..." I said, but he lifted his hands and shook his head.

"I assume that sleeping-bag in that tent is for me?"

I nodded. "All your kit's there, too. Everything you brought to Neyashing."

He stood up and stretched. "I guess we'll be moving on tomorrow?"

"Yes."

"Just out of curiosity, how about showing me where we are, where we'll be going."

I twisted around and reached into the pack I was using for a back rest, feeling down into the side where my map case should have been. It wasn't there. I stood up and dug deeper, rummaging through the whole pack. But there were no maps. In the rush of packing I'd forgotten them. They were lying where I had left them during that last scene with Jenny—on my table, secure in their waterproof pouch.

Gardner laughed when I told him. "Well, isn't *that* interesting! But you know the way, don't you? Travis, you *do* know the way."

"It's an old path," I said. "It shouldn't be hard to find."

An old path: the way my family came to Ningotonjan

172

Lake for the winter, and returned to Neyashing in the spring. I should know it well; I should remember it on some level deeper than memory. But in fact I was not sure I knew it at all. I had travelled it only once when I was eight, with my grandfather. He wanted to show Cutler and me Ningotonjan Lake while he was still able to carry a canoe, he said, and so we journeyed together for two weeks late in the summer, when the bugs were mostly gone and the birds were gathering.

I remembered the strange clarity and stillness of the lake, but I was not clear about the many turnings in the route; I remembered cliffs at the north end, and the ancient paintings on them, but not each of the old portages. I remembered playing with Cutler on this sandspit where generations of others had played before us, swimming far out into the transparent lake, and Grandfather sitting and watching us from among the pines; but the path by which we had come, and the way home to Neyashing were faded and uncertain in my memory, like an old drawing on a scrap of yellowing paper.

"Like this," I said to Michael Gardner.

I built up the fire and smoothed a place in the sand. I began to draw with a pine twig. I was not sure what I would draw, but I thought that if I began with Neyashing and worked my way north along familiar routes that old path would come back to me.

Soon my map left the limits of what I knew and ventured beyond, outlining strange lakes in the sand, linking them to unfamiliar rivers, and at the end of this journey, at the top of this strange map, was Ningotonjan Lake with its sandspit curving from the eastern shore. And then, by a different and more complex route, my stick showed me how we had journeyed back to Neyashing.

"There!"

I straightened up to examine the whole of this map that had been magically revealed to me, and I saw it for what it really was: Grandfather's story-map. I had drawn the map that he had given me long ago, once-upon-a-time when we had sat together on Neyashing beach and he had told a little world into being, his voice weaving through the changes of four days, rising and falling with the cadences of the waves.

Three Visions

I woke at first-light feeling eyes, being watched. I moved my head enough to see the sleeping-bag wrapped around me, and the cold ashes of the fire, and the edge of the pine grove where it met the beach.

There was no-one on the campsite or on the spit. There was no-one on the shore to either side, no-one nearby in the swirling mists of the lake. The canoe lay where we had left it. Gardner was still asleep in the tent. I moved out of the trees and watched the mist grow ever brighter, until at last it billowed like snow away from the sun; but I saw no-one and heard nothing but the calls of loons.

Gardner washed and brushed his teeth as soon as he got up. Over breakfast we discussed the route. "South," I said. "We just keep heading south until we cross the height of land."

"We have enough food?"

"I think so?"

Gardner sipped his coffee and looked south, then east, shading his eyes against the rising sun. "Do you remember the way out of this lake?"

"There's only one way—that river at the south end. There. You can see the reeds at the mouth. Unless you want to go north."

He looked at me quickly. "I think I've come far enough

north, thanks. Let's get started."

All day the meandering little river swung us gently to the left, until by late afternoon we were headed due east, into a network of smaller streams and lakes. All day we searched but found no way south. In the distance we could see the hills that were the height of land, but between us and them lay miles of tangled, impenetrable bush, and no waterways at all.

Gardner worked hard. He was a good paddler. He kept up the steady stroke I had seen the night before, and he didn't complain at several ugly little portages, or at the freezing shallows we waded into as the day wore on. He spoke little that first day, but several times I was unsettled by his laughter—soft, private and incredulous laughter.

That night we camped on an island in a large lake. There were no human signs, but again I felt someone watching. Twice before I slept I went out beyond the circle of firelight and listened, but there was no-one and nothing moving on that lake, or on its dark shore.

The next day we were forced east again, still east, and no way south. Rain began, a steady drizzle.

"We must have missed something," Gardner said that night, his voice taut. "We *must* have."

"No. We've checked every outfall. All beaver ponds, remember?"

"There must have been a portage...."

"No."

"We've come at least 30 miles."

"Not that far. We've circled around a lot. These marshes..."

He was unpacking, throwing things randomly out onto the wet ground, swatting at blackflies on his neck, in his hair and ears, and suddenly he straightened up, thrusting the sheathed head of the axe into my chest. "Goddam you! You arrogant bastard! What right do *you* have? What *right*?"

He caught me off balance. I staggered back against a tree,

175

and he kept coming at me gripping that axe in both hands and shoving the head hard into my chest, just under my throat. "I want *out* of here! Do you understand that? *Do you?*"

I raised my open hands. I blinked the red haze back. "Michael, so do I."

"No you don't! If you wanted out you'd have brought maps, damn you, and we wouldn't be lost in this godforsaken maze!"

"We're not lost. It's just a matter of time. Things will work out." I held his gaze. "You know that."

He turned and strode away, flinging the sheath off the axe as he went. Before long I heard chopping in the woods. By the time he came back with an armful of split cedar I had the tent up and a little fire going, and soon after that we had a hot meal and tea and we both felt better.

He waved his arm toward the rain-pocked lake. "I'm not afraid of *this,* you know."

"I know."

"And I'm not going to apologize to you."

"You don't have to," I said. "Not for that."

Day after day the land forced us east, but there were no more outbursts from Michael Gardner. Instead, little by little as we travelled he circled back to the story he had begun that first night on Ningotonjan Lake. It happened as we talked in the random manner of canoeists. It happened with references to boats, to other summers, to childhood.

It took time for him to continue this strange tale of his coming to Neyashing. It took nights and days for the wilderness to free it from him, but step by step he ventured further on the telling, and the telling became a journey with its own risks and perils. It passed through places in the man I couldn't see, through dimensions other than time and space. It was slowed or hastened by currents I knew nothing of, halted by sudden confluences in the maze of himself and the

176

maze through which we paddled. Small things bore it on—a heron's blink, an owl's call, the visions in the fire, the hiss of rain across a marsh. And other things slowed it—the gut-twisting mire of a portage, the weight of a long, hot day. It moved or did not move in its own time, and in the days, in the nights, I waited and listened and heard the land begin to speak out of him, heard him begin to answer questions neither of us had asked.

At last there came a moment when he pointed with his paddle to the shore of the narrow bay down which we were moving, and we watched a bear, newly emerged and still drowsy with winter, peering out at us through leafless poplars. Silver-green trunks shadowed his gaunt mass. Soon he would remember how to amble toed-in across that slope and up to the ridge where breezes would bring him news—news of fish white-bellied on the beach; news of ants in punky roots; news of a thawing carcass in cliff shadows; news of honey. Soon he would remember, and move, and eat, but for the moment he rested the imponderable gaze from those small eyes on the passage of our canoe. He stared, indifferent to intervening trunks and underbrush, and we returned gazes to meet his own until he vanished in shadows.

"Makwa," I said.

"Makwa."

"No, Mak*wa.*"

"Mak*wa,*" Gardner repeated softly. "Bear."

In the bow there is an oval cockpit with its own twin-paned windshield. He wants to ride there, always. When the launch has been brought out of the boathouse and safely started, its exhaust rumbling and spitting, his mother lifts him over the lacquered deck and the rubber step-plate and lowers him onto the soft, cool seat. It smells of tanned hide, and varnish, and his mother's perfume. Through the cushion and the ribs pressing against his leg he feels the vibrations of the engine. His mother takes off her shoes to follow him in. Her white-stockinged foot presses deep into the cushion, and then

she is beside him with her arm around him saying, "Hold on,
Michael!" and laughing. His father swings the prow away from
the boathouse and presses the throttle open and they veer heavenward
until the boat shudders its whole length to the surface, hits stride,
planes. Always the same giddy mix of sensations sweeps him: the
rumble and roar of engine and wind, the clatter of wavelets against
the hull, the snapping of the pennant, the shouted conversations and
his mother's laughter above all. Sometimes she takes off her hat and
scarf and lets her black hair stream in the wind, and her laughter
reassures him absolutely that he is safe, that nothing in all that
world of wind and sun and water will ever harm him.

Sometimes they are gone for hours, threading through the
islands. Sometimes they meet other launches and they wave, sweep-
ing past. They wave to sailboats, skiffs, canoes. Sometimes they are
alone, only the three of them, and sometimes they are joined by
friends from other cottages, who sit in the wicker chairs behind his
father in the spacious central cockpit. Sometimes they simply ride.
Sometimes they go on picnics, out to the farthest islands....

So, alone with the old album, alone in the cottage, in silence
except for the fire sounds, trembling, unshaven, unwashed, unfed,
knowing that he is journeying now through and beyond himself,
Michael Gardner invites the recollection he has avoided.

"Picnic," he says.

His mother packs a large wicker hamper. They go in a group to
islands in the remote northern end of the lake. There are no cottages
there yet. The shores are wild, the islands quite unspoiled. Some are
wooded, some only wave-washed rocks. Usually his parents go to
one of the larger islands where there are smooth slopes for swimming
and sunbathing, and a good mooring for the launch, and an old
and mossy campsite up among white pines.

He is playing there, on a calm summer afternoon in his pen in the
shade of those trees. He loves being there. Every excursion to that
place has been idyllically happy. His parents are nearby, and
although he cannot see them he can hear their conversation and their
laughter, the plunging of their dives into the flat lake, and the
rhythmic splash of their swimming. Occasionally one of them floats

178

into view and waves to him, surrounded by ripples glinting like diamonds.

His Airedale lies panting beside the pen, his ears twitching now and then toward the mainland, his wiry and reassuring coat always within reach.

Often his mother comes up the rock slope and crosses a space of sun to join him in the shadows. When the child sees her coming he holds out his arms, and sometimes she lifts him, holds him against her breasts, laughs against his neck. She is warm. Her hair smells of sun and water. Sometimes she kneels and touches his head, murmurs to him, offers her finger for him to grasp. Sometimes she checks under his rubber pants, and if necessary lifts him out and changes him on the cool moss.

Then she goes back to the shore, out of sight. He listens for further signs of her. He waits uncomplainingly. He knows that soon she will take him down to the lake and they will swim together. She will fit a little white lifejacket around him and tie it with criss-crossing cotton straps, and he will then float by himself. Already he loves the water. He will splash vigorously, a kind of swimming, imitating the grownups.

But for now he waits patiently. He tours the limits of his pen, tottering, occasionally toppling. Because his pen is set on the high centre of the little island, and because the pine boughs are high and the undergrowth is scant, he is able to gaze in all directions across the silver lake. Northeast, other small islands hover above the surface. Southwest, a smudge floats in the cloudless sky, and beneath it a white speck: a steamboat. In the cove, his father's launch drifts at anchor. East, a few hundred yards away, lies the dark and quiet mainland.

The child exists in this centre, safely enclosed. The island surrounds him, and the lake, and the overarching sky. The woman who holds him against her breast, the laughter from the shore, the whine of cicadas, the drone of a cruising fly, the far-off chatter of squirrels—all these are familiar elements in his comfortable reality. Nothing has ever frightened him at that place.

So, when the bear appears, he is curious but not at first alarmed.

She is simply another interesting part of his surroundings. He and the dog sense her approach in the same instant. The dog stands, quivering, facing north. His hackles rise. He growls, but at the same time backs against the bars. The child grasps the rail of his pen, facing north.

The bear slides out of the lake smoothly for such a large creature. Water sloshes off her. Her claws scrape the rock as she advances. She pauses once to shake, and becomes the centre of a shimmering rainbow in the spray flung off her coat.

The child watches, fascinated, both hands clenched in the neck fur of the dog. He has never seen a living creature so large, even before she rises on her hind legs to see them and scent them better, her forepaws dangling, her snout moving across the breeze. He has never smelled anything like the keen pungency that now drifts over to him, strong and wild. He has never seen such an expression on the face of an animal—curious, calm and intelligent, wary and even amused.

He is unafraid. In fact, he lifts his arms.

But at that moment the dog leaps out of the shade and into the sunlight, a snarling, tawny streak, straight at the interloper.

The bear blinks, drops back onto three feet, and with a swat of the fourth, its left forepaw, snaps the dog's neck.

Stiffening in death throes, the Airedale tumbles back at the edge of the pen, and the child sees the flopping head jerked around until the dog's gaze fixes him in—so it seems to the child—a stare of purest hatred.

Then he screams.

Running up from the water, his mother also screams, and screams, her fists quivering in front of her.

The bear retreats with dignity, back down the flank of the island, back into the lake, back toward the brushy shore less than half a mile away, her coat adrift about her, her furry paws sweeping her along. In a few minutes she will have returned to the forest.

But the men, like the dog, must behave heroically. Pointing, the friend shouts to the child's father, "It's a bear! A bear! My God, the brute's killed the dog!"

"The boat!" his father shouts.

They run for it. By the time they start the engine and dash out of the cove, the bear is halfway to shore. By the time they reach her, she is three-quarters of the way. His mother clutches the child to her breast, but he twists around, compelled to watch this horror. He hears the roar of the bear above the roar of the engine. He sees her, in an astonishing feat of strength, lift the top half of her body out of the water, sees her reach for the prow as the launch rushes down upon her, sees her great claws rake across the varnished mahogany as the stem cuts into her, before she is swept under the boat and the bronze propeller does its work.

They leave the corpse to the lake (it is still a wild place, after all) but not before each man has severed a paw.

There is a photograph in the album of the whole party, even the long shadow of his father hunched over the camera. The child is in his mother's arms. The two unsmiling women are huddled together, separated from the man standing to their right. His father's friend, feigning disgust, proudly displays their two gory trophies.

Only the child is crying.

He is so disconsolate that a doctor has to be summoned, a sedative administered. A new dog is quickly provided, an almost identical Airedale.

But he will not ride in that boat. Never again. He screams when he sees it, howls when he is led toward it. Finally, reluctantly, his father trades it for another.

Many years later, Michael Gardner returns one summer day to that place at the northern end of the lake. He finds a white cottage perched on the island where his dog died. He finds teenagers water-skiing on the bay that once ran red with the blood of the bear.

I wait. I paddle, and watch rain dot the narrow arm down which we are moving southeast. I wait, but there will be no more for now.

After a while, Gardner asks about my mother.

"She's buried in Neyashing. In the graveyard."

"Is there a graveyard? I didn't see it."

"It's easy to miss. It's in the meadow behind the dunes, at

the end of the beach. The markers are small, and if you didn't go close you might think they were just little posts in the fireweed, fenceposts, maybe."

"And your father?"

"Never knew him. I don't even know what he looked like. We don't have any pictures. Mother told me I looked like him when I squinted out at something on the Lake. He left a year or two after Cutler was born. I don't think he ever knew he had me. Mother said Travis was a good name for him because he just moved across Neyashing and then moved on. So he left me two things: his name and his cap. This cap."

"It's too bad you never knew him."

"No, I don't think so. He didn't appreciate Mother. He didn't want to stay and help her in the bad times when she needed someone. No, it's best he moved on."

"Still, no father..."

"Oh, we had many fathers. In Neyashing, all the men were our fathers. They all looked after us. Mother pointed out a few special ones. She told us to watch how they lived, to see what they did and didn't do, to listen to what they said and didn't say. There were good men who kept an eye on us, Cutler and me. Oh sure, we had fathers."

"But your mother raised you, really. Tell me about her. What was she like? Where did she come from?"

What was she like? Not pretty. Just beautiful. Gentle. Where did she come from? The land. I looked down the long beach where we were camped, to the sandbanks and the river mouth at the far end. I said, "Do you want to see where my mother came from?"

Gardner nodded.

"Come. I'll show you."

The rain had stopped. Spindly shadows walked with us down a red beach. People had camped at that place for centuries, for millennia. I knew that even before I began to see chippings and pot fragments in the last of the light, at the base of the eroding bank. I touched Gardner's arm and pointed. The bank was layered like a cake, dark strata going down into time. I brushed my fingers across it, and drew out a bit of pot rim decorated long ago. "Before the Bronze Age," I said, handing it to Gardner. "Before the Iron Age. Before the Smallpox Age. Before the Reservation Age."

He took it in his open palm. "Travis," he said, looking at it, turning it, "I'm not responsible, I'm not personally responsible for..."

"Cutler says I idealize those times. He says they were terrible to live in. When we were younger and we'd find an arrowhead on a beach, Cutler would hold it up and say, 'Travis, imagine you're the poor sucker who made that. You're cold and wet and hungry, and so are your woman and kids. You're 23 years old and you've got rheumatism and arthritis and you'll be dead at 30 from lung cancer or emphysema, or from gangrene or rotting teeth. Here you are, hacking a chunk of rock so you can go out and maybe get a rabbit or duck for supper. The noble savage!'"

Gardner closed his hand on the pot sherd.

"'Or,' Cutler would say, 'maybe you're the woman of the noble savage, and you've just started to give birth when you drop that pot and break it. You know that if the child isn't stillborn it will likely be dead in a month or so, and a wolverine will be pawing it out of a little grave somewhere.'

"And yet, here we are, Michael. We've survived. You know, when I came back from the city, I learned how to do everything in the old way. I made stone knives and used them. I flaked stone scrapers and cleaned hides with them. I cut babiche, bent ash, made snowshoes. I made arrowpoints, and a bark canoe, and baskets and makaks. And I learned enough about medicines so that I could help myself if I were sick and alone.

"Do you know why I learned those things? So I would know where my mother came from. Where I came from. There," I pointed to the lowest stratum. "And so I would know how humans lived with this land from there, to there." I spanned all the strata with the stretched fingers of both hands. "Seven thousand years."

Gardner nodded silently. He held out the bit of pottery, and I took it from him and returned it where it belonged, and we went back up the beach in darkness, to our fire.

Later he said, "I think I begin to see. With you, it isn't just Brightsands Village, is it?"

I said nothing.

"It's bigger. *Much* bigger."

I said nothing. I watched the fire. I waited.

Easter Saturday.

He is entombed. Overnight, snowbanks have formed deep on the south side of the cottage, their glistening tops forming parabolas across the windows. Grainy snow has piled thick against the doors, and has flowed up to seize the drooping boughs of evergreens. The south-western sides of the pine trunks bear tufts of snow in their rough bark. Snow has piled up to the eaves of the boathouse.

Day of stasis, day of ice and cold, day of grey ambivalence. During the night, heat has risen through the uninsulated ceiling, through the attic and the roof, and melting snow has flowed down into long icicles at the eve, a glinting rank of swords closing him in. He stares at these icicles. He considers death. Years earlier he read a murder mystery in which the victim is stabbed with an icicle and the killer goes free because no weapon is found. He appraises death by icicle—the weird perfection in which the weapon enters the heart and is then itself destroyed by the last of the body's heat.

He contemplates death by freezing also, letting the fires languish while he lies still, letting the cold reach in and squelch his spark of life. He imagines the stillness of the cedar tomb in which he would lie with a chaste dust of frost upon his eyes.

He shrugs. He builds the fire and huddles close to it. Life and warmth persist, for reasons not yet clear. He sits, waits.

In time, he returns to the photo album again, angles it toward the light of the fire, turns a page....

Aged eleven, he leans through the window of the boathouse. He

*wears a T-shirt and an oversize US Navy gob hat that one of his
parents' friends has given him. In the photograph, shot against the
light, the brim of the cap flares into arcing protruberances that
might be either wings or horns.*

*The room above the boathouse is now his. It is a lofty space
extending out onto a balcony that overhangs deep black water beside
the dock. From that place, in the night, come the guttural sounds of
the lake. On either side of the central room, under the low eaves of
the building, are stored the marine accessories of other years—
boathooks; lifejackets; oars like curved hands with harp-shaped
locks and leather buffers; paddles of many styles and woods; mast
and boom, rudder and tiller of the beamy old lapstrake sailboat,
long since crumbled to dry rot. For several years the sail had
dangled in its old canvas bag from a rusty nail in a rafter, but one
autumn mice nibbled the string and burrowed nests deep into its cotton folds.*

*The scents of old varnish and old pine drift through that loft,
and other scents mingle with them when the door and window are
open—pine needles in warm shade, wet bodies in the sun on the
canvas-covered dock, tanning-oil, and fish when the men return
from early morning expeditions. Sometimes there is the fresh scent of
rain washing the hot shingles. But underlying all other odours is
the fragrance of cedar; that is the smell of summer—dry cedar in the
rafters and the roofboards; soaked cedar in the cribbings and the
docks.*

*He has slung a hammock across one corner of the room, position-
ing it so that he can lie in it and look through the window to the
southeast. He has rigged a mosquito net above it, and sometimes for
hours he lies there reading, suspended in that gauze cocoon. His
uncle, who spends a furlough with them before going to Italy, worries much about this habit, viewing it as unhealthy introspection,
even withdrawal and retreat.* Action, *that word so much in the
news, is his uncle's favourite, its variants frequently repeated in
monologues and exhortations:* Active. Activity. Activate. *The
boy listens respectfully, his book spread open across his stomach, suspended still in that other world from which is uncle has ordered him*

back; respectful, but old enough now to see through the assumptions behind these entreaties—that to act is absolute good; that action should frequently precede thought; that one can safely rely on instinct.

The boy listens patiently but skeptically to this uncle who even on leave, even on the island, wears some item of military apparel— khaki shorts, or shirt with epaulets, or tartan wedge cap— skeptically, because he has witnessed already in far-off Europe and Asia some of the results of this reliance on instinct, and he suspects that something might be said for the intercession of thought or imagination.

In that loft he spends the nights of his youthful summers, falling asleep to the sound of bugs hurling themselves against the screens or searching for an opening in the netting that draped his hammock. In the night he hears sisal painters creaking on the worn pine cleats of the dock, and ripples lapping against lacquered hulls, and the laughter of adults from the verandah up the hillside. In the night he hears farewells called and engines started, and he often wakens enough to see the stern lights and spumes of launches crossing the lake in the moonlight.

In that loft he constructs cardboard tanks, and warships, and bombers, bending tabs and fitting them into appropriate slots, listening to news of the war on his little battery radio. All his life in those summers is overshadowed by fears for his father and uncle and family friends who have vanished into the vortex of war. The dread of the women left behind is like a kind of weather.

And there, in that loft on a hot afternoon in August 1945, he hears a sound so frail, so tremulous he at first mistakes it for cicadas on the island across the channel, or for gulls in the rookery two miles distant. He hears it but does not listen, suspended in his hammock, absorbed in his book. But again it comes, high and quavering. And again.

He slides to the floor, goes through the creaking screen door onto the little balcony, shades his eyes against the glare and sees a motionless rowboat on the bay. Its oars drift like upturned palms. In the middle, a standing figure gesticulates in some ragged, undeci-

pherable semaphore. Reflections, boat and sun-tattered figure form a
cross. "Ohhh..ur!" The cry is so faint it does not echo. It hovers.
  Squinting against the sun, he recognizes Chrissy Harris, their
mildly deranged neighbour. He waves, leans into the light so he can
be seen, and cups an exaggerated hand to his ear. But she is not
looking at him or calling to him. She is announcing with upraised
arms to the bay, the lake and to heaven, "It's o-o-over...."
  He understands at once. He returns inside and through the static
on the radio learns that a weapon of such ferocity has been used at a
place called Hiroshima that the Japanese must, absolutely must and
will, surrender.
  "Thank God!" his mother exclaims when he runs to tell her.
"Oh, thank God!"
  Three days later Nagasaki happens. Fusion: places become
events.
  The staid little resort town where they go by boat to shop is
euphoric, its streets alive with horns and flags. Someone swirls his
mother into the melee, and she laughs, holding her hat on, dancing.
  His father and uncle soon return, both outwardly unscathed. As
for the child, for the rest of his life the name Hiroshima will conjure
for him the apparition of Chrissy Harris in her boat. In that cruci-
form vision she is only part woman. She is also a wraith of unbear-
able light and heat before whom people can be evanesced to shadows.
She is the herald of an end, perhaps the final end. "It's o-o-over...."
  He leaves the album, leaves the memory of the horror. He goes out
onto the snowy porch of the cottage in the pure, dead light of that
Saturday noon, wondering. Shadows of filigree and icicles play over
him. Wind freshens in the pines. Into that dazzling light he peers
like a miner coming out of a long shift. He searches for clues in the
brilliance, for some sign from the circling fates that have returned
him to this memory and this place on the festival of Eastre, goddess
of East and Earth, oldest of mothers. But he sees nothing but the
land.

A sound. A presence. Someone or something passing on
the lake. I went to the water's edge shielding my eyes
against the reflections of the fire, and saw a shadow move

from the larger shadows of the shore and return, as a single bird might detach itself for one instant from the flock.

"What?" Gardner asked.

"I'm not sure."

He came from the fire and joined me. "Is someone there? Someone out there?" He cupped his hands and called slowly and carefully, "Hel...l-o-w..." and his call echoed and re-echoed off the shores of the lake and dwindled to the hiss of ripples in the sand, dwindled to nothing.

"Go on," I said, returning to the fire. "Tell me the rest."

"I don't know why I'm telling you any of it."

"Don't worry about reasons," I said. "Tell."

He wakes next morning feeling fresh and vigorous, but oddly insubstantial, as if after a long illness. In that clear, bright dawn he has a momentary pang of conscience. He is surprised and ashamed by what he has done. He believes he has behaved impulsively and even irresponsibly, like a deserter who leaves others to bear the weight of action. Old habits admonish him. He runs mentally through the list of cancelled appointments and other matters needing personal attention. He begins to think of going back, perhaps the following morning, perhaps that evening.

But at the same time the thought of returning depresses him, and when he looks out into the day he is filled with childlike delight, even skittishness. It is a lovely morning. During the night the strong north winds have swept the ice clean and the temperature has dropped sharply. The lake glitters, a smooth and bright invitation. Suddenly he realizes that he could skate, something he has not done for many years, not since one cold December when he and Martha spent a week here together.

He pulls on coat, hat, mittens and boots, and dons a pair of ovoid mirror-glasses he has found in a drawer, glasses that give his face the blankness of a skull. He ventures out and wades down through the drifts to test the ice, half-walking, half-sliding. He finds it solid still.

He laughs gleefully. Here is a bright and windless day! Here is a vast and private skating-rink! Only a mile to the north is the narrows, beyond which the lake sprawls away for miles into various arms. Dotted across the narrows he can see the huts of ice fishermen, like black teeth, but beyond them, far to the north, there is only pure light. He could skate all morning, all day! He could skate past the ice huts, through the narrows and keep going.

He hurries back to the cottage and finds his old skates on a closet shelf. The leather uppers are cracked but still pliable, and the laces are good. The blades are rust-pocked but reasonably sharp.

He carries them to the dock, clears away the snow to make himself a seat, and ties them on. His initial strides are very cautious, like those of a small boy wobbling out for the first time. Twice he twists onto his ankles. But soon his confidence grows and he begins to glide, begins to feel again the sense of flying that he had long forgotten. He laughs delightedly, swinging his arms to the rhythm, circling in the tiny bay enclosed by the island. And then he ventures out, turns north toward the line of fish huts across the narrows. Already he is thinking beyond them, imagining the way the lake will open out and he will sail on past miles of shuttered cottages and the opening mouths of rivers.

The huts shimmer and float, lift and settle in the white bright space that is ice and sky and emptiness beyond. A thin pall hangs over them. Small dark oblongs flit between them—snowmobiles, still far-off and soundless. Sometimes a machine will dash for shore, only to return almost immediately. Sometimes two will race out and back on a course oblique to Gardner's line of approach, and when they are closest he hears a sound like angry bees. But for most of the journey he travels in silence except for the whisking of his blades on ice.

Closer, he sees that the huts are not arranged in a line as he first thought, but are dotted haphazardly over the half-acre before the narrows. The ice among them is littered with fishermen's paraphernalia, with snowmachines and sleds, with tethered dogs. The passage at first seems clogged with all of this, but then Michael Gardner spies what he believes is a way through, and he veers toward it.

Three dogs spot him simultaneously and begin to howl in unison, *setting up a yammering chorus that brings squinting fishermen out of the nearest huts. Gardner waves a greeting and calls, "Just passing through," over the uproar of the dogs. He glides on, toward the little zigzagging path that he believes will lead through the narrows and the wide lake beyond.*

But he will not pass through. The clamouring dogs dance out to block his path, and one of the fishermen also runs across in front of him, waving his arms like someone at the scene of an accident. "Thin ice!" he calls.

Gardner sees that he is right. In fact, he sees serpentine patches of black water cutting through where the currents are strongest. Nor is there any easy passage overland. Where the snow is not deep-piled it has melted, leaving raw rock. Regretfully, Gardner sweeps in a little half-circle and curves in toward the nearest hut. A father and son stand beside it, watching him. They are both stocky, bulky in snowmobile suits. The father has unzipped his suit to reveal a heavy black-green flannel jacket and a triangle of red undershirt at his throat. Both men wear peaked caps. Helmets wait on the seat of their snow-machine.

"Don' wanna go through there,*" the father says, squinting at Gardner, "Can't* get *through."*

"Ain't safe!" yells the son, and utters laughter like the cry of a disoriented bird. He is about twenty, scraggle-toothed, befuddled by drink and hapless genes.

Gardner takes a last look at the remote vistas beyond the narrows and then removes his sunglasses and glides closer to the two men. "How's fishing?"

Father and son both laugh. "Pretty good!" the older man says. "Wanna buy some fish today?"

Gardner shakes his head. "Not today."

"Don't blame yuh. Truth is, goddam things ain't worth eatin anymore. Ain't hardly worth cleanin. Look't that there!" He points to stiff forms in the snow.

Gardner glides close and bends down. They are wrong, these fish! For one thing, they are so small. *He has no idea of legal limits, but he recalls the ample trout of his childhood, fish held out in both hands by grinning anglers, proud offerings to the camera. Sometimes, in fact, two men were needed to hold a fish. But these, these are pathetic parodies of those real fish. Worse, some are grotesquely malformed, riddled with ulcerous swellings and lesions. Some have jaws twisted into hideous grins; some, tails stretched like weird fronds. The eyes of some are swollen almost shut with purplish growths.*

"Goddam chemicals, what it is!" says the father. "Goddam stuff in the rain! Still sell 'em, though. Cut the heads off, cut the tails off, still sell 'em."

"But, I remember trout this big!"

"Ha! You and me both! Not him, though. He don't remember fish that big, right George?"

The son shakes his head and grins ruefully, apologetically.

"No sir! Gone for good, them fish!"

Gardner looks again at the flawed trout. One of them still quivers. Its throes have beaten the snow into a tortuous flower, and it lies now with its head near the centre. He peers into its flat eye. He sees his miniature self reflected back, his miniature world. But through those reflections, beneath the spreading mist of death, he sees a look of profoundest hatred.

He trembles.

"Hey!" the father says to him. "You better come in, my friend. Get warm."

"Get warm," the son echoes, holding the door of their hut ajar.

"No. Thank you. I'm all right. I'll just..." Gardner glides backward on his skates. But as he straightens up he is suddenly dizzy, aware that he has eaten very little for three days. "I'll just..."

"Holy Jeez!" the son lunges into the hut and the father lumbers after him. Curious, Gardner glides close, bends down and peers inside.

"Have we got a fish!" the son shouts. "Have we got a fish!" One of the four short rods fixed in sockets around the hole in the ice is bent almost double, its reel screaming.

"Hold onto 'im!" the father shouts, and beckons happily to

191

Gardner. "Come on in! We got some action here!"

Michael Gardner ducks and enters awkwardly on his skates. The hut is small and stuffy, sour with kerosene and fish, whisky and stale sweat. A single window on the north side is clamped and frosted over. When the door swings shut behind him they are in twilight. He is surprised that he is not claustrophobic, perhaps because the clarity of the lake and the fishing-lines refracting into it give an illusion of immense height and space. For an instant he feels that he has been swept heavenward to stare back down at a tranquil earth, no blue and cloud-wrapped globe, but a luminous desert emptied of life.

The boy shouts again as another of his lines dips sharply, and before he can seize it, a third line dips. In his excitement he kicks over a bait pail, freeing several small frogs that begin a frenzied leaping about the hut.

"Frogs!" the father shouts, grabbing for them. "You always gotta use them damn frogs! Nothin' else good enough for yuh!"

"Well," the son says, fumbling with the lines, "they workin, ain't they?"

In the flurry and confusion Gardner gets handed a pole. He takes it, holds it, watching while the two men draw up their fish, pin them with their boots, twist hooks from their jaws, and fling them outside to freeze.

In the same moment, they all realize that Michael Gardner is holding the rod on which the original, and biggest, strike occurred.

He has not fished for decades, but he remembers afternoons when he knelt bare-kneed on rocks or on rotting wharves, and mornings huddled in the bow of a skiff, waiting, his pole clamped in both fists and his head turned as if the strike would be audible. He remembers the feel—at first only a little tugging like a suture needle piercing the lips of a frozen wound, then the lunge, the swallowing of the bait, the rod bending and throbbing as the doomed fish flees.

But this fish does not feel like that. There is no frenzy, no spasm. The end of his rod is slowly and relentlessly drawn toward the eight-inch circle of water. He resists only enough to hold on, and watches fascinated as the handle of the reel continues to spin, begins

192

to blur. Something very large is on the other end; something that does not measure its life in inches or in years, something moving inexorably away, drawing out all the line.

The son gapes. The father curses softly, "Holy Christ! Hold him, man! Hold him!" repeating the same incantations as if by doing so he could conjure a magical weight to counterbalance whatever mass is moving in those depths.

But Gardner cannot hold it. He laughs helplessly and shakes his head. He knows without looking at the blur of the reel handle and the vanishing line that he is linked to something that will do its own will, not his. Perhaps the line will break. Perhaps the hook will straighten out. Perhaps the whole apparatus of rod and reel will be yanked out of his hands to vanish through the hole. Perhaps—he laughs again at this giddy image—he will hold tight and be drawn down and down to begin some eerie flight in that other element.

But when only a few coils of line remain on the reel the whirring stops. The line goes slack. "Reel 'im in! Reel 'im in!" the father shouts, and Gardner attempts to do that. He winds faster and faster but feels no resistance. He whips the rod upward; nothing.

"Broke, goddamit!" The father scowls and spits, beginning a bitter litany of curses while still grabbing at airborne frogs. "Goddam line snapped!"

But no, something far stranger has occurred. The fish has stopped just short of the end and is now circling back. Gardner imagines that long trailing U and knows that he will never wind fast enough, that the creature will move at a pace indifferent to human traps and human striving. He understands that another manifestation will now occur. Intent, expectant, he waits, feeling the grave weight of his body drawing him down and down. He feels as a whale must feel when the living tide ebbs away.

For moments, nothing.

Then, a shadow looms on the north side, from that narrow place in the lake. It is weirdly distorted and magnified beneath the ice, just as the head of the fish, when it appears in the hole, is distorted by the convex lens of water that wells up above it, so that for an instant all three men share the dread of something truly monstrous rising upon them, something that will shatter the ice, shatter the hut, consume them. Some huge version, perhaps, of the diseased victims on the ice outside. All three shrink back.

But the head is unblemished. Silver, luminous in the pale light of the shack, it fills the hole. Immense eyes regard them. Gill covers rise and fall like pewter disks, and jaws set with needle teeth open at such an angle as to give Gardner the hallucinatory glimpse of a smile.

He reaches toward it.

The jaws shut, the fish twists slightly, and when its mouth opens again it is to disgorge a body shockingly like a little man's. A hapless frog, hook still secure in its snout, sprawls belly-up at Michael Gardner's feet. The fish immediately sinks. Kneeling close to the hole, Gardner watches it turn north toward the narrows and the lake beyond.

This happens in seconds.

Still gaping, the young man sits down abruptly, a gaff-hook forgotten in his hand. "Jay-zos!"

Also gaping, the father turns from his son to Gardner and back again. "Well by jeez," he says, "I never seen nothin' like that! You, George?"

"Hell no!"

"Eh?"

"Hell no!"

"By jeez!" The father fumbles in his jacket. "What dyuh figure, George? Thirty pound?"

"More."

"Forty?"

"More! Couldn't uh got him through the damn hole!"

Michael Gardner sits astonished, elated. In those seconds, in the appearance and disappearance of that creature, a world has been revealed that he thought gone for good, a world sublimely beyond the despoiled one he has come to know and accept, a world of promise and of hope, to which this fish is the summoner.

He stands shakily. The father takes his elbow, holding a half-

empty mickey of rye in his other hand. "They're still there, then, ain't they!"

Gardner nods.

"Well sir, here's to em, that's what I say! I hope they never get caught! Here's to em!" Trembling, he removes the cap, drinks, and hands the bottle to Michael Gardner.

Gardner drinks too, and passes the bottle to the son, who is still staring incredulously into the lake. "Thank you," Gardner says, shaking hands with both of them. "Thank you. I have to be going now. Goodbye. Good luck." He opens the door and steps back out into the sun, bedazzled for a moment before he finds his balance and his stride.

"Carry on, my friend!" the father calls from the doorway, arm raised. "Good luck!"

Light, laughing, graceful as a tail-coated skater in some nineteenth-century print, Michael Gardner glides back to his island in the dazzling sun. He takes a long time closing the cottage because he is often beguiled by wonders—the shifting shadow-labyrinth of the pines, the dazzling stillness, the melting sweetness of the breeze.

It is late afternoon when he finishes closing the old place, damps down the fire and packs his few clothes and toiletries. Then, in the dusk, he starts out across the bay to the landing where he can call a cab to take him to the station.

He is going on, going North.

He Hears Spirits Sing

We couldn't get out. The land kept forcing us farther east, then north, then east again, always parallel to the Lake or away from it, with miles of hills between. Several times we thought we saw a passage, but each time the river dwindled

to a sluggish stream and finally to beaver meadows and mus-
keg where mosquitoes rose in swarms and where paddling
and portaging were impossible. Gardner argued once or
twice that we should go south on foot, but I said no; whatever happened we'd stay with the canoe. I'd known of too
many people who set out on an easy walk and were never
seen again. So we circled, backtracked, searched and
researched the land to the south, but found only the bogs,
the lowering hills and the impenetrable bush.

Several times I was sure we were not alone; but I never saw
anyone else or any human sign, except one aircraft passing
far to the west.

By the end of the second week we had used nearly all the
store food, and had begun to live off the land. We fished; we
set snares. I gathered some roots and shoots. We both got
leaner.

Gardner had darkened to my colour. His beard and hair
had bleached almost white. All his movements were surer,
more feral, and on the outside he looked like a healthy man.
But what about inside? I couldn't tell. Sometimes, watching
him stand hands-on-hips at the end of a portage, or on a rock
slope at evening I went cold, he looked so much like some
conqueror, some explorer challenging the wilderness, drunk
with delusions.

But at other times when he laughed at a bear-cub tumbling in the shallows, or at a loon startled by the closeness of
our canoe, or at some child's tale I told about Nanabush, I
would think, Maybe. *Maybe!*

One afternoon at the end of the second week we came into
a large lake that was deep and promising. The hills to the
south seemed very close. "Here we are," Gardner said. "*Here*
we are." But we searched the shore until dusk and found no
way out. We went down that shore and back, and down
again and back, looking for a blazed tree, a fireplace, a scuff
of paint on a rock—any sign of a portage. But there was
nothing.

"Why not?" Gardner asked when we had camped, pointing from the end of the island to a place on the dark shore where the hills were closer, lower. "It should be *there*. Right?"

"It should be," I said.

"Well why isn't it?"

I shrugged. "We'll have another look in the morning." I built up the fire, and then went out in the darkness onto the shelving rocks at the point of the island, looking at that other shore, and listening. After a while I stripped and waded in, breaststroking out away from Michael Gardner, far enough to feel other creatures in the lake with me, loons, and beavers, and deep fish turning, and otters sleek as thought, and someone human passing in the darkness; far enough that the campfire became an orange speck no brighter than any other star. I floated in that ice-cold lake longer than was safe, so that when I got back to the fire I was numb and gasping. I dried, and dressed, and had a large mug of tea close to the fire.

"Someone's out there," I said.

"What? Where?"

I motioned toward the lake, to the place where the portage should have been.

"How do you know?"

"I heard a paddle dripping. I heard a canoe on rock."

"You're imagining it."

"No."

Gardner went out on the rock and cupped his hands and called *Halloooo,* a long call that blended with its echo and circled around and around until it filled the lake. He listened, called again. "Why wouldn't they answer, if they're there?"

"Some people like to be alone," I said.

Again he cupped his hands, and this time he called, "We need help.... Can you help us...?"

We both listened, but there was no answer except the falling, mocking cry of a loon.

"You must have been imagining it," he said, rejoining me at the fire. "If anyone were there they would have answered. Surely. After all, what kind of person wouldn't answer a call for help?"

I sipped my tea. I fed twigs into the fire. I asked, "Michael, who's Martha?"

"What?"

"Martha. Tell me about her."

"Martha is my wife. She was my wife."

"Which?"

He laughed curtly. "Both. She left me, but we're still married. How do you know her name?"

"You've said it in your sleep. And that first night, at Bobby Naponse's cabin. And a few other times, too. Do you love her?"

He glanced up at me and back into the fire. He nodded. "We still love each other," he said.

"What happened, then?"

"Mistakes. My mistakes, I suppose. But I couldn't see any other way at the time." He shook his head. "It's like a dream, all of it at the end, like a dream...."

Many young women come to the cottage at the lake. Some are neighbours, some are guests of neighbours, some are guests or waitresses at nearby resorts. Pictures of several in various summery settings are in the album, but he cannot recall their names. They usher him out of youth, through various adolescent turbulences and into that young stage of manhood when he spends much time aroused and distracted by anticipations—the prospect of festive lights on the water, for example, or music drifting across a glassy bay, or the laughter of women, or a special woman alone in his arms.

The cottage of Martha's parents is also on an island, close to the Gardners'. She is a dark and unpredictable and troubling young woman, swept by moods. Like the evenings through which he paddles to meet her. Like the loon's call. Like a sudden squall that

198

roughens the surface before the sail fills and the boat responds. He is infatuated by her when he is sixteen and in love when he is seventeen. When they are eighteen and nineteen, both working at a nearby resort, they drift apart although they remain good friends. At university they see each other often, laugh together often, although both believe the affair has ended. Their paths diverge—his leading toward business, hers toward art.

Then, late in the autumn after graduation, they find themselves each alone at the cottages where they have spent their childhoods. She has come back to paint the autumn colours; he to close his parents' place for the winter. He is pounding shutters into place on bedroom windows when he hears leaves rustling behind him, and turns. He sees her canoe first, drifting out to the end of its tether at the dock. Then he sees Martha. She is wearing old jeans, an old tartan shirt, an old down vest. Her hair is tied back under a floppy hat. Her hands are in her hip pockets. "Hi," she says. "Need some help?"

They find that they are in love again. Or still.

He cancels a trip to Europe—his last excursion before beginning work—and they stay three weeks alone in that secluded corner of the lake, paddling and hiking in the high, cool days, coming back to the fireplace in the evenings, to her new paintings flowing in the lamplight like spots of forest sun.

They stay until ice begins to form around the islands.

Already the lake has ceased to be North for them both, although they do not realize it or do not admit it. Already by then—the mid-fifties—the wildness had faded from that place like health from an ailing body. The silences went first, and then the darkness of the wild, and then the loons. Even before the shoreline became real estate, and the lake teemed with powerboats, the wilderness had withdrawn.

Still, for a little time after Thanksgiving, when the cottages were boarded up, the docks hauled in and the boats slotted for the winter into their marinas, the feeling of something like wildness returned. At that season at least, if mystery no longer dwelt along the darkened shore, it was possible to imagine it....

Suspended, they spend those three weeks together. For a little time they share again the awe and innocence of their childhood. But they are not children anymore. They are lovers who cannot stop touching one another, who long for this miraculous gift to last forever. And, full of illusions, they believe it will; they believe that they will never be encroached upon like that place which they have loved.

Even after they marry they continue to believe that. Even after they have begun to feel the weight of time and acquisitions....

Michael Gardner paused. He looked into the wind, toward the lake. "Perhaps..."

There is no event or stage to which he can point and say, "Here, exactly here is where things began to go wrong." Rather, he recalls the end of their marriage like one of the slides of his childhood, the kind his father prepared by splashing water down its length, making the hot aluminum slick and cool. He feels that he was helpless on such a slide, spinning in slow motion, too surprised and rapt even to scream, all the disintegration of their life a swirl in memory. He knows where they began, and where they ended, but he does not know what happened in between, or what he might have done to prevent their parting. There were the usual tensions, the unique but predictable difficulties of marriage, but had he not met these rationally, calmly? Had he not resolved them with common sense?

"Perhaps if there had been children..." Michael Gardner said, looking away from the fire, out into the dark lake.

Steadiness. Balance. Rationality. Clearly defined objectives.

He has no difficulty making logical business decisions. He acquires facts, deliberates, decides. He is shrewd, pragmatic, reliable, willing to take calculated risks. His decisions make money; his recommendations work. *His rise first in smaller corporations and finally in Aspen is carefully planned and steady. He enjoys his work and its benefits. Although he is too circumspect to say so, he shares the boyish joy of a stockbroker friend who tells him, clapping his hands, "I just* love *making money!"*

Occasionally he has reservations, niggling misgivings about the larger consequences and implications of some corporate action, but only once is he profoundly shaken by doubt. Only once, early in his

200

career, does he have a personal crisis.

It happens in an unguarded moment when he asks himself why he experiences each decision as a divestment. *His answer: that it is because each choice eliminates all alternatives. Myriad alternatives. With each decision, infinite potential is destroyed. Conscious or unconscious, momentous or trivial, each decision* therefore cre-ates the world.

The duty implicit in this perception strikes Michael Gardner hard enough to terrify and paralyze him. With profound sorrow he understands that to have choice means to be God, and in that instant he is swept to a brink as mariners were once swept to the edge of the ancient world beyond which monsters roamed. Monsters of paradox. Monsters of responsibility. He recognizes why men retreat to rationality, to dogma, to conventional success, and he sees what monsters prowl close there also—monsters of self-deception.

He can't work, can't function. Stupefied, he sits shivering on a couch. His physician says stress, fatigue, nods soothingly at mut-tered explanations, jots prescriptions, frees him indefinitely from schedules and obligations. But it is Martha who knows instinc-tively what must be done; it is she who takes him back to the old cen-tre, to the cottage and the lake.

It is autumn when they go; the bays are restive with flocks and gatherings. The loon's cry searches for him, wraps him, gathers him again into all beginnings....

What she gives him in those days comes in no single statement. She takes no position, makes no reproach, offers no alternatives. Reassurance comes from her silences beside the fire. It comes in her glance, her kiss, her absorbing love. It comes as they walk along the shore, or paddle through October fog. It comes in the way she brushes back a strand of hair as she bends close to her painting. It comes gradually in all their winding conversations. Perhaps, she sug-gests, it would be better to keep asking the questions for which there are no answers, better than choosing the many ways of safety.... Pehaps it would be better to live with mysteries, open-eyed.... Per-haps, she says, gazing at the sad proliferation of securities along the mainland shore, they should go where there is wildness still;

perhaps they should go north....

But they do not. Maybe because he does not respond at that moment, or because she does not insist, their sojourn becomes something merely therapeutic, like a two-week vacation. Gardner recovers. The gulf of misgiving in him heals over. He returns to work. He returns inside, to his executive desk. He executes.

He thinks of that time as an opportunity missed. Afterwards, they diverge. There are successes for each of them—his corporate projects, her questing canvases—but they share less risk as the years pass, and ever less. The space widens.

They are 35. They are 40.

Finally, carried on wholly different currents and tides, she begins to drift out of his sight. She passes through strange storms. She cries often, and laughs in her sleep. For long periods she paints nothing despite the urgings of her gallery, entreaties to which she will respond with notes like: I'm just going to walk for a while, *or* I'm sorry. Everything has become too clear.

She acquiesces to holidays, but they quickly become embarrassments to him. Three weeks at Stowe shrink to five days after she declines to perform the parallel turns of which she was once a master, and rides serenely down on the chair-lift; after she refuses to eat birds, even Rock Cornish hen, no matter how delectably glazed; after she approaches strangers at their drinks and asks, "Excuse me, can you please show me the way back to life?", in the same tone she might use to inquire about the washroom. Frequently she asks such embarrassing questions. She misses appointments because she went to the zoo to watch the gambolling of polar bears and became beguiled by them. For hours she walks alone on the wooded fringes of their estate.

Physicians prescribe drugs she will not take. A psychiatrist alludes to the climacteric, and she laughs at him. At times she drinks too much and grows maudlin and nostalgic, but there is no violence in her. She remains the same gentle person he has known. A phase, Gardner thinks, as he has thought too often; they are in a phase that will pass in time.

But one morning as he is leaving for work she takes his face in her hands and kisses him tenderly, saying goodbye with her smile and her tears, telling him that this marriage has reached its end. He brushes this away. Nonsense. Another excess, he tells himself; marriages end in scenes, not inconvenience.

He cannot stay. He will miss the train, miss pressing appointments. He kisses her, says something about that evening, that night, and then departs, leaving her watching at the window for the last time. He drives out of the driveway, into the country hills and south through the spring morning. He tries not to think of her. He tries to think ahead. He keeps the window down to smell this fresh new morning—the wet bark of maples, the wrinkling ice-skin on meltwater ponds and the vegetable decay of Earth. He parks at the station as usual, crosses the platform as usual with the other commuters and steps aboard the Dayliner, greets the conductor, finds a seat as usual on the north side.

And then, as the train moves, he admits what he knows. He has a vision of himself returning that evening, stepping down and watching the tail-lights of the train recede eastward, listening to its empty whistle while around him doors close, engines start, headlights wash over the gravel of the parking-lot, and other people laugh together at the beginnings of their weekends. He imagines himself returning to an empty house.

Many times in the little spaces between meetings later that day he tries to call, knowing there will be no answer.

And he is right. There is a note on her empty easel that night: "If we could have gone back... If we had had time, or no time...."

He enters then a weird state of suspension that lasts two years, neither life nor death. Everything remains the same, yet everything is radically altered. Their house remains, and he continues to live in it; his career remains, and he continues to live in it. His many church and charitable commitments remain, and he continues to honour them nobly, all the time feeling as if pieces of himself are falling away inside. And so he goes on, performing, until the morning of the swans....

They are whistling swans, 31 of them in a a meltwater pond in the hills. The train rounds a curve and he sees them there, on the

203

north side. Their slender necks are so white in the new sun, against the inky pond, then he gasps. As he watches, their wings spread, they rise together, lifting him out of the talk of morning markets, and the fragrance of tobacco and aftershave, free of the welter of signs and meanings. New life surges through him. His wings brush the others, rising northward into the bounty of the sun.

Then, behind comes the plodding and wondering animal who cancels all appointments indefinitely that Thursday morning and who, in clothes hastily bought, soon boards another train, northbound. He will return to that old centre, that egg-shaped island where in the fullness of time, having been invited yet again, he will find the faith to venture on.

When he finished this story, Michael Gardner turned away from the smoke, and laughed and shook his head—a man embarrassed by a simple puzzle, a puzzle he should have solved with ease. He spread his arms. 'So, here I am! Tell me, Travis, where *am* I?"

He was gone when I woke next morning, and the canoe was gone. I went to the point of the island and looked east down the lake, shading my eyes against the rising sun. He was half a mile away, coming back along the south shore, raising his paddle when he saw me and pointing back down the shore. "I found it," he said when he came close. "I found the portage."

We paddled back together. It was impossible to miss the place now. A strip of khaki cloth fluttered from a branch over the water, and a small tree had been freshly bent over toward the south. Someone had walked through the night before, someone whose boots had been pressed into the soft earth by the weight of a canoe on his shoulders. And there was something else: I bent down and drew my hand across the trail, feeling the slightest resistance. On the tip of my finger I lifted the end of a transparent thread—a monofilament nylon line leading away, over the height of land.

I looked into the tangled woods and lifted my cap to the

man at the other end of that line; the man who was already on the other side, out on the big Lake; the man I knew I would never see.

The portage had not been used for many years. It was dark and overgrown. Big deadfalls blocked the trail every few hundred yards. In some places saplings clustered so close that the canoe jammed in them. I had to back up and search for a way around, or put the canoe down and chop through. Clouds of blackflies swarmed over us. They crawled into my ears and up my nose. I inhaled them. They got under my cap, under my collar, under my cuffs, up my legs. Blood ran out of my hair and down with the sweat into my eyes. Blood clotted under my ears and on my neck. All the way I could hear Michael Gardner coming behind, slipping, wheezing, cursing.

But then, suddenly, we came out into the sun and wind at the top of a plateau that tipped south, and the Lake lay less than two miles away. The arms of the north shore stretched to either side in the clear afternoon, and far to the south the horizon hung faint but clear as a blue line in a child's scribbler. Fat clouds blossomed in the southwest.

Wind swept the bugs away. I set the canoe down and walked around with my hands on my hips, feeling light and a bit dizzy, feeling the blood begin to course back through the muscles of my neck and shoulders.

We portaged the second mile, down into a reedy place where the river was deep enough to launch the canoe, and then we poled toward the Lake, feeling the stream broaden and straighten as the current quickened. I remembered the place then, and heard Grandfather's laughter as we were borne down by that current and into the fast water. Mist rose ahead. There was a sound like rushing wind. "Ginodi-jiwan baotig," I said. "Rapids. Little white water, now."

I remember the three long Vs in the curved black surface, where rocks split the current at the top. I remembered the mist as far as I could see ahead. I remembered Grandfather saying, "You are going to be birds now, boys. You are going to fly...." and a rapid like a long flight of stairs, and the three of us airborne above white water, filling the canyon with warwhoops.

Rapids are living things, never quite the same sason to season. Sometimes rock falls off cliffs. Sometimes trees drop across. Sometimes banks crumble. And the water itself is always working, shifting up or down, changing configurations, and suddenly there will be standing waves where flat pools had been only a month before.

Gardner stopped paddling. "Wait a minute," he said. "That sounds ferocious."

I pointed to the top of the portage and we landed and walked down a ways. It was one gutsy, raging, terrific stretch of water. We looked at it, we looked at the portage and at each other.

I asked, "Well?"

Gardner shrugged, and smiled.

Some people tell their children, *Don't take chances!* but there are times when that is very poor advice. A lot of life is out there on the edge, beyond what is known, beyond any definable risk. I think I will tell my son or daughter, "Go ahead. Be reasonable, but when reason doesn't help you anymore, *take the chance!*"

We did that, Michael Gardner and I.

The first stages were broad and flat and we dropped down cautiously, just far enough on each plateau to see that there were no nasty surprises coming. Then we'd turn downstream and run, eddy out, run again. In the first serious whitewater, Gardner shouted, "Tell me what to do!" and I shouted back, "Whatever's best!" Then spray drenched me and water surged over the gunwale and I got too busy to talk. Gardner said afterward that I hooted and laughed all the way down, and at a place where the bow sank and all we could see was a half-mile of foam under our knees I heard him laughing too, and I saw his paddle in the water, doing the right things.

There was a little pool at the end of that stretch and we eddied behind a curve in the bank and baled out the canoe. Then we were off again, down a smooth, black chute for a quarter of a mile and then into a traverse above some very ugly rocks. I remembered that place, and shouted up to him that it was coming, and when we reached it I said, "Now!" and he leaned out and drew, and we slid across and then down another chute and through a stand of two-foot waves at the bottom. After that the rapid flattened considerably, and there were only two other places where we could have been in serious trouble, where our canoe could have been chopped into kindling and our bodies hung up by the heels and stretched nine feet long by the force of that water. Gardner did well in both places, and we got through with only one or two cracked ribs and two or three little tears in the canvas. And then, too soon, we were on flat water at the bottom and breathing again, being carried by currents around a bend where the river broadened and the cliffs changed into brushy shore, and the thunder of the rapids faded to a sound like soft wind in trees.

We drifted across the strands of foam and down over deep, black water, and finally snagged in some sweetgale on the bank. We were both laughing but gasping too, as if we'd run a race. Gardner laid his paddle across the gunwales and leaned on it, and I collapsed backward with my head on the stern deck and my cap over my face, laughing.

After a while we paddled down to the lagoon behind the beach and had a look at the Lake, although we knew we'd be going no farther that day. A southwest wind lashed the Lake into breakers that rolled right over the low end of the gravel bar and made even the lagoon tricky to cross. Out beyond, Lake and sky were a jumbled turmoil of black and white, grey and pastel, as the clouds shifted and the sun dashed behind them.

We paddled back upstream and camped beside a riffle

near the bottom of the rapid. We patched the canoe there, and bathed, and ate in the dusk beside the fire; and it was there, later in the evening, that Gardner held up a hand and said, "Listen!", his eyes wide. I nodded, hearing what he heard above the dying wind, above the distant pounding of the surf: proud voices singing in the rapid, singing a slow song in a language that neither of us understood, that neither of us needed to understand....

We had only a three-day paddle west. The breeze had shifted by the next morning, and we had a steady tail wind along the shore, all the way home.

Late in the afternoon of the third day I saw the spit again. The Lake was rolling a bit by then, and I went in closer to the point than I should have, finding the spirits on the rock and water and showing them to Gardner. I let the swirling currents of the place catch us and spin us helplessly through a luminous cloud of spray and mist, into the calm of the bay.

Neyashing lay ahead. We drifted in. Children ran down the beach and vanished into the dunes as we approached. Michael Gardner leaned forward, gazing at the beach, and the village, and the hillside in the dusk. He said, "It's good to be back."

The prow touched sand.

We were weaker than we realized. When he got out, Gardner dropped to his knees on the beach, and I had to hold the gunwale until my head cleared.

"Kaa bojo!" And then Cutler was there, Cutler coming down across the beach from his truck, wearing his silly tall hat with the eagle feather and working a toothpick in the corner of his mouth, his hands in his hip pockets and his eyes sizing up everything very fast from under the brim of that hat. He looked at Michael Gardner's torn shirt, and shredded trousers, and bedraggled beard, and he asked, "Have a nice little trip?"

"Lovely," Gardner said, standing up unsteadily

and brushing himself off. "Very relaxing." He pulled on the gunwale but the canoe didn't move.

"Good! Nice time of year for a little trip. Good fishing, usually. Remember that spring, Travis, that time you and I went back..." And he launched into a long and rambling story about some trip long ago, hauling the packs out as he talked, and then picking up the battered canoe with one hand and overturning it high up on the beach, and then slinging a pack on each shoulder and heading toward Bobby Naponse's cabin with Gardner staggering along on one side and myself on the other.

The cabin was just as we had left it the night we abducted Gardner, except that Ellen Naponse had cleaned it and washed the dishes. Cutler gestured to a big saran-wrapped plate of cheese and buns and cold cuts on the red-checkered tablecloth. "My wife Barbara. She thought you might be hungry."

"Thank you."

"Anything else you need?"

"No. I don't need anything."

"Up in the cupboard here there's instant coffee, tea..."

Gardner's unsmiling gaze shot out of the crazy tangle of his hair and beard, and held Cutler. He said, "The last time I had tea with you I lost a piece of my life."

Cutler grinned. "Magic tea, I guess."

"Magic tea." Gardner nodded, still not smiling.

They stared at each other, and Cutler's grin faded. "Now what, Mr. Gardner?"

"I need to sleep, think."

"We'll be hearing from you?"

"Oh yes," Gardner said softly, his eyes bright. "You'll be hearing from me again. No question about that."

Cutler backed toward the door with his palms raised like a man who does not want trouble, who wants nothing but peace and friendship. "N'sheemenh," he said, "I'll just load up that truck."

When he had gone I asked Gardner, "What now?"

"Now the real work begins," he said. He offered his hand and I took it. His face was a white and expressionless Haida mask with sapphire eyes, eyes in which I saw, far back behind the tiredness, a calm union of Lake and sky. "I don't know why I should even talk to you. You kidnapped me, lost me, nearly killed me."

"No charge. Next time I'll have the maps. I promise."

"*Next* time!"

"Free trip then too," I said. "For both of you. Zhawen-dagoziwin. Good luck, my friend."

Outside, my brother looked grim in the shadows of the cab, under his tall hat. He said, "We are for the high jump, n'sheemenh."

"I don't think so, Cutler."

"Listen, that is one very angry man, little brother! When that man gets rested up, he is going to sue us out of our fucking shoelaces!"

I shook my head. "He has changes to make. Work to do."

"When he finishes with us, we'll all be in the cooler—you and me and Jimmy and the Krautlet too."

"Well Cutler, I've done my best. I'm going to bed now. Wake me up in four or five days."

"Eat first. Barbara sent food. It's on your table. I'll let Jimmy know he'll be charged with abduction and narcotic offences. Incidentally, you've lost your job. Sleep well."

I pulled my packs out of the truck and walked up the hill alone. Guaranteed came snuffling out from under the porch, quivering as if he were full of mosquitoes. I twisted his ears and rubbed his belly and put my arms around him when he jumped up to lick my face. "N'dai," I said. "Hello, good old dog."

Jenny had been there the week before. Some split wood was stacked beside the stove and a little jar of withered spring flowers stood on the table beside a photograph of me wearing my cap and old jacket. Underneath there was a note: WANTED. I ate, took a sauna and slept for sixteen hours without a dream.

When I woke up Michael Gardner was gone. According to Bobby Naponse, he had sent one of the kids to make a call to Thunder Bay, and a limousine with smoked windows had come down to pick him up. The car was so long, Bobby said, that when he woke up and saw it going past his window he thought he was back in the old days, living beside the railroad tracks at Jackfish.

That night we picked Jenny up at the station in Schreiber as usual, Guaranteed and I. She said, "What *happened*? You've lost ten pounds!"

"It was hard work."

"Travis, what do you think?"

"It depends on things I don't understand. Corporate things. Power. But I think maybe, Jenny. I think maybe. We'll just have to wait and see."

We waited a week. Then two. Then three.

Every day we waited, surveyors in their 4X4 came down to the beach and went to work in the long grass with their transits and their stakes, and if it was quiet you could hear them calling. Every two or three days a van with BRIGHT-SANDS VILLAGE DEVELOPMENTS on the door would arrive, and men wearing ties and white hardhats would walk around in the grass with large rolled plans, pointing to the stakes, or up at my place, or at Cutler's or at someone else's.

One morning I heard them very early, and when I looked out they were in the graveyard. Five of them. Right in the middle of it, as if it were just another corner of the field. And they were doing what they usually did, pointing at plans, pointing at places where they saw imaginary buildings.

I was halfway down the road before I even realized it. Guaranteed came racing up behind me and passed, running as if he were three years old and had all his teeth and no arthritis. We crossed the meadow, and a hundred yards away from those boss engineers I kicked one of their posts out of the ground and lifted it by the tapered end so they could see it plainly above the grass, and I told them loudly and clearly that if they were not out of that graveyard by the time I got to them I was going to test those goddam hardhats.

Guaranteed helped, too. Guaranteed went through that grass like a jet-propelled badger, so fast that if you could see only the grass swaying you might think that something twenty feet long was coming at you. By the time he got to the edge of the graveyard he had worked up an awful snarling deep in his throat. He was frothing at the mouth and his eyes had gone red. "That dog," Jimmy Pagoosie said once, watching Guaranteed chase some drunks off the beach, "that dog can go rabid whenever he wants."

"Call him off!" one of them shouted. They were bumping into each other in their hurry to get to the truck, and Guaranteed was after all their ankles at once, making terrible sounds. Even when they had clambered inside and shut the doors he didn't give up; he kept chewing at the tires for a quarter of a mile down the road.

It nearly finished Guaranteed, that performance. He had to stop often on the way back, and we went up the hill a lot more slowly than we had come down. "Damn fool," I said. But he was laughing, a lopsided and toothless laugh, and I was laughing too. "N'dai," I said, and rubbed his ears. "You smell like a bear." And he did. He was pumping so much adrenalin it was coming right out of the ends of his hairs.

Later that day he growled again, but without moving this time, just enough to tell me someone was coming. I was repairing my canoe on the Council Rock and hadn't heard anything, and when I looked up, there was Alex Wilkinson with his policeman's cap and his sunglasses fixed on in a very businesslike manner. Little claws went to work in my stomach.

"Bojo, Alex."

"Bojo, Travis." He pulled his notebook out of his tunic pocket, licked his thumb and flipped over a few pages. "Vicious dog," he said.

I looked around. "Where?"

"Five employees of Brightsands Village Developments have laid a complaint. The say they were attacked here by a vicious dog. Possibly rabid." He looked at Guaranteed.

"Alex, that dog doesn't even have teeth anymore. What are you going to charge him with?"

Alex looked at me and then back at Guaranteed, very flat and indifferent in his place under the porch. "They also claim that the owner of the dog threatened them with a dangerous weapon. A survey stake." He slid his glasses down and gazed very sternly at me. "Travis, you and I and Cutler have talked about survey stakes. If someone takes one of them out of the ground, that is a misdemeanour. If someone waves it around and threatens to split white skulls..."

"Hats. I didn't say skulls, I said hats."

"Doesn't matter. It's still assault."

"Alex, did those gentlemen mention where they were standing when we asked them to move?"

"On Company property, they said."

"In the cemetery, Alex. They were standing on Mother's grave."

Alex's eyes went cold and dark as the winter Lake. He folded the little notebook slowly and put it back into his pocket and buttoned the flap. He took his hat off. "Something been chewing on your canoe, Travis?"

"I took a little spring trip. With a friend. We came down some rapids."

He nodded. He checked out my work and ran a finger down some of the gashes I still had to repair. Then he asked, "Well, Travis, what do you think?"

"I think maybe, Alex," I said. "I think maybe."

He turned and looked at me a long time. A long, long time. I cannot describe how he looked at me except that it was a look of hope and something else. Pride, maybe. Trust, maybe. It was a look that travelled across a lot of human time, across a whole generation.

Then he settled his cap squarely and turned away to go back down the hill to where his car was parked with its radio squawking. Over his shoulder he said, "Better tie up that vicious dog. Anything that smells that bad doesn't need teeth."

The next Friday, I knew.

I knew when I saw Aja on the beach. At first light when I went out on the porch to watch the sunrise, I saw a commotion of gulls above the water's edge. Underneath was Aja. I thought at first she was ill, maybe having a stroke or a heart attack, but when I got my telescope and focused it I saw that she was dancing. Dancing to some ancient music. Dancing the jubilant dance you could imagine braves performing when they came home with many trophies, feet going, head now down, now back, turning little circles on the edge of a larger circle. Sometimes her hands were cupped in front of her as if she were making an offering, and sometimes they stretched like wings, and when she felt me looking at her she jabbed her forefingers above her head and did a little quick-step like a fullback who has just scored.

I sat down on the top step. I felt light, and clean, and cool. I didn't breathe for a while; I let the Lake do that for me.

And I was sitting there still when I heard an aircraft coming low and fast from the west, the Krautlet, and I realized that he must have taken off at first light, maybe even before. He came over the western point and swept around to the right in a great banking turn that enclosed all of Neyashing in a cone of sound and took him around and back out of sight to the west. I knew from the sound that he was banking again, and climbing. I went out onto the Council Rock and lifted my arms. Other people came out of their houses too, roused by the clamour of that old Wasp engine—the Trowbridges with their arms raised, and Albert Penassie running down the road, and Meg Sugedub with all the kids. In a few minutes everybody in Neyashing was out, looking up. He went over again, this time pulling out of a steep dive that rattled every stovepipe and windowpane, and then he rose over the spit, over the Lake, waggling his wings all the way up, and up, until, brilliant yellow in the new sun, he tipped the old Beaver over on its side and over the top and around again, still climbing.

You may have seen many beautiful things in your life, but until you have seen a float-plane perform a victory roll, you have not seen anything.

All day the news came in other ways. It came with Isaac Kohotchuk passing on the highway and giving us a blast of his airhorn. It came with Alex Wilkinson and a touch of the siren just long enough for everyone to hear, and with Maynard skipping school and running down through the woods shouting, "Hey! Uncle Travis..." and with Weass Faille, just home from Thunder Bay, coming up the hill with two large mugs of Scotch coffee.

I wouldn't have gone to work even if I'd had a job. Guaranteed and I went out to the end of the spit, to the very end, and we sat there alone all that afternoon, until the time came to pick up Jenny at the station.

She came off the train waving a newspaper, and when she hugged me she crumpled it against my back and pressed her face into my chest, getting my shirt wet.

She read to me as we drove back, windows open in the evening:

RESORT PLANS SCRAPPED
Aspen Corporation announced late yesterday that it has shelved its plans to build a world-class resort hotel at McDonnell's Depot, east of Thunder Bay.

B.T. Weir, Aspen vice president and chairman of the Resort Division, made the announcement in a telegram received at press time. Weir confirmed by telephone that the decision to delay construction indefinitely probably means the end of Aspen's plans for the resort. He cited economic factors for the decision, and shareholder opposition at the corporation's recent annual meeting.

MP Jim Cottingham called the decision tragic. "We were looking at a hundred new jobs in the first year and at least fifty more in the second. What will those people do now?"

Cottingham noted that in backing away from the project, Aspen was forfeiting 12.4 million in federal and provincial assistance. "It was a very attractive package," he said, "and a golden opportunity to tap the human resources of our region."

Eric Morrow, Aspen's attorney who has assembled the company's real-estate holdings at McDonnell's Depot, was bitter at news of the decision. "No imagination, no guts, no willingness to take risks!" he said. "Just another example of why this country is going down the tubes." He added that he was planning to move south of the border.

Once a thriving fishing community in the twenties and thirties, McDonnell's Depot has stagnated in recent years. Asked about the value of Aspen's holdings in the area, Weir said they were now "negligible" and added that in his opinion it was unlikely the corporation would even try to dispose of them.

When Jenny finished reading, I trailed my arm out the window. "I like that story. It has point. It has...symmetry."

Jenny smiled. "Your mother would like it too," she said.

It was Minookami, Spring. I had a new job that didn't pay any more than the last one, but it was enough. In June, Jenny said, "I have a maternity leave, Travis. I can stay here. I can come and stay with you."

It was summer, Neebin, time of fruit, time of seeds and berries, time of gathering-up. One morning Jenny came in from the porch looking puzzled, small objects cupped in her hands. "Look. They were hanging on the railing."

"Old, old," I said, taking them from her one by one.

"Older than Aja, even." The loon's foot for grace and power in the Lake. The tern's wing for magical fleetness between the rollers and the storm. The bear's ear to listen for safety. The frail rawhide spiderweb to entrap evil. And something else: a little doeskin pouch for the umbilical cord of a human child.

"But what *are* they?"

"They are gifts for the baby. For the bar of the tikanagan."

She touched the loon's foot. "What does it mean, Travis?"

"It means that she is getting ready to go back," I said.

It was fall, Digwagi, the time of the falling leaves, time of tamarack like molten gold in the hills and waterfowl gathering in the bay. There was the smell of spruce smoke in the nights, and dawn frost sparkled on all the roofs of Neyashing.

One morning Bobby Naponse came to the door of his house and stopped me as I was passing on my way to work. "Letter," he said, grinning, waving a sheet of paper. "Retired fella and his wife, they want to rent my cabin. All October. Maybe longer."

"Good."

"Fella says here he wants to see you right away."

"I'm not guiding anymore, Bobby. Tell them to try Richard."

He was shaking his head, still grinning. "They don't need a guide, these folks," he said. And he passed me the letter so that I could see the signature: *Michael Gardner.*

The car came down very slowly, halting often so that the people inside could see Neyashing clearly, from several levels and several times.

I watched them park beside Bobby's cabin and walk up into the dunes with their arms around each other. I watched him pointing out places in Neyashing to her—the old campground, and the graveyard, and the western end of the beach. I watched him point to something I couldn't see high above the Palisades, an eagle, maybe.

I found my cap where I had tossed it on the woodpile, and I put it on, put my jacket on and whistled for Guaranteed. He came snarling out of a bad dream and flew off the porch like a furry mat. "Easy," I said. "No lawyers, No surveyors. Friends."

I found them on the beach, at the edge of the Lake. Michael Gardner came forward and took my hand in both of his.

"I expected you sooner," I said.

"There was a lot to do. A lot to finish."

"And now you begin."

He laughed, and took me over to the woman making friends with Guaranteed at the water's edge. "Martha," he said.

She also took my hand in both of hers. Her eyes were pale green, clear, calm and sane, the colour of the Lake where it lies over quartzite shoals. She looked at me as if we had known each other from a place before all time. "Thank you, Travis," she said. She wore the crowsfeet on her temples, and the silver in her black hair, and the creases in the corners of her mouth like proud badges. It was an honest face, the face of a woman who had been swept by many storms and had endured.

I laid my free hand on top of hers. "You're welcome," I said. "Ni minowendam wabamin naan, Martha. You're welcome here."

I watched them walk in the dusk until they reached the end of the spit and went down the farthest slope and out of sight. But I could see them still as I folded the tripod and carried the telescope back inside. I could see them together in the growing darkness, the cold wind rising and the Lake beginning to roll, going out to the very end, out to that place where granite and Lake are one, and where the footing

218

is most perilous. And there, I think, Michael Gardner's story really begins....

Inside, Jenny had lit the lamps. She was humming, dancing a little dance beside the stove. I went to her and laid my hands on her belly, and we danced together like that while the night came on, singing a quiet song for the baby, for all the babies.